Prelude conveys the peak oil problem via a story that's both artful and compelling. Attention Hollywood: Option this novel! If you've been trying to explain your concerns about our energy future to friends and family who just can't manage to slog through pages of depletion analysis, this book might prove to be your best teaching tool.

— Richard Heinberg, Senior Fellow,
Post Carbon Institute and Author of
*The Party's Over: Oil, War and the Fate
of Industrial Societies*

Kurt Cobb treats us to a riveting suspense story in an authentic Washington setting. All the while he effortlessly slips in background about peak oil that will introduce many readers to a new, more realistic way of looking at our energy-challenged future.

— Tom Whipple, Editor, *Peak Oil Review*
and Former CIA Analyst

PRELUDE

≈ about PRELUDE and Peak Oil ≈

While *Prelude* is a fictional story, peak oil is anything but. Peak oil refers to the time when the worldwide rate of oil production will top out and thereafter begin an irreversible decline. This phenomenon is of the utmost seriousness because oil provides the largest share of our energy. As of now there are no good substitutes for oil that can be produced on a scale large enough to make up for such a decline. Without proper preparation for the transition from a society in which oil supplies are growing to one in which they are declining, humankind could face tremendous hardships.

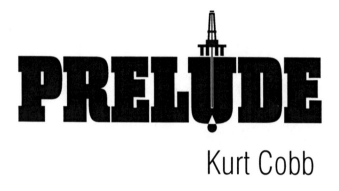

PRELUDE

Kurt Cobb

PUBLIC INTEREST COMMUNICATIONS

ISBN 978-0-9831089-0-0

Published by
Public Interest Communications
P.O. Box 671
Portage, Michigan 49081-0671

For additional copies visit: *www.preludethenovel.com*

Cover and book design by
Keith Jones, n-Dimensional Design

To the members of the peak oil community

≈ **acknowledgements** ≈

A work of fiction about an important public topic such as world peak oil production requires long periods of exposure to the minds of others deeply involved in the issue. In my many years of writing about energy issues I have had the pleasure of such exposure which has now solidified itself into the story that constitutes this novel. To the many who have written and spoken on peak oil, I owe a debt of gratitude. Unfortunately, these people are too numerous to mention here individually.

There are some individuals, however, who deserve special mention. Jim Armstrong offered early advice in the outline stage. He also offered important criticism of the first draft that strengthened the characters, improved the dialogue and led to the addition of some scenes and the expansion of others. Beth Johnson offered insights that helped to enliven the interactions of the main characters and provided validation that the story would have appeal to women readers. Bart Anderson, Steve Andrews, Donna Anton and Debbie Cook all offered valuable editing suggestions.

Dmitri Orlov's slide show *Closing the Collapse Gap* and his follow-up book *Reinventing Collapse* provided the basis for a discussion of the differences between the circumstances Russians faced during the collapse of the Soviet Union and those that Americans might face during a similar economic collapse.

Dave Cohen reviewed the technical information in the manuscript. B. J. Doyle read through glossary entries related to the oil and gas industry to ensure that I properly defined important industry terms used in the novel. He also introduced me to his colleague, Don Snow, who provided an excellent tutorial one afternoon on 3-D seismic computer models used to evaluate oil and gas prospects. Any technical errors that remain in the text are solely mine.

Andy Leonard lent me his condo for an extended stay in Washington, D.C. This allowed me to travel the paths of my characters repeatedly and at various times of day and night just as they would have. Steve Anton and his family provided me with their hospitality while I was in Houston doing research. Steve, a Houston native, gave me special insight into the city's culture and landscape.

Finally, I wish to thank my sister, Tracy, for the use of her very tranquil condo where I wrote the first draft.

≈ chapter 1 ≈

Cassie Young kept scanning the horizon from her seat
beside the pilot of the black Eurocopter as the engine
droned and the rotor blades filled the cabin with the noise
of their rapid-fire thumping. To her right she could see the
Athabasca River, which appeared to be a muddy gray through
the haze that had beset the landscape below. The river was
flanked on both sides by the deep green of the great boreal
forest, a vast, densely wooded wilderness that encircles the
northerly reaches of the earth from Scandinavia through
Siberia and from Alaska to the Atlantic seaboard of Canada.

She imagined that bobcats and moose and elk and maybe
a grizzly bear or two wandered below her along the forest
floor. The scene reminded her of trips she had taken with her
father in northern Minnesota in the summertime, just the
two of them in the wilderness paddling a canoe across lakes
you could dip your cup into and take a drink.

The helicopter was ferrying Cassie from Fort McMurray
to the tar sands operations of SandOil of Canada. SandOil
was one of the first companies to coax bitumen, a black, tar-
like substance, out of sands which sit under 54,000 square
miles of forest in northern Alberta, an area the size of New
York state. She knew these facts because she worked as an
energy analyst who had written many reports that included
information on the tar sands, or rather oil sands, as the industry preferred to call them.

With oil prices this high — oil had moved above $100 a

barrel earlier in the year—the oil sands were having their day. It was finally profitable to dig them out. Just how profitable was part of what she came to find out. On this June day in 2008 Cassie was visiting the oil sands as an analyst for Energy Advisers International, a prestigious energy consulting firm based in Washington, D.C. At age 31, she was the youngest analyst in the firm.

"Ever been up here before, Ms. Young?" the pilot asked.

Cassie detected a distinct Scottish brogue through the headset she was wearing. "No, this is my first time," she replied. "But I've written a lot of research that included the oil sands."

"Well, that's your business, isn't it?" he replied. "Of course, even though the stuff's really more like tar, everyone here calls it oil sands…marketing and all that."

"Of course," Cassie said. She knew that using the words "tar sands" in Alberta could easily be interpreted as a sign of contempt for those working in the industry.

Cassie pulled a camera from her khaki travel vest, put the strap around her neck, and fired off several shots of the landscape below.

She noticed that her scruffy, black-haired pilot had a rather young-looking face. "When did you arrive here?" she asked him.

"This morning?" he asked.

"No, when did you move to Fort McMurray?"

"About three years ago now," he said. "I started out working as a chopper pilot in the North Sea."

"Were you flying Super Pumas out of Aberdeen?"

"Yes, those were the only things we flew. And they were sturdy. But I'd rather fly in a bad snow up here than in a howling storm over the North Sea."

"So, it was the wonderful weather that brought you here," Cassie said with a smirk.

The pilot turned toward her and smiled. "Not exactly the

weather," he said. "But after six years in Aberdeen, I could see that the fields were going to do nothing but go downhill. So, I decided to go where the future is. And that's here. There's enough oil here to last at least another 40 years, and probably a hundred when they ramp up production of all the stuff that's too deep to get at from the surface."

"So, you're planning on staying?" she inquired.

"Oh, I'm planning on staying as long as the oil lasts, and that's gonna be long after I'm dead."

"And you don't think the environmentalists or concerns about global warming are going to limit the development of the oil sands — at some point, I mean?"

"Ms. Young, there's more than a trillion barrels of oil down there." He turned his gaze to her for a moment. "Even if they only get half of it out, that's enough to last the world — the whole world — for 16 years. Right here!" He was pointing down at the ground. "In this one place!" His eyes returned forward. "Nobody's gonna stop that. Not with all the people in China and India wanting to live like you and I do…not with big oilfields like the North Sea drying up…not until they've done all the digging that can be done." He looked toward her again with his eyebrows raised and his head tilted at an angle as if to ask, "Do you really think anything can stop it?"

Mirroring him, Cassie raised her eyebrows and tilted her head in his direction. "I suppose you're right," she said.

The SandOil site was now coming into view. Cassie could see a vast dark pond streaked with oily stains. Purifying the wastewater from oil sands operations had turned out to be trickier than anyone had anticipated. She had read that some of the ponds had been around for decades waiting for the industry to find a solution. She reached for her camera and started taking photos again.

Just ahead smoke was drifting upward from the tall towers of the upgraders and seemed to blend with the haze in the grayish-white sky. The upgraders were the final processing stage in which the bitumen, now separated from sand and water, was turned into something resembling oil.

"Mr. Weller asked me to take you for a little spin around the site," the pilot said. "Is that okay?"

"Please do," Cassie responded.

The helicopter descended until it seemed as if she could almost touch the tops of the circular gray metallic upgrading towers with their long, twisting vertical pipes hugging the sides. Near the top of one tower she could see a man in a blue hard hat standing with his hand on the safety railing of a walkway that ran the circumference of the tower, one of several such walkways at various heights. Closer to the ground the pipes ran so thick and in so many directions that Cassie thought it looked as if someone had deposited a large helping of giant-sized spaghetti there.

"What's that yellow stack that looks like the beginnings of a pyramid?" she asked.

"That's the sulfur they extract from the oil," the pilot said. "They haven't been able to figure out what to do with it until recently. They've finally found a contractor who will haul it away and sell it."

Now they were over the open pit mine. The sand was deep black. The operation looked more than anything else like a vast strip mine in coal country. Enormous dump trucks were being filled by large hydraulic shovels that scooped tons of sand with each bite. A tangle of makeshift roads crisscrossed the mine surface which now sank deeply into the former forest floor.

As they circled back, Cassie saw several large funnel-shaped vessels. Inside them bitumen was being skimmed off the top of the hot water used to separate it from the sand.

The helicopter was soon hovering over a parking lot and closing in on an adjacent helipad. As the pilot set down, Cassie could see a man and a woman waiting at the perimeter.

A half a minute later they were advancing toward her as the pilot reached over, unlatched the door and told her it was now safe to exit.

The man rushed toward the helicopter with his hand outstretched as Cassie climbed out. "Terry Weller, Ms. Young," he said, wearing a broad smile as he shook her hand. "We're honored to have you here to review our operation." Cassie had found during her travels for the firm that whenever EAI came calling, people seemed to stand at attention. She turned back temporarily toward the door of the helicopter, pulled out her burgundy-colored shoulder bag—which she found much handier than a briefcase—and put the strap over her shoulder.

She thanked the pilot and then pivoted to face Weller, a short, stout, middle-aged man with sandy hair combed straight back. He was in shirtsleeves and a tie and wore a blue hard hat. He handed a hard hat to Cassie. "You'll be needing this," he said. He looked behind her at the pilot, but his words seemed addressed to her. "Did Gavin take you for a nice look-see of the site like I asked?"

"Yes, Mr. Weller, he certainly did," the pilot responded.

"Good," Weller said. He gave the pilot a thumbs-up and with that Weller was back attending to Cassie and guiding her away from the helicopter. "Pretty impressive, isn't it?"

"Yes, it is," Cassie said.

"The oil sands are just about the biggest engineering project on the planet right now, and you can see why," Weller continued. "It takes a lot of equipment and know-how to move enough earth every day to fill Rogers Centre…or, in your case, Yankee Stadium. But that's what the oil sands operators do on a combined basis every 24 hours."

They were now at the edge of the helipad. Weller turned and waved as the helicopter roared to a liftoff. The rotor wash caused Cassie's pants and shirtsleeves to flutter vigorously and stirred up a thin veil of dust. She rubbed her eyes to relieve the irritation. After the helicopter hovered away, Weller introduced Cassie to the woman who was accompanying him. "Ms. Young, I'd like you to meet Kelly Waverly, my assistant."

Cassie shook hands and exchanged greetings with Waverly, a tall, thin brunette whose face seemed full of sharp edges.

"Let's all get in the car, shall we?" Weller said.

After everyone was situated in the car and Weller had the vehicle moving, Cassie asked Weller what his position with SandOil was.

"Vice president for public affairs," Weller answered.

Cassie was hoping for someone other than the company's public relations people. She resented the way most of them treated her — as if she were part of their image management team instead of an analyst whose job was to gather information and offer objective advice to clients. Still, she was getting the perfunctory tour, and she really did need to understand in a more concrete way how the oil sands projects worked.

"It's a good thing you came up here in the summer," Weller said. The car tires began to crackle against the gravel as they moved off the pavement. "In winter it can get down to 30 below and just stay there for weeks." Shortly, they arrived at the edge of the pit Cassie had seen from the air.

All of them got out of the car. Weller looked over at Cassie and tapped his hard hat.

"Oh yes, of course," she said and donned the hard hat Weller had given her. Cassie advanced toward the edge of the enormous pit which was guarded by huge bald tires lying on their sides, tires larger than she'd ever seen. A smell like fresh asphalt wafted up from below and completely enveloped her — not surprising, since bitumen is mixed with aggregate to pave roads.

"The tires come from the big trucks you see down there," Weller said as he approached Cassie. "Those trucks can carry 400 tons each. The tires alone are 13 feet high."

In the distance the drivers in the cabs of these partially

blackened, yellow-orange dump trucks were tiny, shadowy figures. "The trucks cost five million dollars each," Weller continued. "Way back, you can see a shovel." Cassie could see the red cab of the huge shovel, but the bucket was temporarily hidden behind it as it scooped up another load of black sand.

Weller began coughing. It was a terrible fit, maybe four or five deep coughs followed by several smaller ones. His assistant extracted a bottle of water from the bag she was carrying and handed it to him. Weller opened it and took a long drink.

"Sorry about that," he said. Then he continued his narrative. "Our shovels can pick up 100 tons at a time. That one there cost us 15 million dollars." Weller paused for a moment, and then as he started again, he drew both hands apart to bring attention to the entire expanse of the pit. "All that you see here is surface mining. This mine goes down about 80 meters; that's about 260 feet for our friends south of the border," he said smiling and looking toward Cassie. "But surface deposits are only 20 percent of what's available in Alberta. The other 80 percent are too deep to dig out."

"SandOil has some SAGD, don't they?" Cassie pronounced the abbreviation *sag-dee*. She was referring to a method for mining reserves deep underground by piping in steam to melt the bitumen and then pumping the liquid out via wells drilled for that purpose.

"We've got some working SAGD operations already," Weller responded.

"What do you think of toe to heel air injection?" Cassie queried. This method actually sets some of the bitumen on fire underground. The heat from the fire liquefies the remaining bitumen and also creates gases that push the liquid to the surface through recovery wells.

"We think it's a very promising technique for underground recovery," Weller replied.

"And?" Cassie probed. She believed Weller was holding something back.

"And what?" Weller looked down, a sure sign he was uncomfortable with the question, she thought.

"So, you're not ready to tell me that SandOil is in negotiations for a licensing agreement and joint venture with the patent holders."

"Well, I can't confirm that," Weller said.

"You just did."

"No, I didn't," Weller said with a chuckle even as he wagged his finger at Cassie. Then she knew she was right. She regarded it as a game to try to get anything remotely useful out of public relations people.

"Fine," Cassie said raising one hand in a conciliatory gesture. "I'm sorry I brought it up. Please continue with the tour."

Weller's smile had shifted to a frown, but he caught himself and quickly reverted to smiling. "Over there is the crusher," he said pointing to where all the trucks filled with the black sand were going. "Everything gets crushed to a size that allows us to more easily extract the bitumen." He paused. "Would you like to feel a sample of the oil sand?"

"Yes, I would," Cassie said.

Weller motioned to his assistant, and she produced a small jar with some lumps of blackened sand in it. Weller took the jar from her and opened it, jiggling a lump onto Cassie's waiting hand.

"Rub it around a little," he said.

"It's sticky and much more coarse than I imagined," Cassie remarked.

"That's why it wears down those big tires in a year or less," Weller explained. "And it sticks to the trucks so badly in the summer that we have to wash them frequently. Sometimes the trucks weigh 10 tons less when we get done. And speaking of washing, just throw the sample you have on the ground there, and Kelly will give you some wipes to clean your hands."

Weller's assistant handed Cassie some moist wipes ripped from a foil pouch. Cassie wiped her hands, handed the soiled wipes back to Waverly, and then thanked her.

"Let's get in the car and drive over to the separation facilities," Weller said. Cassie climbed into the front seat, and Waverly got in back. As they moved slowly toward pavement again, Weller explained that the crushed "ore," as he called it, is mixed with warm water and caustic soda—what most people know as lye—and piped to separation facilities, the gigantic funnels Cassie had seen from the sky. There the sand, clay and other matter are separated. The bitumen floats to the top and is skimmed off. The sand drops to the bottom. And in the middle, a cloudy mixture of clay, bitumen and water is piped off to be processed further. After all this, the bitumen is moved to an upgrader, one of the tall, metallic towers Cassie had seen from the helicopter. There it is further processed into a flowing synthetic oil, Weller explained. Then it can be refined just like regular crude oil into gasoline or diesel or any number of products, he added.

Soon they pulled up beside one of the huge funnel-shaped processors. A smooth low hum was emanating from it. "No need to get out," Weller said. "Not much to see. But let me say that we now get 90 percent recovery of the oil out of the sands using advanced technology. That's up from 75 percent. And after we upgrade it to synthetic crude, we send most of it south to you folks in the U.S."

"Aren't you going to build a pipeline to eastern Canada at some point?" Cassie asked.

"Too expensive," Weller replied. "It's just easier and cheaper for eastern Canada to import their oil from abroad and for us to send this stuff down to you through the western pipeline system."

Cassie already knew the answer to her question, but she wanted to see exactly how Weller would handle it. Of course, he was right on purely economic grounds. As a result though, Canada, which could easily be energy independent, had now tied its own energy security to that of the United States.

They drove a bit farther to the upgrader and then got out of the car again. Cassie detected the odor of burning matches which she knew came from sulfur compounds expelled by the upgrading towers.

Weller began explaining in detail the chemistry of SandOil's particular upgrading process. For the first time, Cassie retrieved a notebook and started writing. This information was new to her since she only had a general idea of the chemistry involved. He said that most of the heat needed for the conversion came from natural gas, but that in the not-too-distant future he expected nuclear power to be the main energy source driving oil sands development. There was talk of perhaps a dozen nuclear plants being built.

Then he added, "Yep, Canada's going to be the biggest supplier of imported crude oil to the United States from here on out. You can thank the oil sands for that. And we're doing it without significantly affecting water quality or fish and wildlife." He looked over at Cassie and emphasized the next point with a shake of his index finger. "That's been confirmed by all the studies we've done in conjunction with the government of Alberta."

Cassie couldn't believe that he had had the audacity to say the last sentence to her with a straight face. No one actually believed the phony reports put out by these joint government and industry bodies that were supposedly policing the environment around the oil sands. But she knew it was part of the pitch. And naturally, it was unacceptable to say that the government and the oil industry were colluding to sacrifice northern Alberta for oil. But that's what they were doing, and everybody knew it. She hated being treated like a simpleton; but, she hated the hypocrisy even more.

Her job, however, wasn't to judge the wisdom of such

projects—only their likely success, their place in the oil supply picture, and any possible technical, financial or environmental obstacles that might prevent them from expanding. From the looks of things, her helicopter pilot was right. Nothing was going to stop the development of Alberta's oil sands.

With the tour concluded, Weller left his assistant behind and drove Cassie to SandOil's corporate offices just south of the mine. They entered the parking lot of a sleek, low-slung, glass-faced office building. Weller escorted Cassie into the building and then into a conference room. There two men rose to meet her and Weller as they entered. One was bald on top and had a handlebar mustache. He introduced himself as Randall Taylor, the company's chief engineer. Taylor was maybe 40 and wore a red plaid shirt but no tie. The other man was SandOil's chief operating officer, Harrison Cole. Cole had a droopy face and oversized ears and seemed to be in his late fifties. He wore a blue tie over his white dress shirt and a pair of blue dress slacks.

After the introductions, everyone sat down and Cole started. "Ms. Young, we're pleased you could meet with us. We know you have a very busy schedule. Now what can we tell you?"

"I'm most interested in the cost side of your operations," Cassie began.

"Wait a minute—you're the one who wrote the report two years ago on...what did they call it?" Cole was looking at Taylor for the answer.

"The law of receding horizons," Taylor said.

"But you weren't working for EAI then?" Cole inquired.

"No, I was working for a brokerage, Atlas Group, out of Chicago," Cassie replied. At the time her conclusions were not warmly received by the firm. In fact, her boss had to fight to get management to release the report. Brokerage firms simply didn't like putting out bad news because they felt it might hurt business. Fortunately, her candid style hadn't caused any similar problems at EAI, at least not yet.

"You pissed off a lot of people up here by saying that our profits would get squeezed." Cole spoke calmly and with a smile.

"Yeah, I said the price of natural gas and other inputs could rise faster than oil prices," Cassie said. "And that the cost of capital would go through the roof."

"Unfortunately, you were right," Cole said. "Natural gas prices shot up so much in the last six months, it's been killing us. Right about now I could use those nuclear power plants."

"Any word on when you'll get them?" Cassie asked.

"Our CEO is at an industry meeting today working on just that," Cole responded. "He sends his regrets for not being able to be here."

"I understand you're in negotiations for a toe to heel air injection joint venture," Cassie said.

Cole glared at Weller.

"I didn't tell her," Weller said. "She already had it figured out."

Cole turned back to Cassie. "We're not quite ready for that to get out."

"But you'll let me know, right?" Cassie asked.

"I'll give you a heads-up when we're ready to make the announcement," Weller responded.

Cole and Taylor spent the rest of their time with Cassie discussing in detail their plans for lowering mining and processing costs through management efficiencies and new technologies. Cassie took careful notes. This is what she had really come for. The results, the two men explained, would only accrue over time. But little steps here and there, they assured her, would eventually bring down the cost of producing oil from the oil sands substantially.

As soon as Cassie indicated she was finished with her interview, Cole and Taylor were on their feet making apologies for having to run off right away. "The oil around here doesn't squirt out of the ground," Taylor remarked. "We have to do a lot of coaxing."

≈

That evening as Cassie sat in bed in her hotel room in Fort McMurray watching the news, she noticed that financial forecasters were expecting oil prices to pull back from their record levels. They said the fundamentals couldn't sustain these prices. She agreed and was astounded that the price had gotten this high. The view of the future from Fort McMurray was one with a lot of new supply. Add to that new oil supplies coming from deepwater drilling off Africa and expanded production in the Middle East, and the price was bound to go back down, she thought.

She switched off the television and began to ponder the last 12 months working for EAI. She thought about all the trips and extra work she had volunteered for, trying to make a good impression, trying to lay the groundwork for a partnership in the firm. Still, she wondered if she was doing enough. Yes, she had a valuable ally, her mentor, Evan, who was a managing partner. But she was taking nothing for granted. She would be in line for a promotion to senior associate in six months. And then, if she were lucky, she'd maybe make partner two or three years after that.

Then she thought about Paul Hendler, the man she'd been seeing for the last four months. She had met him at a party given by an associate at the firm. Paul had tagged along with one of the invitees that night, so he wasn't really a friend of anyone at EAI. In some ways that was a relief. Cassie never felt obliged to talk shop with him, and so she could leave her work behind whenever she was with him.

But both of them were so busy traveling that it was hard to plan time together. Still, he was such a sweet man really, and that was an almost nonexistent commodity in the cut-throat town of Washington, D.C. Maybe two people with busy careers just weren't meant to be together. She didn't know whether to hope that their relationship would somehow work out or that it wouldn't. If it didn't work out, she thought she would probably look for someone who was less obsessed with climbing the career ladder than she had to admit that she was.

Enough ruminating, she thought. She was too tired for this. She shut off the light on the nightstand, pulled the covers over her and tried to get some sleep for the long day of travel ahead.

≈ **chapter 2** ≈

The next morning Weller came to fetch Cassie at the hotel to take her to the airport. He met her in the lobby and insisted on carrying her bags to his car. Once the two of them were in the car, he thanked her profusely for coming. Too profusely, she thought. But he had some welcome news.

One of SandOil's corporate jets was flying to D.C. that day via Toronto. It would save her about four hours of travel time if she wanted to ride along, compliments of SandOil. She jumped at the chance. When they got to the airport, she cancelled her ticket, and Weller escorted her to the SandOil jet, a large Gulfstream, which was sitting on the tarmac with the stairway extended waiting for her to board. She climbed the stairs and was greeted at the top by the steward. Once she was in, he immediately pushed a button that retracted the stairway and sealed the aircraft.

Cassie surveyed the cabin, but it seemed curiously empty. "We're going to pick up our legal and trade team in Toronto," the steward explained. He took her suitcase, and she went to sit down. She sank into a large, high-backed seat facing the rear of the aircraft. In front of her was a table big enough to spread out both her papers and her laptop. What a pleasure!

She worked in solitude until the plane stopped in Toronto and six people boarded, four men and two women, all in business suits. One of the men stood next to the table she was working on and looked as if he might be ready to sit down in the seat facing her.

"Let me move some of my things so you can use the table," Cassie said.

"No need," said the man who was wearing a charcoal gray pinstripe suit. His black hair was perfectly combed, and he had a dark complexion.

"Clay Thompson, Ms. Young," he said, offering his hand. They shook hands as he continued. "I'm SandOil's VP for government relations. Weller said you would be on the flight. Do you mind if I sit with you?"

"Not at all. Please do," she said removing her papers from the table despite Thompson's assurances. She preferred to talk with him rather than work anyway.

Thompson introduced Cassie to the others who had boarded and then sat down across from her. Soon the plane was in the air, and after some small talk Cassie got to the point.

"What's the political climate in Canada like these days?" she asked.

"With the Harper administration, we—I mean we in the oil sands—have basically got the wind at our backs," Thompson said. "He's an Alberta boy, you know."

"I guess I knew that," Cassie said. "What takes you to Washington?"

"Ostensibly, we're testifying before the House energy subcommittee on the future of North American oil supplies," Thompson replied.

"And your real mission is?"

"Look, whoever becomes president in the fall is going to be pushing climate change legislation," he began. "It's starting to look like oil from the oil sands will be disadvantaged under the rules Congress is contemplating. Our team is going to fan out to try to make the relevant committee chairmen see the disconnect between *that* and the wisdom of getting substantial oil supplies from a politically stable neighbor."

"Sounds like you have your story down."

"I'd like to think so."

"What about those nuclear power plants I keep hearing about?"

"It's a great idea," Thompson said without enthusiasm.

"There's a 'but' in there somewhere," Cassie said.

"Between you and me…" Thompson leaned in toward her. "Off the record?"

"Sure, off the record."

"No, I mean really off the record. Nothing at all in your reports."

"All right," she replied. She didn't understand why he was taking her into his confidence so readily, but it piqued her interest.

"This nuclear power thing isn't going to happen. We can't get the cooperation of the other companies to finance a joint project. It's a real cowboy mentality in the oil sands."

"So, this is why you're worried about climate change legislation."

"Without those plants we can't get our greenhouse gas emissions down to what they are for processing conventional oil. It just takes a lot more energy to separate the oil from the sands, and that's going to generate higher emissions. So we're making the rounds in Washington." He paused for a moment and then returned his gaze to Cassie. "Look, it's okay to mention the climate legislation stuff in your reports, on background, not attributed to me or the company. But my views on the prospects for nuclear power in the oil sands need to stay under wraps."

Of course, Cassie knew he didn't really mean what he said about the nuclear power issue or he wouldn't have told her anything at all. Then it dawned on her. SandOil was pushing other industry players to support nukes for the oil sands. Now, if she used the information Thompson gave her in an EAI report, he'd never talk to her again. But what he really wanted was for someone from, say, a prominent energy consulting firm, to mention to energy policymakers in the

United States, a country heavily dependent on Canada for oil, that the industry is stalling on nuclear power for the oil sands. Then maybe those U.S. policymakers would give the big industry players a little shove in the right direction. And all of this would be completely free of SandOil's fingerprints. This guy doesn't miss a beat, she thought. She would pass the information on to Larry Hilliard, the chairman of EAI. He had a lot of relationships with energy people in the Congress and at the various agencies and, of course, in the industry. She'd let him figure out what to do.

The fatigue was catching up with her as she continued her conversation with Thompson. She had flown to Calgary on Sunday, met with oil sands executives from several companies all day Monday, and dined with three of them until late into the evening. Then, early in the morning she had caught a flight to Fort McMurray where she met the helicopter that took her to the SandOil site for a tour and a meeting with the two SandOil managers. She was exhausted now and anxious to get back home to a nice warm bath and then relax for the evening.

It was late afternoon when they started their descent into Washington. The cloud layer below looked like a snow-covered landscape of small mountains. As the plane sliced through the clouds, the Potomac came into view. She could see tree-covered neighborhoods on the east bank punctuated by green fields. That gave way to the U.S. Naval Research Laboratory, its signature radio telescope mounted on top of the main building with the dish pointing straight up.

As she gazed out the window, she remembered a trip to Washington with her parents during which her father, a geologist, had explained that four geologic provinces meet in the Washington area: the Triassic lowlands and the Blue Ridge out in Virginia, the coastal plain in the area around the Jefferson Memorial, and the Piedmont, the transition from the coastal plain to the Appalachian Mountains.

It had been almost three years since her father's death. She had been the stoic one at the funeral, not crying, trying to be strong for both herself and her mother who was falling apart that day. But now whenever she thought about him — his death was premature and a bitter loss — she couldn't help but tear up a bit.

She rubbed her eyes and then reached for her cellphone and flipped it open. She found a message from Paul waiting for her. The steward signaled her to close her phone, which she did, feeling a little embarrassed.

Soon the plane bumped down on the runway and then reversed engines to slow its momentum, pushing her back against her aft-facing seat. As the plane taxied toward the gate, she strained to see something beyond the airport through her now rain-streaked window. She could only barely make out the thin white spire of the Washington Monument against the gray gloom.

She pulled out her cellphone again, retrieved Paul's message and held the phone against her ear to listen. He was inviting her to a concert that evening, one his boss had invited him to. Paul's boss wanted to meet Cassie and also introduce his new wife to both of them.

Cassie was determined to say no. But she decided to wait until she was inside the terminal to make the call so that she would be out of earshot of her fellow travelers.

Once inside, she said her goodbyes to Thompson and thanked him for the ride and for the conversation. Then she dialed Paul. Before she could get a word out, Paul took control of the conversation.

"Cassie, I am soooo glad you called. I know you're coming back from a long trip. But I really, really want you to come to this concert tonight. It's a fundraiser for the Northern Virginia Opera organized by my boss's new wife. Both of them are very anxious to meet you." He said all this practically in one breath.

"Paul, I—"

"Look, I promise that I'll meet you right away at your place. I'll rub your shoulders and then you can take a nap while I go out and bring us back some dinner. What's not to like?"

"Paul, I'm really exhausted from this trip," Cassie said.

"Hence the nap," Paul retorted. "You'll be as good as new, especially after I bring us back some spring rolls, some massaman curry and some tom kha gai soup from Regent Thai."

Cassie sighed. "The person who invented the idea of putting lime juice in soup should get a medal," she said. She couldn't believe how quickly her resolve had melted in the face of Paul's superior salesmanship. He was, after all, a salesman, a pharmaceutical salesman, in fact. But really all he had done was make her realize just how much she wanted to see him despite her fatigue.

"All right, I'll go on one condition," Cassie said.

"What's that?"

"We skip the shoulder rub, and I get to take a nice, long, hot bath."

"That works for me. You can even take a rain check on the massage."

"I'll do that," Cassie replied. "Pick up the food on your way and come about six, okay?"

"I owe you one for this," Paul said.

"And you know I'm going to make you pay for this big time."

"It makes me hot just thinking about how you're going to do that."

Cassie laughed. "I'll see you at six."

She hurried through the airport to a cabstand. Normally, she'd take the Metro home. The station at Dupont Circle was just five blocks from her condo. But today she wanted to treat herself to a cab, and she could use that extra time to relax before Paul arrived. When she got to the condo, she ran a hot bath pouring some lavender-scented oil into the water. She went back into the bedroom and undressed.

When she returned, she stopped to look at herself in the mirror. She pinched her side. She thought maybe all the travel and restaurant food was putting a little extra weight on her normally trim figure despite the time she devoted to riding her bicycle. She took a deep breath, and then turned around and stepped into the tub as it continued to fill. She adjusted the faucet to make the water hotter. After she had slipped down into the tub, she realized she'd forgotten her bath pillow. But she didn't really want to get out. She reached up, pulled down the towel hanging above her and folded it to create a makeshift headrest. A minute later the tub was full. She turned off the faucet, leaned back and closed her eyes for what she expected would be maybe a 30-minute soak. Why had she agreed to go out with Paul this evening? This soak in the tub was all she wanted besides getting a bite to eat.

Cassie was awakened by the intercom buzzer. She rose up and realized she had fallen asleep and for a lot longer than 30 minutes.

She climbed out of the tub, grabbed a fresh towel from the linen closet and tried to pat herself dry as she dashed across the living room to the kitchen to press the intercom.

"Paul, is that you?" she asked.

"Yes," he replied.

"Come on up and let yourself in. I'm just getting out of the tub."

"Okay."

Cassie buzzed him through the front entrance and then reached over and unlocked the door to her condo. She finished drying off and was still brushing her hair when she heard Paul come through the door.

"I'll be there in a minute," she called out. There wasn't much hair to brush really. She wore her brown hair short and her bangs reached less than halfway down her forehead. It was a good thing that Paul was 6' 4" for she herself was 5' 11". When it came to dating, her height had seemed like a disadvantage. But in the mostly male environment she worked in, it was clearly an asset. She thought her square jaw perhaps made her look a little masculine; but the narrow contours of her face, high cheekbones, and blue eyes seemed to restore femininity to her visage.

"Don't let everything get cold," Paul called to her. "I know how much you hate it when your food is cold."

"I'll be right there," Cassie replied as she laid her brush down. She went back to the bedroom and put on a blue dress that she sometimes wore to work. She popped into the bathroom for another look in the mirror and then walked out into the living room and toward the kitchen. Paul had all the cartons of food open and plates and silverware laid out on the black granite kitchen bar. He was sitting on one of the stools, and Cassie sat down beside him.

"Sorry," Cassie said. "I fell asleep in the bathtub."

"Don't worry about it," Paul said. "I'm just glad you're coming." He leaned over and gave her a kiss. "It's good to see you."

"I *am* tired," she responded. "But it's good to see you, too." She stared at him for a moment. A patch of Paul's curly brown hair dipped onto his forehead and seemed as if it might lead back to a part. But his thick hair piled up so that, if there was one, it never showed. Paul was only a year younger, but his dark brows, bright eyes, and eager smile framed an unblemished face that lacked the careworn expressions of his professional peers. In fact, he looked as if he might have recently finished college. Tonight he was wearing a blue sport jacket, white dress shirt, and khakis, but no tie. He was just plain sexy, Cassie thought. For a moment her energy surged, and she imagined undressing him and dragging his tall, trim body into the bedroom. But they had to be going soon, so she just returned his kiss.

"What were you thinking just then?" Paul asked.

"I was thinking about making wild love with you," she responded.

His eyes lit up. "Too bad we have to go."

After they finished eating, they made their way down from the third floor using the steps and then exited through the front entrance onto 16th Street. Parking was always difficult in that neighborhood, and they had to walk practically all the way down to O Street from her place between P and Q before they reached Paul's green Toyota Land Cruiser. At least the rain had stopped, so they weren't getting wet on their way.

Once they were in the SUV, Paul drove into Scott Circle and then veered onto Rhode Island Avenue. When he got to M, he turned toward Georgetown and passed right through, finally stopping at the entrance to Key Bridge. Traffic coming off the bridge into the District was backed up waiting for the light to change. But going out, things looked clear. Paul had his left blinker on indicating he was about to turn onto the bridge toward Virginia.

"Where exactly are we going?" Cassie asked.

"The concert's at George Mason University," Paul said.

"Arlington?" Cassie queried as Paul turned onto the bridge.

"No, it's at the Fairfax campus," he replied.

"Wait a minute! You didn't tell me the concert was all the way out there."

"I thought if I told you, you wouldn't come," Paul said sheepishly.

"Paul, I don't like it when you don't give me the full story." Cassie folded her arms. She wasn't going to pursue it. Paul had gotten his way with a little subterfuge…again! But there was no point in complaining now. She might as well make the best of it.

"I'm sorry, I'm sorry," he said. "But you're going to like this concert. It's all music written by Philip Glass."

"Who?"

"Philip Glass…uh, he does a lot of movie music. He did the music for 'The Hours.'"

"He did that?"

"Yeah, you love that movie," Paul said. "You have the soundtrack, don't you?"

"I listen to it all the time," Cassie responded. "So that's Philip Glass."

They were moving along fine until an accident on I-66 slowed traffic to a crawl. Paul was afraid they might not arrive before the performance began. But they finally got going and made it to the theater with five minutes to spare. Paul picked up the tickets and then led Cassie toward two people standing near the theater entrance.

Paul's boss, Ron Jamison, was balding and squat and carried a jolly expression on his face. He looked fiftyish. Darlene, his new wife, was a petite blonde, probably in her early forties. Paul made the introductions and then Jamison motioned for everyone to go into the theater.

"The show starts any minute," Ron said. "We'll get a chance to talk at the reception afterwards."

There was a reception! Paul hadn't mentioned that either. Cassie just bit her tongue. She took a program from the usher as she entered and followed behind everyone else. She and Paul had to sidle past several people already seated, but ended up sitting in the center just a few rows back. Cassie had only a brief moment to glance at her program which said "A Tribute to Philip Glass" on the cover.

The concert lasted about an hour and a half with a short break. Several groups performed including one from D.C. Paul had previewed the concert as "movie music," but Cassie thought that it was really much more than that. What some people might have found repetitive, she found hypnotic. And she was intrigued by the vocals from operas written by Glass, including one piece in which the singers recited numbers over a narrator.

Afterwards several of the musicians appeared at the reception in the lobby. Cassie wanted to talk to some of them, but found herself immediately cornered by Darlene.

"Honey, you've got a fine lookin' man there," Darlene said in a soft Virginia accent as she approached. Cassie nodded. Darlene was carrying two plastic cups with a red liquid in them and offered one to Cassie. "I thought you might like some punch," Darlene continued. She was wearing a long, lemon-colored dress with an empire waist and bow.

"Thanks," Cassie responded as she took the cup from Darlene's hand.

"Are you guys serious?" she asked.

Cassie was taken aback. "You mean Paul and I?"

"Well yes, dear." Darlene's tone indicated that she thought her meaning was obvious.

"I think so," Cassie responded.

Darlene raised her eyebrows. "Well, it's really none of my business," she continued. "But you know how newlyweds are, even retreads like me. They think it would be great if everyone else shared in the bliss they're feeling."

"I understand," Cassie said in an especially solicitous tone.

Darlene asked Cassie about the concert, and Cassie replied that she liked it very much. Cassie inquired about the piece in which the singers recited numbers. Darlene explained that it came from a very long opera called "Einstein on the Beach."

"I probably shouldn't say this," Darlene continued, "but my brother emailed me a couple of links—because he knows I'm involved with the opera—spoofs of Philip Glass. And when they did that piece from 'Einstein on the Beach,' all I could think of was PDQ Bach's spoof. I think it's called 'Prelude to Einstein on the Fritz.'"

"PDQ Bach?"

"Peter Schickele. He spoofs classical music mostly. Very funny stuff. And then there was this short play called 'Philip

Glass Buys a Loaf of Bread.' I had tears in my eyes from laughing." Darlene paused for a moment. "As funny as they were, I wish my brother hadn't sent those links to me *before* the concert."

Cassie discerned what she was in for and determined not to spend the rest of the evening talking with Darlene. "Look, ah, I need to talk to one of the musicians, so—"

"Oh, that's all right, honey, you go right ahead," Darlene said. "We'll talk later."

Darlene had a big smile on her face, but Cassie sensed that she was a little disappointed. Nevertheless, Cassie moved toward one of the musicians she recognized from the D.C.-based group. He wore a sport jacket, turtleneck and dress slacks, all black. His short brown hair spiked up a bit at the top of his forehead, and he was graying almost imperceptibly at the temples. His unusually smooth face made the intensity of his brown eyes stand out. At that moment he appeared lost in thought. He looked like a mannequin into whose hand someone had wedged a plastic glass filled with the same red punch she was carrying.

"Thank you for a wonderful performance," Cassie said as she approached him.

He jerked his head in her direction awakening from his momentary reverie. "You're very welcome," the man said in an accent Cassie thought was probably Russian. "So, you liked all the pieces?"

"All the ones you did," she responded.

"So, there were ones you didn't like?"

"Well…the piece with just two notes and those unexpected crashes on the drums…"

The musician chuckled. "Yes, I think to a lot of people it sounds like a cellist tuning while someone occasionally throws a firecracker at him. I admit it is an acquired taste to like music that simple and crazy. It's not Philip Glass, so I'm not sure why they played it."

"Do you play here often?"

"This was the first time, but I hope we get asked back," he said. "People actually listened."

"Did you ever meet Philip Glass?"

"Several times, mostly at concerts. I would get myself invited backstage to fawn over him a little bit." He took a sip from his punch glass.

"Is that a Russian accent I hear?"

"Yes, what's left of it. I've been here 18 years now. I don't suppose I will ever actually get rid of it. But why should I? People seem to find it charming when you speak English with a funny accent."

"Well, *I* find it charming."

The musician snorted mildly and put on a broad smile.

"I am so rude," he said as he gestured with his free hand. "I haven't even introduced myself. Victor Chernov. And you are?"

"Cassie Young."

They shook hands. Through the glass wall directly behind Victor, Cassie could see the last bit of summer dusk fading into night. An exterior light attached to an overhang started to flicker on, and under it several concertgoers were enjoying a long awaited smoke.

"What brings you to George Mason University tonight — I mean other than an interest in Philip Glass?" Victor asked.

"Actually, I came with friends." She couldn't believe she was saying this. But for some reason she didn't want this man to know that she had come with her boyfriend.

"And you're from this area?" Victor asked.

"Yes, I live in the District."

"So do I," Victor responded. "Would you like a card with our website so you and your friends will know where we are playing?"

"That would be great," Cassie responded. Victor pulled a card from his coat pocket and handed it to her. "When did you come to the United States?" she asked as she slipped the card into her dress pocket.

"In 1990 when things were falling apart in Russia, my family and I emigrated."

"Have you been back?"

"Several times. I have many friends and relatives still there, mostly in Moscow."

"Are you glad you came here?"

"Some days, yes. Like today, I get to meet a beautiful new fan who likes my music."

Cassie smiled. "And on other days?"

"Other days I remember that what I saw in Russia is coming here, too."

At that moment Cassie felt someone clasping her arm from behind. It was Paul, and he had startled her a bit. But she recovered herself. "Victor, I'd like you to meet Paul Hendler," Cassie said. "Paul, this is Victor Chernov."

"You must be one of Cassie's friends," Chernov said maintaining a charming half-smile.

Paul looked a little puzzled as the two men shook hands. "I really enjoyed your music," Paul said.

"Thank you so much," Chernov replied. "Cassie has a card for our website. Perhaps you can come to see us again some time."

"That would be great," Paul said. "Well, I need to introduce Cassie to some people, so if you'll excuse us?"

Cassie didn't want to end her conversation with Victor, but now she found herself being pulled away. She waved politely to him as she walked with Paul toward a group of people that included Ron and Darlene.

Paul did, in fact, introduce her to several of the other salespeople attending the concert. But they all seemed more interested in talking shop than talking with her. She turned from the circle to see if Victor was still there, but he was gone. She surveyed the lobby, but couldn't find him.

After enduring another half hour of conversations in which she was basically a mere bystander, she suggested to Paul that they drive back to the city. He looked at his watch and agreed.

They left the lobby, found the Land Cruiser in the parking ramp, and were soon on the highway. A heavy rain started up. The metronomic beat of the wipers accompanied sheets of water that were pelting the windshield.

"How did you like the concert?" Paul asked.

"I really liked it," Cassie said.

"See, I knew you would."

"And you?"

"It's not what I expected," Paul replied. "Ron told me a Philip Glass knock-knock joke that I think gets it perfectly."

"Which is?"

"Knock, knock. Who's there? Knock, knock. Who's there? Knock, knock. Who's there? Knock, knock. Who's there? Knock, knock. Who's there? Philip Glass."

Cassie laughed. "Still, I liked the music."

"I saw you talking to Darlene, but not for very long," Paul continued.

If he was going to register a complaint, so could she. "I would have liked to have finished my conversation with that musician."

"Part of the reason for coming was to introduce you to people. I wish you had talked to Darlene a little longer."

"Oh, don't be so whiny, Paul," Cassie replied.

"I'm not being whiny," he said. "I'm just telling you what I want."

"I'm not a babysitter for your boss or his wife or your friends at work. These people are all grown-ups. I think they can take care of themselves."

"Ouch!"

Paul was silent after that. In fact, he didn't say another word the whole way. That's how he got when his feelings were hurt. Mute. She knew it wasn't so much to punish her as to nurse his injuries in solitude.

When they were parked in the drop-off area in front of her condo building, Paul leaned over and gave Cassie a perfunctory kiss on the cheek.

"Don't be mad at me," she said.

"I'll be over it by tomorrow," Paul responded without turning to look at her.

Cassie patted him on the knee and got out of the car. When she reached her condo, she could think of nothing but sleep, and within five minutes she had her nightgown on, climbed into bed and quickly dozed off.

≈ **chapter 3** ≈

On weekends Cassie often pedaled her bicycle to Rock Creek Park to ride the trails there. Today, she reveled in the cool, cloudy quietude of the Saturday morning streets. The pavement was still wet from an early morning rain, and passing cars splashed water from the puddles. She got going so fast on the stretch right before the park that a little splatter from her tires sprinkled her face.

When she reached the P Street bridge over Rock Creek, she made her way down onto the bike trail which paralleled the parkway and creek below. The thick, arching canopy of green over the trail soon gave way to a tan-colored stone arch that served as a footing for one of the bridges spanning the park. The underside of Washington looked as much like Rome as the topside did like Greece. The ideals of ancient Greece on the surface, she thought, but the decadence of ancient Rome underneath.

Joggers, walkers, cyclists, and couples with baby carriages crossed her path as the low chirping of the cicadas and crickets competed with the loud hum of the traffic roaring along the parkway nearby. When the arched underside of the Connecticut Avenue bridge appeared, her chain slipped off while she was changing gears, and she was forced to stop.

She set her bike against one of the signs next to a circuit training station, one for sit-ups it seemed. She was about to kneel down to fix the chain when she spotted Victor Chernov riding a bicycle in her direction. Cassie waved to him, but she could see on his face that he wasn't sure who she was. Then his face lit up, and he slowed as he approached.

"Having problems?" he asked as he stopped.

"The chain slipped off," she said.

"Cassie, right?"

"Right."

"Where is your friend?" Victor asked.

Cassie had to think a minute. "Oh yes, Paul. He doesn't particularly like biking."

"Do you come here often?"

"Almost always on the weekends when I'm in town. And sometimes on the weekdays if I don't stay at work too late."

"I like it here, too," Victor said. "Did you know that in the Washington area four geologic provinces come together? For instance, you can see the Piedmont right here, which is coughing up all the large stones in this creek, and below us — "

"Yeah, I know," Cassie said. "Are you a geologist in addition to being a musician?" she asked.

"My uncle was one, and he used to take me rock hunting," Victor replied. "Say, have you had a chance to see the gems and minerals exhibit at the Smithsonian? It's one of my favorites."

"No, I've been traveling so much since I moved here that I haven't had time to see the city really."

"Would you like to see it today?"

"The city or the exhibit at the Smithsonian?"

"Maybe a little bit of both," Victor replied.

Cassie thought for a minute. "Sure, why not? When?"

"How about right now?"

"Okay," Cassie said nodding. "I suppose there's no particular dress code at the Smithsonian."

"I often get around on a bicycle, and I can assure you, they have let me in looking like this," Victor said. That was a good thing because she was wearing a black and yellow striped top and matching bicycle shorts. Victor wore a top with large black and white checks, and he had on black bicycle shorts and black shoes. He stood with his bicycle under him—a carbon-fiber Cannondale, nicer and a lot more expensive than her Trek. He seemed to be about the same height as Cassie. Strange, she hadn't remembered looking him more or less in the eye when they'd met at the concert. But that's how it must have been.

"All right," Cassie said. "Let me reset my chain and we'll go."

Once she was done and had cleaned the grease from her hands using some wipes that she carried, they were off to the museum.

When they arrived, Victor suggested they tether their bikes to the railing on the steps facing the National Mall. Not far away a juggler appeared to be keeping a tennis racket, a basketball and a bowling ball aloft. Cassie pointed him out to Victor and wondered aloud if the bowling ball could be for real.

After securing their bikes, they walked up the steps and through the museum entrance. A guard searched their backpacks, and they both passed through metal detectors. After retrieving their backpacks, Victor led Cassie directly to the gems and minerals exhibit. On the way Cassie told him that her father had been a geologist, and although she had never had any formal training, she learned a lot of geology from him.

As they entered the dim gallery, Cassie spotted a piece of leucophoenicite. She'd seen it before on field trips with her father. This piece looked like a slice of chocolate cake with pistachio and raspberry filling. She mentioned the resemblance to Victor, and he concurred. After that their eyes scanned for mineral samples that looked like food. A mineral called scheelite, transparent and pinkish brown, looked like a piece of crystallized ginger to Victor. The calcite, they agreed, seemed to be made of marzipan. Something called elbaite gave the appearance of great sticks of hard candy, both lime and raspberry. Lots of raspberry, Cassie noted. The gypsum looked like flakes of milk chocolate, Victor suggested. It was as if the flakes had been piled up on a plate in random positions and then been melted slightly and resolidified. Cassie said she wanted to take a piece of fluorite home since it looked like raspberry cake with raspberry frosting.

There were huge topazes that were bluish, amber and clear. One amber topaz was as large as a tree stump. There was a specimen of aragonite that looked like the open jaws of a shark. And there was pyrite, fool's gold, some of which was formed into such perfect shiny cubes that they seemed to have come from a factory rather than nature.

They wandered through the gem collection as well, but Cassie thought that only the Hope Diamond had beauty that rivaled that of the natural crystals they had just seen.

As they walked out of the exhibit, Victor launched into a disquisition on the wonders of geology. It determines where waters flow, and thus where cities are founded, he said. It determines which land is fertile and which is barren. It deposits minerals in concentrations useful to human civilization. Indeed, those minerals are like food—as Cassie had so aptly imagined them to be—as essential to the complex workings of modern society as real food is to the survival of human beings. On top of this, geology has a role in regulating climate through its interactions with the atmosphere.

"Geology does all this so slowly and imperceptibly," Victor concluded, "that it is easy to forget that geology is destiny. There's simply no getting around it."

It was early afternoon when they finished their tour. Victor said that all the imagined desserts in the minerals gallery had stimulated his appetite. He suggested that they ride up to one of his favorite restaurants, The Iron Gate, and have lunch. Cassie recognized the name. The restaurant was not too far from Dupont Circle where she worked.

When they arrived, they locked their bikes to the namesake black iron gate at the entrance. Then they walked under an arch and through a passage between two buildings until they reached an outdoor brick patio covered by trellises draped in a sinewy tangle of leafy grapevines.

A waiter escorted them across the patio to a table next to the trunk of a tree that was growing up through the trellis. After the two of them were seated, Victor ordered a glass of red wine.

"Any wine for you?" Victor asked.

"No," said Cassie. "I want to be awake for lunch." She turned her attention to the waiter. "I'll just have some iced tea." The waiter nodded and retreated toward the kitchen.

"Have you eaten here before?" Victor inquired as he picked up the menu.

"Just had some drinks after work one time."

"I hope you didn't fall asleep."

"I hadn't been riding then. Just sitting all day."

"How about I order us a couple of appetizers to share?" Victor asked.

"That would be fine."

Victor said he would get the stuffed grape leaves and the goat cheese torte, which he called "magnificent." The waiter came with their drinks, and Victor ordered the appetizers, indicating that the two of them would order entrées later.

"Tell me about yourself," Victor said.

"What do you want to know?" Cassie asked.

"You said you work near here."

"Yes, on 19th Street, just off the circle."

"And what do you do on 19th Street just off the circle?" Victor had a slight smile on his face as if to acknowledge that Cassie was forcing him to ask for each bit of information.

"I work for Energy Advisers International as an oil and gas analyst."

"You work for them?"

"You make it sound bad."

"No, no. You must be a real big shot to work there."

"I'm not really a big shot."

"Oh, don't be so humble."

"The truth is I got the job because a longtime friend of my father's recruited me."

"He must think you are good."

"I suppose so." Cassie paused for a moment as the waiter lowered the appetizer plates onto the dark red tablecloth. "Oh, that torte looks good." Cassie served herself a piece, as did Victor. She took a bite. He was definitely right about the torte. She noticed that Victor was looking intently at her as she chewed.

"I'll let you have the rest of it just to see that look on your face," he said.

"You're sounding almost lewd," Cassie retorted.

"I enjoy other people's enjoyment. It makes my life twice as enjoyable." Victor finally took a bite of the torte.

"Now, getting back to our conversation," Cassie continued. "How do you know about EAI? That's the kind of thing usually only industry insiders know."

"Well, I suppose you could call me an industry insider," Victor responded. "I used to trade oil futures in New York."

"No kidding." Cassie sat up in her seat.

"Yes, I worked for one of the big commodity houses, first as a computer guy and then as a floor trader. After that, I managed commodity funds for them; and finally, I started my own hedge fund."

"And that's what you are doing now?"

"Oh, no," Victor said shaking his head. "I disbanded the fund two years ago."

"So, now you're making a living as a musician?"

He laughed. "That would be very nice. But it's really just a hobby."

"So you're—"

"I'm hanging out in Washington with some musician

friends because I'm a good pianist; and yes, with what I made on the hedge fund, it doesn't matter whether I make a living as a musician."

"Oh, I see."

"Does life seem a bit unfair now? Even from where you work at the fancy consulting firm?"

"I didn't mean *that*."

"It's all right."

They both concentrated on finishing the appetizers for a couple of minutes. Cassie looked beyond the half wall of red brick that defined the edge of the patio and could see that the sun had finally broken through the clouds. A delicious, light breeze was blowing on them. The city's usual summer mugginess was taking a break.

The waiter approached and asked for their orders. Victor got the lamb shank and Cassie ordered the tuna kabob. She also asked the waiter to set aside a piece of raspberry cheesecake so she could make sure she got one.

"Perhaps we should go straight to dessert," Victor said after the waiter had gone.

"Well, I have been known to do just that," Cassie replied.

"All right, so, what can you tell me about oil?" Victor asked.

"You mean that you don't already know," Cassie retorted.

"Are you doing some kind of report now maybe?"

"I just got back from the oil sands in Canada."

"Are they going to save the world?"

"*They* think they are."

"What do *you* think?"

"I think they're going to wreck northern Alberta trying to."

"And will they succeed at saving the world?"

"Do you think the world needs saving, Victor?"

"It most certainly does. But the world doesn't even know it."

"You said the other night that what you saw in Russia is coming here. What did you mean by that?"

"Collapse…financial collapse, peak oil collapse, climate collapse, take your pick."

Cassie focused in on the words "peak oil." The concept was really the product of some fringe petroleum geologists who theorized that the world was coming to the point where it wouldn't be able to grow petroleum supplies anymore. Some of them predicted that production would decline rapidly after the peak and that that would cause a financial and social collapse. Surely someone as intelligent as Victor, an oil trader no less, wouldn't fall for this apocalyptic claptrap.

"So you think oil is peaking?" Cassie asked.

"Yes, very soon. Maybe even this year," Victor responded. "That's why I closed down my fund. Our focus was oil, and I don't think there's going to be much oil trading in the future. Oil will be too precious. Everything will be locked up with contracts. No freely trading oil, and so, nothing for a trader like me to do."

"I can't believe someone of your intelligence would buy into such a crackpot idea."

"So, what do *you* think?"

"Well, our firm forecasts that we have at least three decades, maybe more, before oil production hits a plateau. And we believe that plateau will go on for several more decades," she explained. "That's plenty of time to develop new energy sources."

"I already know what your firm believes. I want to know what *you* believe."

"I think they're right."

Victor snorted mildly as he smiled, shook his head and looked down.

"What?" Cassie said.

"Let's take your tar sands," Victor began. "You don't go looking for oil in gunky tar sands unless all the easy-to-get stuff is gone. And yet, this is what is going to fill the gap 20, 30, 40 years from now according to you?"

"Yes, I guess you could say that."

"And how many millions of barrels a day are these tar sands supposed to give us?"

"We project five million by 2030."

"And that's out of how many the world will be using by then, that is, according to your calculations?"

"Out of approximately 113 million."

"Even if they do it—which I doubt, because they'll run out of water or natural gas to process it—it's a drop in the bucket. Oil from tar sands is so hard to get that you can't produce it very fast."

Victor was starting to infuriate her. He wasn't looking at the whole picture. Sure, he was an oil trader. But oil traders look at the very short term for the most part. That's not the same as studying the long-term trends which she had done for years.

"But Victor, you're just looking at a small piece of the puzzle. What about all the deepwater deposits? We've only just begun to explore those all over the world. That's where the big growth is going to come from."

"All right, okay," he said. "Take this Mooney-3 discovery well. It's supposed to be the first of many that will bring us 15 billion barrels of oil from the middle of the Gulf of Mexico. Well, you don't go 200 miles out into the gulf unless you've basically found all the easy stuff on land and close to shore."

Victor was getting agitated now. He had been calm up to that point. But Cassie had obviously hit on something that pushed a button. "And even if there are 15 billion barrels there, that's only a *six-month supply* for the world," he continued. "And they never mention the low estimate of three billion barrels; it's too depressing. Now, I predict the oil they found in the Mooney-3 well will turn out to be too costly to produce, and they'll end up capping it." He emphasized this last point with a wave of his finger.

"But Victor," Cassie said, "you're underestimating advances

in technology. You're acting as if we're still in the Stone Age. And if people like you were in charge, we still *would* be." Cassie didn't mean for the last sentence to come out. But she was getting agitated, too. She couldn't abide sloppy thinking like Victor's.

"Technology is like fairy dust to you," he retorted. "You sprinkle some on the tar sands and magically their output goes up four times." Victor was wiggling his fingers like a magician, first to one side, then to the other. "You sprinkle some on the ocean and magically oil that is 30,000 feet down becomes easy to produce." Victor leaned forward. "Yes, Cassie, we have technology. But now geology is winning the contest between the two. Remember: geology is destiny. You can't get away from it no matter how much fairy dust you spread around."

"Victor, maybe we should talk about something else."

He raised both hands as if to surrender. "Okay, okay. That's fine."

"Tell me about your family," Cassie said. At this point the waiter laid their entrées on the table.

Victor explained that he and his younger sister came to the United States with their parents. Fortunately, the family already had relatives living in New York City, and so they had a place to stay while Victor's father, a computer programmer, found work. Victor's mother taught piano lessons and had performed in Moscow many times when they lived there. His sister was now married and living in Vermont. His parents were living in New York still. His father was semi-retired though his mother was still taking the full complement of piano students.

"And what about you?" Cassie asked.

"What do you mean?" Victor responded.

"Do you live alone?"

"Oh, yes. But I didn't always. I married a Russian woman soon after my family arrived in New York. It didn't work out.

We lasted six months," he explained. "And how about you?"

"No brothers or sisters. My father died three years ago," Cassie said.

"I'm sorry to hear that."

"We were devastated. It was a heart attack with no warning. But he had a good life." She could feel a lump in her throat, but she pressed on with her explanation. "He wanted to teach geology at the university, and that's what he did until the day he died. And he got to travel and be outdoors a lot when he did his research." She paused for a moment to recover herself. "My mother still lives in Chicago. She works as a bookkeeper."

Now what will the two of them talk about, Cassie wondered, if they can't discuss the one thing they both know the most about? Cassie asked Victor about his group and the kind of music they played. She found him interesting, but his crazy views on energy chafed at her, even made her feel uncomfortable, since she would have to avoid the one subject that was at the center of her life.

When the bill arrived, Victor insisted on paying. When Cassie protested, Victor said she could pay next time. Except Cassie didn't think there would be a next time. After the bill was taken care of, they both got up and made their way to the entrance. As they freed their bikes from the front gate, Victor asked if the two of them might have lunch again sometime. Cassie only managed a "maybe," and she could see that Victor was disheartened by her response.

"Thank you for a wonderful day," he called out as she rode off.

"Bye, now," was all that came out of her mouth as she pedaled away into the street.

≈ **chapter 4** ≈

Cassie was filing into the conference room behind several colleagues for the 9 o'clock Monday morning meeting at EAI. At the same time a man who had just finished talking to Larry Hilliard, the chairman of EAI, came toward her and the others, excused himself as he squeezed past, and exited the conference room. A minute later the wall clock registered nine, and people quickly sat down in the brown leather chairs on either side of the long, dark walnut conference table.

Hilliard remained standing at one end. He was dressed in a black suit with red pinstripes and a red tie over his white shirt. Hilliard was medium height — Cassie had to look down slightly when they stood face to face — and he had a somewhat corpulent build. In his mid-fifties, Hilliard's thinning wiry reddish hair never seemed to be quite in order. When Cassie first met him, she thought he had a slightly nerdy look, and his round face, rectangular black-rimmed glasses and perpetual grin only accentuated this impression. But this was definitely revenge of the nerds, for he was now one of the most influential energy analysts on the planet.

"Good morning," Hilliard began. He leaned on the conference table and looked at his notes. "All right." He looked up again. "First, we've got an invitation from Breckenridge Oil for a visit and briefing on the Mooney-3 results."

"I thought we had the Houston office on this," said one of Cassie's male colleagues.

"We do," Hilliard responded. "But they really want somebody from our main office to be briefed. And I think, as big as this thing is, we ought to have someone from this office go down and look things over. So Cassie, would you like to take a trip to Houston this week?"

Cassie was a bit surprised. Something this important was usually assigned to a senior analyst. "Sure, Larry. I'd love to go," she said.

"Great, great!" he said, bobbing his head up and down a bit. Hilliard always seemed to project a cheerful countenance. But he appeared more animated than usual over something as routine as a junior analyst accepting an assignment. He turned to his assistant who was standing behind him. "Cecilia, please take care of Cassie's travel arrangements." Cecilia made a note as Hilliard was speaking.

The meeting lasted for another 20 minutes or so which was about average. Nothing else caught Cassie by surprise. But being assigned to visit Breckenridge Oil to discuss the Mooney-3 discovery was all the surprise she wanted for now.

After the meeting Evan Grant approached her and asked her to come into his office. Evan had met her father when they were in graduate school together. They became and remained friends until the day Cassie's father died. Unlike her father, Evan had chosen to use his geology Ph.D. to pursue a career in the oil industry. That career had brought him to EAI more than a decade ago.

Evan, like Hilliard, was in his mid-fifties, but trim and more nattily dressed. He preferred suits made in London, the city of his youth. He had only come to America in his twenties to pursue his doctoral studies. His graying wavy blond hair seemed almost to match the linen suit he was wearing. His well-preserved face and natural glad-handing disposition allowed him to project an energetic and youthful spirit.

Cassie had known Evan since she was a child, and in some ways she regarded him as an uncle. But now he was her boss, and she felt she needed to respect their new relationship.

"Have a seat, love," Evan said as he ushered her into his office and closed the door. "Love" was a British term of endearment which Evan often used when talking to her because he knew her so well. But he was careful not to use it with any of the other women in the office lest they take offense.

Cassie sat down in one of the oxblood leather chairs facing Evan's burgundy-stained walnut desk. Behind it was a tall matching credenza filled with books that were visible through the glass-paned doors. There were several floor-to-ceiling bookcases and wainscoting along the walls which made the office look more like a study than a place of business.

Evan walked behind his desk, began to sit down, but then straightened up again and clasped his hands together. "I have some good news for you," he said sporting a wide, somewhat toothy grin. "Congratulations, you're now a senior associate." He reached across the desk and offered his hand. She rose and shook hands with him, and then Evan continued. "Larry didn't want us to wait the full 18 months, and I agreed. We both thought you deserved the promotion now."

"I don't know what to say," Cassie replied.

"You don't have to say anything, love. Just keep doing the great work you're doing."

"That's what I intend to do."

"There he is now," said Evan pointing to one of the four television sets recessed into the built-in bookcases. Cassie turned around and looked. One television was tuned to CNN, another to CNBC, a third to C-SPAN on which Hilliard was currently filling the screen, and a fourth was off. Cassie remembered that Hilliard had given testimony before Congress the week before.

"Turn it up for a minute," Cassie requested.

"Sure," Evan replied as he reached for the remote.

What Hilliard had to say was no surprise. He was telling Congress that the oil price spike was only temporary, that there was plenty of oil for decades to come, and that he was forecasting prices to return to around $55 a barrel within a year. If there were any problems with oil supplies in the next two to three decades, they would be due to aboveground factors, not the availability of oil under the ground, he said. And the crawler over on CNBC was proving his point as a report came across about an attack by rebels on Nigerian oil installations, just one of the many aboveground factors that had sent the price of crude to $106 a barrel that morning.

Evan muted the sound, and Cassie turned back to face him. "Great visibility. That's why we love him. He keeps us in work." Evan then leaned toward Cassie. "I'm going to tell you something I'm not supposed to," he said.

"Which is?" Cassie leaned toward him.

"EAI is working on a possible merger deal with GCC, you know, the old General Consulting Corporation. It probably won't go through this year, so that means we may have time to make you a partner. Then you could share in the windfall that will come from that merger," Evan explained. "Now Larry likes you so much that I think he'll support an early partnership. And I think his support would bring along enough partners to make it happen."

"Do I need to do anything?" Cassie inquired.

"No, love. Just keep going in the direction you're going. Let Larry and me do the rest."

"Okay."

"And don't breathe a word."

"Absolutely not."

"All right. Go knock 'em dead in Houston." Evan looked away from her for a moment. "Did I get that right?"

He was always teasing her and pretending he didn't understand American idioms even though he'd lived in the United States for 30 years.

"That's the ticket, mate," she said in the best English accent she could muster. Evan laughed.

≈ **chapter 5** ≈

Two days later Cassie was on a plane to Houston. She had to get up at 4:30 in the morning to catch an early flight that would put her at Breckenridge headquarters for a noon briefing and luncheon.

As her plane approached Houston, she could see the shoreline of Lake Livingston through the wispy clouds. Tightly spaced houses with boat docks jutting into the lake were interspersed with long, undulating stretches of wooded shoreline. The Trinity River had been dammed here to store water for Houston and the surrounding communities. Just beyond the lake was a large patch of green which she knew was the Sam Houston National Forest. In the forest Cassie spied the San Jacinto River lazily cutting S-curves that had helped to deposit some of the miles-deep sediments which characterize the Texas coastal plain—sediments that created ideal conditions for the formation of oil and natural gas.

Once inside the airport she rode down an escalator into Intercontinental's baggage claim area and spied a driver holding a sheet with her last name on it in large, bold letters. When she reached him, she introduced herself, shaking the hand of this man who had salt and pepper hair and a goatee. He wore a black suit and tie which Cassie thought looked altogether too warm for Houston.

He took her suitcase, escorted her to a black Lincoln Town Car outside, and opened the door for her. After she was in, he closed the door and then put her bag in the trunk. They drove out onto a pleasant green boulevard, but soon got up onto I-45. This road Cassie regarded as the ugliest in Houston. An almost seamless stretch of strip malls, I-45 from the airport to downtown was lined with fast food restaurants, car dealerships, discount furniture places, 24-hour newsstands — which were nothing more than porn shops with peep shows — and, of course, strip joints with names like Moments, Ice Cream Castle, and Fantasy Plaza. Judging from the billboards alongside the interstate, however, the owners preferred the term "gentlemen's club."

Insurance offices abounded as well. Someone had explained to Cassie on one of her previous trips to Houston that these offices thrived on selling auto insurance — which is mandatory in Texas — to the many poor who could only afford to pay a month at a time. And, of course, these customers ended up paying two and three times the true cost of the insurance.

Everywhere signs on long skinny poles shot up to announce the stores and service stations along the interstate. For the first time Cassie noticed some Spanish-language billboards, though she thought she must have missed them on previous trips.

About 20 minutes after leaving the airport, the downtown became visible, a tightly packed set of mostly glass and steel towers that looked to Cassie like a tall but lonely grove on an otherwise barren savanna. Houston, she had once read, had tried to make its downtown look like Manhattan. But whereas much of Manhattan is rock, Houston sits on soft clay and other sediments that are miles deep. She remembered writer John McPhee describing the skyscrapers as duckpins sitting in clay — clay which turns to jelly when it's wet. Houston is sinking year after year into that jelly, and there's nothing anyone can do about it.

The driver exited onto McKinney Street and stopped at a light across from city hall, a sturdy art deco affair. Opposite it was the public library, a modernist tan block building with a bright red metal sculpture in front. Someone had told her the sculpture was supposed to be a mouse. She could see the ears now, but the poor thing appeared to have fallen on its side.

The light changed and soon they reached Smith Street where they turned right passing in front of the Wells Fargo Plaza, a sleek glass skyscraper with rounded edges. The buildings on Smith now towered above them forming a narrow canyon. Along both sides, live oaks of various heights were growing. Some reached maybe 20 feet in the air; others, much shorter and probably recently transplanted, had guy wires to support the trunks.

The car passed a pink granite building that housed pipeline giant Enbridge. Along the front stood men and women smoking, some leaning with their backs up against the granite, others standing and talking in groups of two or three.

The car halted again at the next intersection. A group of men in shirtsleeves and women in summer dresses crossed in front. They were probably headed for lunch, Cassie thought. In Washington, even on hot summer days, she would often see men in suit coats on the street. Nobody seemed to be bothering with that here. Just then two bicycle messengers sailed by, one right after the other. The light changed to green, and the driver pulled up to Allen Center, her destination. In front of the two Allen Center towers, Kinder Morgan, another pipeline giant, and Devon, the shale gas driller, had both planted signs in a small strip of grass. The towers were essentially boxes with concrete lattices and windows which gave the impression of a computer punch card with all the punches taken out. Farther down the street she could see the shiny, oval towers that used to be owned by Enron before it collapsed. Now these towers were occupied by Chevron. She had arrived at the heart of the energy city.

Cassie opened the car door, and the broiling downtown heat hit her face. She got out before the driver arrived to help her, and so he retreated to the trunk to get her suitcase. She thanked him and then proceeded through a glass entrance, up an escalator and into a lobby with cream-colored marble floors and walls. She turned down a corridor which led to the elevators. She had been in this building before, just not to visit Breckenridge Oil. She got onto the elevator alone and pressed 29. Just as the doors were about to shut, someone reached in with a clipboard, and the doors bounced open. A messenger wearing an orange helmet and blue shorts got on.

"Sorry, ma'am," he said. Cassie smiled and nodded.

She got off on the 29th floor and left the messenger behind. At one end of the hall Cassie saw the Breckenridge name on a glass entryway and headed toward it. As she went in, the receptionist got up to greet her. Cassie asked if she might leave her suitcase at the front. But the receptionist said she'd been asked to run it over to the hotel connected to the center, check her in, and bring back her key card. How nice, Cassie thought. She abandoned her suitcase, but kept her shoulder bag, and the woman escorted Cassie to what she recognized as a 3-D seismic visualization room where she was introduced to several Breckenridge people by Julian Voss, the company's vice president for exploration. Standing in Voss's vicinity were Breckenridge's chief geologist; another staff geologist, the only other woman in the room; the vice president for communications; two computer specialists who apparently had responsibility for putting together today's presentation; and the chief financial officer.

After everyone sat down, Voss, a tall, lanky man with deep divots in his cheeks and thinning black hair, moved to the front of the room. He was dressed in a white, long-sleeved shirt and a red-and-black striped tie. Cassie thought he might be in his fifties.

"We want to welcome Ms. Cassie Young from EAI. She has come to take a look at our work on Mooney-3, the deepest successful well test so far in the Gulf of Mexico," Voss said.

He spoke with a Texas drawl as thick as she had ever heard. "Now, I'm gonna get right to the presentation 'cause I know that everyone's gonna want to eat lunch soon, especially Ms. Young here who has traveled all the way from Washington today to be with us."

Voss told everyone to put on their 3-D glasses as he began. The images started to appear on the large screen that filled one side of the room. Cassie felt as if she had stepped into the earth itself. Suspended in space were flowing shapes of deep green and splashes of red and blue, all of which seemed as if they were features on a topographical map that could be touched. Voss explained that the green area represented oil reservoirs, the red, gas reservoirs, and the blue represented water under the seabed. It was a color scheme Cassie had seen used before in other similar presentations. A long thin line piercing a large green zone represented the Mooney-3 drill path. He let everyone wander for a couple of minutes through the virtual maze. Then a large gray cube suddenly showed up and covered the area around the drill site. Voss asked everyone to notice the numerous green areas that appeared as the gray cube slowly retracted, revealing slice after slice of the deep seabed. This, he explained, represented potential finds near the already discovered reservoir.

He then changed the presentation and discussed two other nearby unexplored areas for which seismic data had become available. He put on a similar show but without, of course, any drill paths displayed. Again, everyone had a chance to wander in the virtual subterranean canyons. As they moved, he explained why he thought these areas had excellent potential.

He then had everyone take off their 3-D glasses, asked them to sit at the table behind them, and continued his presentation with conventional slides, several of which contained information on the Mooney-3 well. He included a summary of other deepwater exploration efforts in the gulf and finally reviewed the results of the Mooney-3 flow test, the one that gave the company great hope that it had found a major field in the deepwater gulf. Voss added that Breckenridge was evaluating its results and would announce plans for delineation wells in the near future. Cassie took some notes, but the presentation was pretty much what she had expected.

When Voss seemed to have finished, Cassie began asking a question, but he cut her off. "Ms. Young, why don't we bring in lunch, and while we're all eatin', we'll answer any questions you like?" he said.

"That's fine with me," she replied.

Voss signaled to someone standing near the door. A minute later several servers, men and women in black vests, appeared and began setting elegantly prepared spinach salads in front of everyone. Voss gestured to one of his associates—the head geologist, Cassie realized—and the man got up from the chair next to her. Then Voss walked over and sat in the vacated chair.

By this time there were several conversations taking place around the table as both she and Voss put fork to salad.

"What do you think of our little discovery?" Voss asked as he put some of the spinach salad into his mouth.

"I'm impressed," Cassie replied. "But I have a number of questions if you don't mind."

"Go right ahead," he responded in a slightly muffled tone as he finished chewing his salad.

Cassie asked him about the quality of the oil, something he hadn't mentioned in his presentation. The numbers Voss then gave her meant that the crude oil would probably be acceptable to most refineries in the United States. Cassie began jotting down some notes. She then asked about the sulfur content, something that had to be reduced if it were too high in order to meet auto emission standards. Voss said the company had gotten inconsistent analyses and was rechecking them. He'd get back to her on that.

Cassie queried him about getting the oil to market. Voss

admitted that there weren't any undersea pipelines nearby to hook into, and so any oil produced would have to be loaded onto tankers for storage and transport. That would, of course, be more expensive. Voss added that there was some natural gas dissolved in the oil, but without pipelines there was no practical way to get the gas to market.

As they talked, the entrée arrived, a Dover sole, Cassie discerned, a first-class meal definitely designed to impress her. A wonderful lemon-sage scent rose off the plate as the server placed it before her. While everyone ate, Voss went on at length about the great potential for the deepwater gulf and why Breckenridge was positioned to benefit from the boom he saw. Cassie probed Voss about what he knew concerning the results of other companies exploring the deepwater area, but his answers were strangely general. It was as if he wanted to avoid details at all costs.

When the dessert arrived — a triple-layered mousse of dark chocolate, milk chocolate and white chocolate in a parfait glass — Voss gulped it down like a hungry child eating ice cream. He pronounced it "very good" as he wiped some excess from his mouth with his white cloth napkin.

Voss told Cassie that he understood that she wanted to see one of the company's deepwater drilling projects firsthand. Since the platform from which the Mooney-3 well had been drilled was no longer on the site, he had made arrangements to fly her out to another exploration platform that was currently drilling. He said he would be unable to accompany her, but that the drilling foreman would meet her there and show her around.

After Cassie had finished her dessert, she thanked Voss for the presentation, and he motioned to the only other woman in the room who came over to them. "Heather is gonna make sure that you get over to the heliport and on your way," Voss said.

Cassie rose from her chair. "When do we go?" she asked.

"Right now," Heather responded.

With that Cassie put her notebook back into her bag, put the carrying strap over her shoulder, and said goodbye to the people in the room, giving a special thank-you to Voss. Then she and Heather made their way to the elevator.

Heather did have a last name. It was Johnston, Heather told her. Cassie had noticed that many Texas men, especially those in the oil business, often seemed to forget that women had last names. Heather was dressed in a blue business suit and wore her blond hair in a ponytail. She was probably about Cassie's age. As they rode down on the elevator, Heather told Cassie that she was Breckenridge's only female petroleum geologist, not surprising given how few women were in the field.

When they reached the street, Heather guided Cassie to a waiting car, and the two of them got into the back for the ride to the heliport.

"Are you a native of Houston?" Cassie asked after the car began moving.

Heather swiveled her body toward Cassie. "Yes, I'm a Houston native, but what I want to say is that it's so nice to meet another woman professional in the oil business." She said the word "oil" as if it were spelled "awl."

"Well, I feel the same way," Cassie said as she chuckled slightly.

"I'm glad you do," Heather replied. "Look, I know that you're here only for today. But you get to Houston often, don't you?"

"Well, so far I've been here three times since I started my current job about a year ago. But this is my first chance to go out on an offshore exploration rig."

"Oh, really," Heather said. "I would have thought with all your experience you would have been out on an offshore rig by now."

"I've visited a lot of land rigs and even been out on an offshore production platform once," Cassie said.

"Well, it's exciting to be on one of those rigs when they're drillin'. All kinds of things goin' on."

"Yes," Cassie replied.

As the two of them continued to chat, Cassie noticed the Houston offices of several major energy companies along their route. Total, the French oil giant, and Eni, the Italian major, were sharing offices, judging by the sign in front of a building at the corner of Louisiana and Dallas. The car turned up Louisiana passing by CenterPoint, the big Texas utility, and The El Paso Corporation, a huge natural gas pipeline company. They turned right on McKinney and soon passed RRI Energy, an owner of power generating stations in several states. The driver paused as Houston's light rail train passed in front of them, a silver-colored, two-car affair with a streamlined nose and tail. Soon they were moving alongside the Houston Center, a huge, two-building complex with a brown anodized aluminum exterior so popular in the 1980s.

"Look, would you let me know next time you're comin' for a visit, and maybe we could go to lunch or somethin'?" Heather asked.

"I'd love that," Cassie said.

The two of them exchanged business cards. Shortly thereafter they arrived at the old Chevron Tower, now called the Fulbright Tower, a soaring glass and steel skyscraper situated diagonally within an entire city block. Heather rode the elevator up to the roof with Cassie where a helicopter was already waiting on the pad.

"Oh, I almost forgot," Heather said as they stepped out onto the roof. She pulled out a hotel key card. "Mandy, our receptionist, gave this to me to give to you. You're all checked in." Cassie took the key card, put it in her pocket and thanked Heather.

"Now, do call me when you come back to Houston," Heather reiterated.

"Yes, I promise."

An attendant opened a low gate at the edge of the helipad and signaled for her to go through. She walked perhaps 15 yards, tossed her shoulder bag into the open helicopter, and then climbed up into what she recognized as a Bell 206. She was getting pretty good at identifying helicopters. The attendant had followed her, and he closed the door behind her. This time she would be alone in the passenger compartment behind the pilot.

The pilot looked to be in his late fifties or maybe early sixties—Cassie couldn't see his whole face to judge properly. He signaled to the attendant that he was ready to go and started up the engine as the attendant hurried to the edge of the pad.

Once they were aloft and drifting away from the towers of Houston's downtown, the pilot said that they would be in flight for a little under two hours. Cassie had gotten used to helicopter flights because so much oil prospecting was done in remote areas. But she'd never had to ride two hours to her destination. She knew that the platform she was visiting was in the deepwater part of the gulf, but hadn't really realized just how far out that was until now.

It took about half an hour before they reached what she knew was Galveston. Then they were finally cruising over the gulf. The sun shone brightly on the gently heaving waters. After they had passed well beyond land, Cassie spotted a few oil and gas platforms and a ship here and there. But mostly what she saw was open water flickering below.

Cassie chatted with the pilot a little, but it was difficult to do so from the passenger compartment. He didn't appear to have much to say about the state of oil exploration in the gulf other than that he was very busy ferrying crews back and forth these days. A deepwater platform like the one he was taking her to would normally have around 120 crew members who would be on for two weeks straight, he explained. Then they would take two weeks off while another crew of

120 relieved them. "Lots of trips back and forth," the pilot said. "Lots of trips."

Finally, she spotted a platform emerging off the horizon. The pilot confirmed that this was their destination. She remembered that she had brought some shoes for walking around on the platform. She pulled them out of her bag and exchanged her unassuming black flats for a pair of multicolored sneakers built from strips of material in purple, black, yellow, and a milky green—a bit garish, but extremely comfortable. She had wisely worn her dark gray pantsuit that day, knowing that she would be touring the platform.

As the helicopter got closer, she saw what looked like something concocted from a child's Erector Set mounted on squat yellow tin cans under each corner. The "tin cans" were the floating legs of this semisubmersible and were anchored to the seabed for stability. The topside was an intricate latticework of metal which included all the necessary drilling equipment and the living quarters for the crew. Two crane booms rose up from the platform on either side of the derrick. And a flatbed service boat of some kind was moored to one of the yellow legs. The helipad, also a bright yellow, jutted off one corner of the platform.

Once the helicopter had landed, Cassie was greeted by a man with curly gray locks flowing freely from under his white hard hat. Dressed in a blue jumpsuit, he had a short gray beard and a tanned, well-lined face. He introduced himself as Conrad Turner, the drilling foreman.

"Welcome aboard the Leopard II," he said as they shook hands.

"Thank you, Mr. Turner," Cassie replied. The smell of the sea filled her nostrils as she looked up at the derrick. It had seemed so small from far away, but now it towered over her even though she was on the next highest spot on the platform.

"Would you like to tour the rig now?" Turner inquired.

"Yes, let's do that," Cassie replied. From Turner's accent she judged he was probably another Texan.

He handed her a white hard hat which she put on. He suggested that she leave her shoulder bag in the helicopter since it would be easier to maneuver on the platform without it. Cassie agreed and deposited the bag back in the helicopter.

Then Turner led her down a metal stairway and along a short walkway where she could smell diesel exhaust that had to be from the engines powering the rig. She looked out beyond the edge of the platform and saw nothing but water all the way to the horizon. When Turner opened a gray metal door at the end of the walkway, the low din she'd been hearing in the background became a loud roar. She entered the room and saw a man in safety glasses and a hard hat who was inspecting something on a huge generator that stood twice as high as he did and extended maybe 40 feet at the base. Cassie counted six of them in the room, all painted bright blue. Turner caught the attention of the man, and he walked over to them.

"This is our motorman, Doug Smith," Turner said in a loud voice. "This is Cassie Young, an oil analyst from Washington." Cassie shook hands with Smith.

"What can I tell you about the power plant, ma'am?" Smith asked.

"How many horsepower do you have available?" she asked.

"When all the engines are runnin' we can generate almost 60,000 horsepower," he replied. "Of course, that's all turned into electricity to run everything from the drawworks all the way down to the refrigerators in the galley."

She thanked the motorman, and then Turner led her through an exit at the far end of the room and out into the open air. From there she could see a gaggle of pipes dangling off the end of one of the cranes. Below it was the flatbed ship from which they'd been plucked, the one she had seen on her approach to the platform. Nearby was a red escape pod that those on the rig could use in case of an emergency. It reminded her of a small cartoon spaceship.

Turner shepherded Cassie down a steep metal stairway past one landing and then down another similarly steep flight of stairs until they reached the pipe deck. Pipes were laid out on racks that took up much of the area. Cassie could see that workers in hard hats on the drill floor above were using a pulley to drag a length of casing pipe from the pipe deck up a steep, almost vertical ramp. Once the casing was dangling in a vertical position above the drill floor, they grabbed it with huge, red power tongs suspended from the derrick and moved the pipe over the wellbore in order to marry it to another piece of casing pipe.

"They just finished pullin' the drillstring," Turner said. "You do know what a drillstring is, don't ya?"

"Of course I do," Cassie replied.

"I ask because we get analyst types out here who don't know the difference between a drillstring, a drill bit, and a drill their daddy uses at home," Turner said.

"I've met them," Cassie said.

"Now they're runnin' pipe to the openhole," he added.

Having been joined together, the two casing pipes were now lowered into the wellbore to make room for more pipe, and then the entire procedure was repeated. The purpose was to seal the well from seepage and protect it from a cave-in.

"They'll be at it for a while," Turner said. "Why don't we go to the mess and get somethin' to drink?"

Turner led her back up two flights of stairs to the living quarters. As they entered, the air conditioning felt downright cold after the hot, humid deck. While they walked, Turner pointed occasionally and announced what they were seeing. They passed by the infirmary, which was empty; the laundry, which had a couple of men folding clothes; a recreation room in which a spirited match of Ping-Pong was taking place with several onlookers cheering the participants; a workout area, where both of the treadmills were occupied and several people were straining in various postures around the weight machine; a lounge with a large, flat-screen TV where a worker in a baseball cap was sitting on a cushioned bench strumming a guitar; and finally the cabins. Cassie paused to look into one that was open. It had a metal bunk bed with a ladder, a small desk with a lamp, and a tiny bathroom.

"That one's unoccupied," Turner said. "I could rent it to you cheap." He smiled.

They arrived in the dining area, a windowless room with tubular metal chairs and round, blond-colored Formica tables. The galley staff was setting up the salad bar, but otherwise the place was deserted.

"Please have a seat, Ms. Young," Turner said. "What can I get you? Juice or coffee, maybe? Sorry, no alcohol allowed on the rig."

"Coffee would be fine," Cassie replied.

"Sugar or cream?"

"Both, thank you."

Turner came back holding two mugs of steaming coffee in one hand and set them down on the table. From his other hand he produced several packets of sugar, plastic containers of cream, and a wooden stirrer.

"We don't get too many ladies out here," Turner said as he seated himself.

"There aren't many in the industry, period," Cassie replied as she poured cream and sugar into her coffee and stirred.

"Well, now that's somethin' that I for one am ready to see change. But what woman in her right mind really wants to live with these animals for 14 days straight?"

"Maybe some of us are tough enough to make the grade."

"May*be*," Turner said as he took a sip from his cup.

"Did you by any chance supervise the Mooney-3 well?" Cassie asked.

"Yes ma'am, I did."

"What can you tell me about it?"

"Well…here and now I can tell you it was a raging success."

"And if you were someplace else?"

"There was a time long ago when I did sales for a custom fabrication company," Turner began. "And the manufacturin' department kept givin' us very quick delivery dates so as to get orders. Well, we didn't always make those dates, and I lost some business. So, I started promisin' longer delivery times, and that cost me some business up front. But when I delivered early, my customers were happy. I built up quite a bit of business over time."

"You don't like people who overpromise, do you?" Cassie said. She finally took a drink of her coffee.

"I think it's better for business when customers are pleasantly surprised." Turner leaned forward almost lifting himself off his seat and spoke very quietly. "How about you and I have lunch?" He was moving his index finger back and forth in a friendly fashion as he spoke.

"Aren't you worried?" Cassie asked. "Talking to somebody like me?"

"Should I be?" He stared her right in the eye.

"No, you shouldn't."

Turner leaned back. "I'm flyin' in tomorrow mornin' for the day."

"Where do you want to meet?"

"You like sushi?"

"I love sushi," Cassie replied.

"Let's go to Sushi King. Not so many oil people there," Turner said. "How about 1:30? Won't be so many people of any kind there then."

"Great," Cassie said.

Turner gave her the cross streets which she wrote down on a small pad she retrieved from her pocket.

After they were done with their coffee, Turner showed her the wire line unit, a small trailer-like affair with windows, where several people were busily engaged monitoring the drilling operation which had resumed. As Turner and Cassie proceeded, they passed by a white, tube-shaped capsule big enough for a person to crawl into. Cassie recognized it as a hyperbaric chamber for divers who needed to decompress to prevent the bends.

They eventually made their way to the driller's cabin. Inside, it was air-conditioned. They stood behind the driller who sat in a chair that reminded Cassie of something out of a science fiction movie. He looked back briefly, smiled and waved with a small twist of his hand. Then he returned his attention immediately to the drill floor directly in front of him through the windows. The drillstring was now turning at a steady rate. Cassie returned her attention to the driller's chair which had a joystick attached to each of the broad flat arms, and each arm had a panel with several rows of square buttons. There was a two-screen display in front of the chair and another display off to the right.

"A little more comfortable than the old days," Turner remarked. "I could show you more, but it's gettin' late, and I don't like my pilots to fly at night if they don't have to."

"I'm done," Cassie replied nodding. She thanked him for taking so much time with her, and he said he would accompany her to the helipad. They returned via a welter of catwalks and stairways, past pipes and cables, tanks and pumps, dials and more dials, and digital readouts.

They also passed the mudlogging cabin, another small trailer that looked like it had been plunked down on the deck. Cassie could see through a window that one man was looking into a microscope. In all likelihood he was examining cuttings from the drill bit brought up by the drilling mud which was circulated in the well both to cool the bit and to keep oil and gas from traveling back to the surface and causing a blowout. Two others, a man and a woman—the only woman Cassie had seen on the entire platform—were looking at racks of monitoring equipment and several computer screens. Turner used the pause in their journey to radio ahead to the pilot. When they arrived, the pilot was already sitting in the helicopter.

≈

As Cassie exited the cab in front of her hotel, she looked around to see if there was a place she might get dinner. All she wanted was something quick, but the sandwich shop across the street was closed and so was the Mediterranean deli. The street looked deserted, and it was only 8 o'clock. The Italian restaurant directly in front of her seemed to be open, but she didn't really want to sit down to a meal. She decided she'd just get something from room service.

She entered the hotel and made her way to her room. It was on the top floor as it turned out. She was puzzled when she got there because the entryway had double doors. She inserted her key card, the light turned green, and she opened the door into a huge room. It had a large dining table and wet bar on one end and a set of couches ringed in front of a big screen TV on the other. The bed was in a separate room off to the side. This can't be right, she thought.

She put down her things, and then walked toward the phone which was on a table next to the television. She called the front desk and said that she thought the hotel had made a mistake. The clerk looked up her reservation. She told Cassie that there was no mistake. Dr. Voss had arranged for an upgrade. There would be no additional charge for the suite. She thanked the clerk and hung up. Voss, it appeared, was bucking for a good review even in absentia.

She didn't really need all this space, especially for just one night. But it would be nice to have a large table to spread out some of the work she had brought along with her. Cassie noticed she was chilled, so before she did anything else she checked the air conditioning. She discovered the temperature control in the foyer and found that it was set to 65. On a previous visit someone had joked that Houston was the coldest place on earth…in the summer!

After she moved the temperature up to 70, she turned and saw a small table near the entrance that had a folder thick with paper. She opened it and inside were what appeared to be a media kit for reporters about the Mooney-3 discovery and then page after page of technical information about the well. The packet must have been delivered to the hotel by Breckenridge Oil in her absence. She would look at it more closely later.

Then she went back to the phone and called the airline to change her return flight the next day to a later departure. She wanted to spend as much time as possible with Turner. She had sensed that something wasn't right at the presentation that morning, and he might be able to explain why.

The next morning Cassie stayed in her hotel room examining the materials delivered by Breckenridge the previous day and catching up on other work. At 1 o'clock she checked out, left her suitcase with the bellman, and caught a cab to Sushi King.

The restaurant wasn't what she had expected. From the name she had assumed that it might be a storefront operation with a few tables. Inside, she found an elegant, upscale dining room. From where she entered she could see a long black granite bar which had white napkins folded neatly in triangles sticking up from plates that were all in a line. No one was seated there at the moment. A couple of chefs were milling around behind the counter, and one of them waved her in. She walked to the end of the bar and was about to engage the chef when she spotted Turner peering out from behind a translucent glass partition that had hidden him from view. He rose as she approached the table, and they shook hands. After they both sat down, Turner took a sip from his glass of beer.

"I wasn't sure you'd come," Cassie said.

"I wasn't sure I would either," Turner replied.

A waiter appeared, handed Cassie a menu, and asked for her drink order. She wanted to be fully awake for her encounter with Turner and asked for iced tea. The waiter left.

"Anything you get here is good," Turner said. He pulled out a pair of reading glasses, put them on, and then opened his menu and started glancing at it. Cassie picked up her menu as well.

"There sure has been a lot of hype about this whole thing, don't you think?" Turner asked as he looked at Cassie over the top of his menu.

"You tell me if it's hype," Cassie responded.

"What are you plannin' on tellin' those bosses of yours back in Washington?"

"I haven't decided yet."

"I like my job, and I'm good at it."

"As far as I'm concerned, this meeting never took place."

Turner put his menu down and removed his glasses. He was about to continue when the waiter came, set down Cassie's iced tea, and then took their orders. After the waiter had gone, Turner tried again. "If you thought you had just made a major find in the deepwater Gulf of Mexico, what would *you* do?"

"Well, I'd drill some delineation wells to figure out just what I had," Cassie responded. "Then, I'd analyze those results, evaluate the economics of extracting and transporting the stuff—existing pipelines versus having to carry it by tanker. If it was a go, then I'd line up the financing and build the production facilities."

"So, you wouldn't sell part of what you just found?"

"Not unless that was the only way to finance it."

"But Breckenridge already has two major international oil companies as partners for this project, both with very deep pockets."

"You're telling me that they're trying to sell their share!"

Turner grimaced while moving both hands in a downward tamping motion to signal Cassie to lower her voice. Then he craned his neck and surveyed the restaurant before restarting the conversation. "Now, how would it look if you sold the biggest deepwater Gulf of Mexico find to date almost immediately after you found it?"

"It would signal that you've got no faith that you've really found something worth developing," Cassie replied. She took a sip of her iced tea.

"So, what I'd do is drill a delineation well and hope to find somethin', anything to justify the hype." Turner looked around the restaurant again. There were only two other groups that Cassie could see, and they were in booths 20 feet away. Turner continued. "Then, I'd tell the world that I am looking for another partner to help with the development of this new field because it's gonna require a lot of money. So, I salvage part of my investment up front by sellin' maybe half my share. Then, if things don't work out, I've cut my losses, *and* I've moved money into somethin' I know is actually there like...the Canadian tar sands."

"You know this is Breckenridge's plan?" Cassie queried.

"I know what I'm hearin'."

"What makes you think it's true?"

Turner took a long drink from his beer glass. Then he put the glass down. "You met with Julian Voss yesterday, didn't you?"

"Yes."

"Did you have a hard time figurin' out what kind of oil came out of Mooney-3 during the flow test?"

"Yes, I did," Cassie said. "The tests on the sulfur content were, I think he said, 'inconsistent.'"

"Well, I can tell you that that was some of the stinkier oil I've brought out of the ground," Turner said. "It ain't sweet crude—that's for sure."

"Well, they can't keep that a secret."

"Of course, they can't," Turner replied. "Any potential

buyer would have to verify the oil characteristics before makin' a deal. But Breckenridge can keep the hype goin' a little longer. They can emphasize the flow rate. They can announce plans for delineation wells. If the find is big enough, hell, they can sell the stinky stuff and make it worthwhile. But that's a big 'if.' A lot of refineries just can't refine it, or don't want to. And so, of course, they pay less even if they can refine it."

"So, you think it'll be too expensive to bring this field online?"

"Too early to tell," Turner said. "But what I've told you is a far cry from what's in the press." Turner took another sip of his beer.

Their lunches came. They both ended up with one of the sampler plates. A little extravagant, Cassie thought, but why not? Her plate had a brightly colored assortment — red, orange, pink, white, yellow, and brown — that included tuna, salmon, salmon roe, shrimp, crab, octopus, squid, mackerel, and eel, all perched on clumps of rice. Some of it, she guessed, had come from the gulf she had flown over the day before. She poured a little soy sauce into a small dipping dish. Using her chopsticks she levitated the piece of glazed eel with rice and placed it into the dipping dish. She picked up some slices of pickled ginger, putting them on top of the eel. Finally, she added some green wasabi mustard, too much as it turned out. Shortly after the ginger, eel and other flavors hit her mouth, they were obliterated by the wasabi fumes which created an excruciatingly painful sensation deep in her sinuses. She closed her eyes. It took a moment to recover.

"Little too much, huh?" Turner said smiling. "Personally, I don't really feel like I've had sushi unless I almost black out a couple of times."

Turner had already told her what he wanted to tell her, so the conversation turned to day-to-day life on an oil platform, the amazing run-up in crude oil prices, the increasing number of helicopters in Houston as the oil wealth flowed in, and the cuisine around town — as good as any major city in the world, Turner said, and he'd lived in or traveled to many of them.

≈

Cassie boarded her flight back to Washington around 7 o'clock. Once aloft, the plane veered sharply to the left revealing a last glimpse of Houston's downtown towers through the hazy sky. Her ears popped as the plane swiftly gained altitude. When the aircraft turned away from the sun and headed toward Washington, the sky took on a misty, yellowish color.

Cassie began to reflect on what she'd heard and seen. Mooney-3 wasn't an unequivocal success. In fact, it would be some time before Breckenridge and its partners knew for sure whether it would be worth developing. Its main significance lay in the fact that it demonstrated large flows of oil from some of the deepest waters ever drilled in the Gulf of Mexico. It marked the opening of a new offshore frontier. But frontiers, she thought, are always full of unforeseen dangers and possible setbacks. And frontiers can sometimes be fatal.

≈ **chapter 6** ≈

Over the next few days Cassie worked on and off writing her report about Breckenridge Oil's Mooney-3 discovery and the prospects for deepwater drilling in the Gulf of Mexico. Still feeling uneasy, she decided to call Heather Johnston at Breckenridge to run some things by her before submitting the final version.

"Heather, this is Cassie Young," Cassie said when she reached Heather on the phone.

"Cassie, I'm so pleased you called," Heather responded. "Are you comin' to Houston again so soon?"

"No, I'm afraid not. But I would like to talk to you about my report on Mooney-3 and the deepwater drilling program at Breckenridge."

"Well, Julian Voss is probably the one you should be talkin' to about that."

"I was hoping I could just talk to you," Cassie said. "What if we just keep this between us?"

"Well, if it's just between us. I mean I could get into trouble if somebody found out I talked to you without authorization."

"I'm not going to tell anyone, and I'm not going to use the information in the report. I just need someone to tell me if I'm on the right track. Now, do you know something different from what Voss told me?"

"Well, not exactly," Heather replied. "I wouldn't say different—just, in addition."

"Please go on."

"Naturally, we're always havin' discussions about various projects and whether we should move to the next step or not. Well, there's a group of us geologists who think that proceeding with the Mooney development isn't worth the risk. We think we ought to cap it and just move on."

"But what about the seismic data? It looks so promising."

"Not necessarily."

"What do you mean?"

"Well, when you're standin' there in the 3-D presentation room feelin' like you're walkin' through the geology below the seabed, it all seems so clear. But, you know, a lot of assumptions and interpretations and adjustments go into creatin' those models of the geology. And that's all they are — models. The raw data never says anything so clear as what you think you see in those three-dimensional visuals."

"What are you getting at?"

"Some of us — and we're in the minority, mind you — think that Voss has made assumptions that are too optimistic in this case, unwarranted by what the data says. Look, if all these computer simulations were nothin' but a representation of exactly what's down there under the seabed, we'd never hit dry holes or worthless reservoirs. But we've hit plenty of them. And so have many others doin' this kind of work. I probably shouldn't say this..."

"Go ahead," Cassie reassured her. "It's just between us."

"Well, do you know what we call the kind of presentation we showed you?" Heather asked.

"No, what?"

"We call it the idiot presentation, aka, the management presentation. And you can make those presentations show pretty much anything you want them to."

"I see," Cassie replied wondering why she had never heard this term before.

"A lot of what we do — and I hate to admit this — is guesswork," Heather continued. "Very sophisticated guesswork aided by very sophisticated computer models. But guesswork none-theless."

"Heather, you've helped me out a lot," Cassie said. "When we meet for lunch next time I'm in Houston, I'm buying."

With that Cassie concluded the call and was off the phone. Her instincts had proven correct. Heather's information jibed with Turner's story. Even people at the highest levels at Breckenridge were having doubts about Mooney-3. Cassie picked up her latest draft of the report and stared at it for a moment. She decided to submit it without further changes.

≈

Two days later Evan Grant called Cassie into his office. When she arrived, she noticed that all four televisions were dark. Evan and Larry Hilliard were chatting across Evan's desk, and Hilliard's presence made Cassie wary.

"What do you want to see me about?" Cassie asked as she stood at the door.

"Have a seat, Cassie," Evan said motioning for her to come in. Cassie sat down next to Hilliard in one of the oxblood leather chairs. Evan continued. "Well, Larry and I are little concerned about the tone of your report on Breckenridge and the whole deepwater gulf phenomenon."

"In what way?" she asked.

"Now, I'll be the first one to say that we can't take every-thing oil companies tell us at face value," Evan said. "But you've got a very low URR for the Lower Tertiary for starters."

"Evan, even Breckenridge gives a range of 3 to 15 billion barrels ultimately recoverable," Cassie responded.

"Cassie," Hilliard said, "clients pay us to provide some-thing more definitive than what they can get off a company website."

"What was the offending phrase?" she asked.

Evan thumbed through his copy of the report, and then stopped. "Here it is: 'Given current technology, we should expect the URR to be nearer to the low side of the Breckenridge estimate.'"

"Well, that's a *little* more definitive," Cassie said sheepishly.

Hilliard turned to look at Cassie more directly. "Cassie, it's not that I'm expecting you to pull a number out of the air," he said. "But you know that technology is a moving target. The E&P companies are going to get better at isolating reserves and at boosting recovery rates as new technology is developed."

"Well, we'll revise our estimates upward when they do," Cassie replied. "They're going to develop these deepwater fields with the technology they have now. I think we've got to use that as our baseline."

Evan chimed in again and made Cassie feel as if she were at a Ping-Pong match—only she was the ball. "Your recovery rates are going to end up being too low in this report. I mean 10 to 15 percent of the original oil in place is very pessimistic."

"I just think we need to be careful not to become an extension of the PR departments of the E&P companies," Cassie replied. "Wait a minute, that's what this is about, isn't it?"

"Now hold on," Evan interjected. He had both hands in the air.

"You're worried because Breckenridge Oil is a client," Cassie retorted.

Evan pulled back a bit. "You make it sound like a bad thing."

"Well, it's a bad thing when we don't give the rest of our clients our best judgment," Cassie said forcefully.

"I agree, Cassie," said Hilliard as he flashed her one of his compulsive big smiles. "Evan and I just think your judgment is a little flawed on this one."

She turned back to Evan. "Evan, I'm giving you my best judgment. Isn't that what you hired me to do?"

"Well, yes, of course it is," Evan replied. "It's not so much *what* you say as the *way* you say it. Naturally, there are all kinds of uncertainties with deepwater exploration. But this is a huge new frontier. We've got to expect there to be quite a bit of oil where people haven't drilled before."

"I'm not saying there's no oil," Cassie said. "I'm saying I'm not sure it's going to be economical to get as much of it out as the companies are hyping. Maybe later. Maybe with new technologies. Maybe with additional development of the underwater pipeline system."

"Cassie, you must realize—how can I put this?"

"Look, Evan, I know that we can't afford to alienate a client as big as Breckenridge," Cassie said.

"I'm not asking you to lie about anything you saw or heard," Evan continued. "I'm only asking you to be..." He paused, looked up at the ceiling for a moment, and then back down at her. "More evenhanded. That's what I mean to say. You can do that, can't you?"

Cassie glanced over at Hilliard who gave her another big smile and nodded his head several times. Then she returned her attention to Evan. "Of course, I can."

"Good, good," Evan said as he leaned back in his chair. Now *he* was smiling, too. "Take a few more days to rewrite it, won't you?"

"Certainly," Cassie said.

"Now, on another note, we didn't hear from you about Larry's open house. Did you miss the email?" Evan asked.

"I must have," she replied.

Hilliard spoke again, and he was still smiling. "I realize you've been very busy and probably just forgot about it. But Julia and I would love it if you could come this Saturday to see the new house we've built."

"Of course, I'll come," Cassie responded.

"And bring a friend if you'd like," Hilliard added.

"Okay, I'll do that."

≈

Later in the day Cassie came back from the copy room to find Evan standing next to her desk. "What brings *you* here?" she asked as she walked behind her desk and put the papers she was carrying down.

"Well, love, I just wanted you to know that you're probably right about Mooney-3 and Breckenridge Oil and the whole Gulf of Mexico deepwater," Evan said. "My performance this morning was for Larry's sake. You *do* want to become a partner sooner rather than later, don't you?"

"Yes, of course," Cassie said. "But not at the expense of compromising my work."

"No, of course not. But I had to let Larry know that I'm going to keep you on the straight and narrow. After all, I'm the one who brought you in, and so I'm the one who's responsible for you."

"I'm sorry, Evan," Cassie replied shaking her head. "I don't mean to be ungrateful."

"I know you aren't," Evan said. "But I so want to see you as a partner in this firm. After all, I need allies. And I made a pledge to your father that if anything happened to him that I would look after you. So, how am I doing?"

Cassie walked around from behind her desk and gave Evan an affectionate peck on the cheek. "You're doing fine." She pulled back. "You saved me on this one, and I owe you for it."

"Cassie, you don't owe me anything," Evan said. "Well, I know you've got your work cut out for you, so I'll let you get to it."

"Thanks, Evan," Cassie said.

"You're welcome."

As Evan exited her office, Cassie searched for the censured Breckenridge Oil report which she now had to start revising in earnest. She found it, flipped through it and then set it down again. Frustrated, she slipped her hands into her dress pockets as she contemplated how to approach the changes she would have to make. She felt something in one of the pockets and pulled it out. It was a business card, the one that Victor Chernov had given her at George Mason University during the reception after the concert. It was the card for his group, The Washington Ensemble.

She was reminded of their conversation over lunch. Victor specifically mentioned Mooney-3 and predicted that it would probably be capped because it wouldn't be economical to produce. And that's the conclusion she had come to as well—though she knew better than to go that far in her report. She found herself wanting to talk to Victor some more. Yes, he was infuriating. But she wanted to find out how he knew so much about Mooney-3. Did he just make a lucky guess or was there something else to it?

She sat down and typed in the website address for Victor's group on her computer. She found individual email addresses for each of the group's members. She emailed Victor telling him that she wanted to meet with him sometime soon.

Within a couple of minutes he phoned her. She asked if he could meet that evening, but he said he couldn't because the ensemble had a performance. The next day didn't work either because he would be out of town all day.

"Are you around on Saturday?" she asked.

"Yes. I usually take a bike ride in Rock Creek Park in the morning, but after that I'm free until evening."

Then Cassie got an idea. "Victor, would you mind accompanying me to an open house on Saturday afternoon? Paul is out of town until next week, and he doesn't like to go to these things anyway—"

"I'd be delighted," he said. "Whose house?"

"Larry Hilliard," Cassie replied. "He built a new one out in Falls Church."

"I can't wait for this," Victor said.

≈ chapter 7 ≈

On Saturday afternoon Cassie picked up Victor—who claimed not to own a car—at his home near 30th and Porter. He had said it was the one with tomato plants in front, and she quickly found it as a result. Victor exited the house as she pulled up to the curb. He was dressed in black—black sport coat, black dress shirt, black slacks—as if he were going to perform.

He opened the door of her white Volkswagen hatchback and got in.

"Do you always dress in black?" Cassie asked.

"This is who I am," Victor replied. "Victor Chernov. Victor Black. That's what it means."

"I didn't know."

"How could you?"

Cassie made her way to Wisconsin Avenue and headed toward Key Bridge.

"Now, you've got to promise to lay off the peak oil talk while you're with this crowd," she said.

"I promise to be a good boy," he said with a sheepish look.

"But I do have some interesting news for you about the Mooney-3 well."

"How do you come by this news?" Victor asked.

"I actually visited the company and got a briefing," Cassie responded. "And then I got an earful from a couple of insiders which, of course, you can't repeat."

"Of course. And these insiders said…"

"They said almost exactly what you said. That the company might end up capping the well because the oil will be too expensive to produce. And the quality isn't that great either. How did you know?"

"I see hype like this all the time in the oil industry," Victor said. "Of course, I don't have any inside knowledge. I just read the newspapers and the trade journals, and in my head I cross out all the lies. It makes things easy because there's so little information left over to process."

"Maybe you should take *my* job," Cassie said. "You wouldn't even have to travel. You could just write the reports from your office."

Victor laughed.

"I was all ready to prove you wrong," Cassie said.

"But I'm right."

Cassie changed the subject. "How are your tomato plants coming?"

"The tomato plants are fine, but the neighbors don't like me growing vegetables on the front lawn," Victor said.

"Why don't you just grow them in the back?"

"Too much shade. And I've got other things planted there anyway."

"I wouldn't have pegged you as a gardener."

"It's a lot of bother."

"Then why do you do it?"

"Can I say the words?"

"What words?

"The prohibited words today?"

"You mean 'peak oil?' "

"There, you said them," Victor responded. "We're all going to have to grow more food ourselves. So, I'm learning how."

"That's nonsense, Victor."

"Someday you'll be begging me for one of my tomatoes."

Cassie couldn't tell whether the look on his face was mock

seriousness or not.

"So, you don't own a car for the same reason?" She was about to turn onto Key Bridge and cross the river.

"Cars are evil," Victor said.

"But you're riding in a car right now."

"*Your* car is *not* evil."

"So, my car gets a pass."

"Yes, good for one day only. So I can go to the house of this fool of a man who thinks the earth is a magic pudding from which you can get endless barrels of oil...and everything else you want, too."

"Please don't hold back, Victor. Tell me what you really think."

"My friend, Sasha. He says the U.S. is going down just like the Soviet Union. And it will take the world with it."

"You're in a fine mood today."

"I know it's pointless to talk to you this way." He crossed his arms and leaned back.

"You're right. It is pointless," Cassie said.

By then they were across the bridge heading toward Falls Church. Within 15 minutes Cassie was pulling up to the Hilliard homestead.

A semicircular drive was filled with black limousines and an assortment of cars. The house itself was a mammoth, two-level red brick Federal-style building with a two-story portico supported by four round white columns. Large Palladian windows ran along both stories. The lot included a substantial lawn with many newly planted trees. In fact, the landscaping appeared to be still underway as one worker was planting trees along the drive.

Cassie and Victor climbed out of the car and walked toward the entrance along a sidewalk that traced the same arc as the drive.

"That's got to be 12,000 square feet," Victor said. "They built this from scratch?"

"That's what I hear," Cassie said.

Cassie stayed focused on the gargantuan home as she continued to walk toward the entrance. Evan happened to be there and had just finished talking to a couple who turned to go inside as Cassie came up the steps.

"Hello, love," Evan said. He gave Cassie a kiss on the cheek. "A little bigger than you expected?" he added in a low voice.

"Well, yes," she said.

"Every man's home is his castle." Evan looked in both directions as a substitute for pointing out the large dimensions. "For some it's more true than others."

Cassie didn't see Evan's wife anywhere near. "Where's Martha?" Cassie inquired.

"Home entertaining relatives," Evan replied. "I've got to make a quick appearance here and then get back to help her, so I better go in. Enjoy the party, love."

Cassie nodded, and Evan turned to go inside. She now realized that she had lost track of Victor. She turned around and saw him talking with the landscaper they had spotted when they had arrived. A moment later Victor turned away from the man and trotted toward the entrance.

"Sorry about that," he said as he mounted the steps.

The two of them then proceeded together toward the door where a man in a gray cutaway complete with vest, ascot tie and white wing collar shirt opened it for them. Once inside another man in a waiter's uniform motioned to them and said, "Right this way." He pointed straight ahead under a curving staircase beyond which Cassie could see people standing near a long table stocked with hors d'oeuvres and wine.

The white marble floor led into a great room with a dining area on the left where the refreshment table stood and a sunken living room area on the right. Victor looked up at the ceiling.

"It must be 25 feet," he remarked.

Shimmering gold curtains had been opened to allow light

in through the Palladian windows which reached almost to the ceiling. Outside Cassie could see a pool, a large fenced pasture on which two horses were grazing, and a small lake.

The room was fairly well filled with people. Most had drinks in their hands and many held small plates filled with goodies from the lengthy hors d'oeuvre table. Hilliard was standing near an opening in the railing that separated the living and dining areas. He was wearing a dark blue suit and a blue club tie. When he saw Cassie, he broke away from the group he was with and took his wife, Julia, with him.

"Cassie, I'm so glad you made it," Hilliard said displaying his broad signature smile. "Of course, you know Julia."

"Yes, Mrs. Hilliard, it's good to see you and your beautiful new home," Cassie said.

"Thank you so much, Cassie." Julia said. "And who is this?" she asked nodding in Victor's direction.

"May I present Victor Chernov," Cassie said. "Larry and Julia Hilliard."

"Nice to meet you both," Victor said as he shook their hands in succession.

"We're planning on doing a lot of entertaining here," said Julia, who was wearing a royal blue cocktail dress. Her bright red hair looked as if it might be dyed, Cassie thought. Her aquiline nose gave her a domineering appearance, and the few times Cassie had encountered her, Julia seemed always to get her way.

"Now, if you don't mind, I'd like to borrow Cassie and introduce her to a couple of people," Larry Hilliard said.

Victor nodded and with that Hilliard put his hand on the small of Cassie's back and guided her down the steps into the sunken living room. Hilliard and Cassie stepped onto the wood floor and then walked across a large Persian rug toward two men holding drinks and conversing next to one of the couches. The two men turned toward Hilliard as he approached them.

"Senator," Hilliard said, "I'd like to introduce you to one of my senior associates, Cassie Young. Cassie, this is Senator Phillips."

"Pleased to meet you, senator," Cassie said as they shook hands.

"The pleasure is all mine," the senator said. Phillips towered over her. His shiny gray mane and friendly face made him perfect for the part of senator from Virginia, she thought.

"And this is Congressman O'Connor from Maryland," Hilliard added. O'Connor was a small, portly man with a large, veiny nose. He had a few strands of hair on his balding top and was perhaps in his early sixties.

"Nice to meet you, congressman," Cassie said.

"Nice to meet you, Cassie," said O'Connor as he took her hand and shook it vigorously but with a strangely loose grip.

"I'll let the three of you get acquainted," Hilliard said as he withdrew.

"Cassie," the senator said. "I keep telling O'Connor here that we need to open up more federal land to drilling, and he keeps going on about windmills and solar panels. Maybe you can talk some sense into him."

"Senator, why don't you give Congressman O'Connor what he wants, and maybe he'll give you what you want?" Cassie said with a sly smile.

O'Connor seemed mildly amused.

"That's just the problem, my dear," Phillips replied. "He won't make a deal. He wants his windmills and solar panels, but won't allow me to open up more federal land to drilling."

Cassie turned toward O'Connor. "Is that true, congressman?"

O'Connor looked down at the floor and then up again. "I'm afraid so," he said. "But I keep telling the senator that we won't need any of that drilling if he'd just give me my windmills and solar panels. And so, we go round and round."

O'Connor seemed oddly pleased with the state of affairs

he had just described. At that moment the crowd shifted. Cassie could now see a fireplace at the end of the room, and it was lit. It was probably 80 degrees outside, the air conditioning was on, and there was a fire in what appeared to be a gas fireplace.

"Gentlemen," Cassie said. "I think I have something we can all agree on."

"What's that?" Phillips asked.

"We can turn off that fireplace," she said as she pointed to it.

"You've got my vote, Cassie," O'Connor said raising one hand.

Phillips looked over in Larry Hilliard's direction. "I think you'll have to consult the management," Phillips said. As he turned his attention back, he added, "Larry always was a bit of a show-off."

Then the senator craned his neck slightly and seemed to notice someone coming under the staircase and into the room. "A senator's work is never done," he said to Cassie. Then he looked over at O'Connor. "I need to go talk to Joe." Turning back to Cassie, Phillips continued. "Cassie, it was so very nice to meet you. I do hope I have the pleasure of seeing you again. But right now I have to go talk to somebody I've been trying to talk to for a week. Will you please excuse me?"

"Of course, senator," she replied.

He shook hands with her, and then so did O'Connor. "I gotta see him, too. Nice to meet you, Cassie. Come by my office anytime." And then O'Connor was gone as well.

Cassie tried to see whom they were aiming for when she found a cold drink thrust into her hand. It was Bob Ulrich, an analyst who had the office next to hers at EAI.

"You looked like you might be dying of thirst," Ulrich said.

Ulrich couldn't have been much older than Cassie. His thick blond hair was parted on the left side and stayed perfectly in place, probably by means of hairspray, Cassie thought. His square-jawed face was deeply tanned. He was solidly built, and Cassie had heard him say that he lifts weights three times a week. Over that solidly built frame he had draped a blue sport coat, white dress shirt and gray slacks, but no tie.

"Thanks," she said. She took a sip of what turned out to be white wine, ice cold white wine, it seemed.

"How's Paul?" he asked.

"Paul's fine," she said. "Why do you ask?"

"Well, he's *not* here and you *are* here...with somebody else."

"You are about as subtle as a freight train, Bob," she said. "Okay, for the record, Victor is just a friend, and Paul had to go out of town for 10 days."

"So, you're still seeing him."

"Yes, but I don't see how that's any of your business."

"Well, I worry about you," Ulrich said.

Cassie let out a laugh that caught the attention of people nearby. When they had turned back to their own conversations, she spoke. "Bob, the only thing you worry about is getting ahead at the firm."

Ulrich's mouth dropped open.

Cassie immediately regretted what she had said. "I didn't mean that. It wasn't fair," she told him. "I apologize."

Ulrich had a pained look on his face. "It's okay," he said shaking his head slightly. "Don't worry about it." He turned and walked away.

At that point Cassie could see Julia Hilliard motioning her to come over. She and Victor were standing near the grand piano in a corner of the living room. When Cassie arrived, Julia turned toward her.

"I've just been telling Victor about this dreadful little newspaper we have out here that has been printing these columns about the *end of oil* and the *end of the world*," Julia said delivering the last two phrases with great mock drama. Cassie looked over at Victor and put her finger to her lips to remind him of their agreement. He shrugged his shoulders, cocked his head, and put his hands up to indicate that he hadn't pursued the issue.

Julia continued, "Larry has tried to set them straight, but they just don't listen. They're even sponsoring a peak oil conference next week in Washington. Of course, nobody serious will be going to that." She paused for a moment and then started again. "Anyway, that's not what I called you over for. I found out Victor's a musician, and I want you to convince him to play the piano for us." Julia turned her gaze to Victor.

"I told her I didn't think this crowd would appreciate my music," he said.

"I told him I love Philip Glass," Julia said putting her hand on Cassie's shoulder.

"It's all right, Victor," Cassie said. She knew he was trying to keep his promise to be a good boy.

"Okay, I'll do a few pieces," Victor said.

He sat down at the black Steinway grand and began playing a slow, quiet, almost dirge-like tune that seemed far different from the kind of music Cassie had heard him play at the George Mason concert. A few people gathered around the piano to listen, and when he had finished, they clapped politely.

Victor went on to a somewhat more energetic piece which attracted more listeners. Julia leaned her head in Cassie's direction and whispered, "I think that's from a movie I saw, but I can't think of the name."

" 'The Hours,' " Cassie whispered back.

"Oh, yes," Julia said. "I love that movie."

Victor finished not with Philip Glass, but George Gershwin, playing part of "Rhapsody in Blue." Toward the end his hands were hopping across the keyboard, and his head was jerking occasionally with staccato movements of the kind one expects to see in a classical recital. After he had finished, the room erupted with applause.

Victor stood up and took a bow. When the applause had abated, he went over to Julia and Cassie. "I guess I was wrong," he said.

"You certainly were," Julia replied.

"Gershwin," Victor added with a confident nod of the head. "It's always a crowd pleaser."

"Now, I want you to meet a friend of ours who is the dean at Peabody," Julia said. She turned back to Cassie. "You'll excuse us for a moment, won't you?"

"Yes, of course," Cassie said. She sipped some more of the wine she'd been nursing since Ulrich had given it to her. It had now reached a more palatable temperature. She then turned to walk up the steps to get something from the hors d'oeuvre table. Standing in her path, however, was a man, perhaps in his early forties, with a dark complexion and searing eyes. He was dressed in a perfectly tailored black business suit and wore a Rolex.

"May I introduce myself?" he said. "Bashir Al-Jamil."

Cassie detected something of a British accent. "Cassie Young," she responded as she shook his hand.

"Lawrence has really outdone himself," Al-Jamil said.

"What do you mean?"

"You are by far the best looking associate he has ever hired."

"Since he hasn't hired that many women — and I'm assuming you're not the type who likes men — aren't you sort of damning me with faint praise?" Cassie retorted.

"I'm sorry. I meant no offense," he replied, gently gesturing with one hand.

"None taken," Cassie said. "How exactly do you know Larry Hilliard?" As she was asking the question, Cassie could see Hilliard moving with some velocity toward them from behind Al-Jamil. Before Al-Jamil had a chance to respond, Hilliard intervened.

"Cassie," Hilliard said with a big smile. "I see you've met his excellency, the ambassador of Ammar."

"He didn't tell me he was an ambassador," she said alternating her glance between the two of them.

"My apologies again," Al-Jamil said. "Sometimes I like to

have a normal conversation which is difficult if you are an ambassador."

"I'll try to be as normal as possible," Cassie said. She could see Hilliard wince slightly as she spoke.

The ambassador continued. "You know, we Ammaris are always looking for top energy talent." He turned his head toward Hilliard. "Is she one of your top people?"

"Most definitely," Hilliard said.

Al-Jamil turned back to Cassie. "Someday you may want to make a move."

"I'm very happy where I am," Cassie responded.

"Things change," Al-Jamil said.

"Ambassador," Hilliard said, "there are some people I want you to meet."

"Yes, of course," Al-Jamil replied. He turned toward Cassie again. "I find myself apologizing a third time—this time for my hasty exit. But I'll try to make it up to you sometime."

"It was nice meeting you, ambassador," Cassie said as she shook his hand. Hilliard then led the ambassador along a twisting route through the crowd to the other side of the room.

She was glad to be rid of him. What a creep, she thought. Certainly, Hilliard could manage a business relationship with somebody like that. But if she were the head of the firm, she wondered how she would handle Al-Jamil, a key contact with the firm's biggest client. She shuddered to think about it.

Cassie finally was able to make her way over to the hors d'oeuvre table and found Victor there sampling the cuisine.

"Very good caviar," he said as he took a bite from a cracker bearing a clump of the tiny black jellied eggs. "It's almost impossible to get really good stuff, given all the restrictions on harvesting these days."

"You were the toast of the town," Cassie said as she reached for a canapé, one with a light orange-colored spread on it.

He shrugged his shoulders as he continued to chew.

"Aren't you enjoying yourself?" she asked as she popped

the canapé in her mouth. It was topped with a tasty salmon mousse.

"Yes, quite a bit," he said. "This has been very instructive."

"What do you mean?"

"I can't tell you here. Later in the car," he said.

After Cassie and Victor finished snacking, they decided to say goodbye to the Hilliards. As they drove away from the house, Cassie asked what was so "instructive."

"You remember I talked to the landscaper on the way in," Victor said.

"Yes, I saw," Cassie replied.

"Well, he told me that his company had done $200,000 worth of landscaping for the house."

"So?"

"And he said it was lucky for Hilliard that Hilliard's company was paying the bills."

"EAI is paying for his landscaping?"

"No," Victor said. "Some company called Century Associates."

"What's that?"

"The landscaper assumed that it was Hilliard's firm. Very strange," Victor said. "Very strange, indeed."

"Maybe he's got some other business interests," Cassie said.

"Maybe," Victor responded. "But still, how can he be legally paying for the landscaping of his personal home through his company?"

"You've got me. But I'll bet he has the best tax lawyers in Washington."

≈ **chapter 8** ≈

The following Monday morning as Cassie walked to Dupont Circle on her way to work, she was thinking of Victor and his crazy apocalyptic ideas. When she arrived, the circle was humming with cars and groaning with diesel buses. And in every direction people were jammed together at crosswalks and bus stops as the pulsing sound of a lone car alarm rose above the street noise. Cassie couldn't imagine all of this coming to an end—at least not anytime soon. Yes, the oil age would end, she told herself. But when it did, no one would even notice. Civilization would go on, powered by other sources of energy.

As she walked around the circle toward her office on 19th Street, she thought she just might drop in on the peak oil conference that was being held in Washington that week. What could these people possibly be thinking? She wanted to find out.

Soon she was at the entrance to her building, a cheerless, gray concrete box with large square openings for windows. Inside, however, the lobby had a pleasant art deco décor with a black and white diamond design on the floor and translucent seashell-shaped lamps inverted to bounce their light off the ceiling.

As she waited at the elevator, she contemplated the brass doors which included a set of eight square bas-reliefs, one of which was a depiction of Vulcan, the Roman god of fire and also, as it turned out, a blacksmith. She had looked it up after asking the building manager one day about the doors. Vulcan, she discovered, seemed to be the singular example of a god who had a job. But he also presided over destructive fire such as volcanoes. Opposite him was Ceres, the Roman goddess of grain. The other six squares, two above and four below, depicted the cornucopia, the horn of plenty, often signifying fertility and abundance. It was a supernatural horn which would give those who possessed it whatever they wanted.

Right now what Cassie wanted was for the elevator to come. It seemed especially slow today. Finally, it arrived empty, and she got on and hit the fourth floor button. When she reached her destination, the doors opened and she was greeted by Dhanesh, the firm's IT manager.

"Hello, my one and only," he said with a smile on his face. He seemed to have a minor crush on her and was always saying such things. She didn't take offense because it had now become more like an inside joke. At 25 Dhanesh was one of the youngest people in the firm. While he was clearly the son of Indian parents, he was born in the United States and thoroughly Americanized. He sounded like any American male his age, maybe more so, Cassie thought.

Cassie could have made a stink about his behavior, but she liked Dhanesh. And he wasn't doing anything overt like pressuring her for a date. Besides, there were practical considerations such as surviving in a mostly male organization and having a good relationship with the person who runs all the computers.

She entered the door of EAI and made her way to her office. It was a simple office with a modest wooden desk, some overstuffed wooden bookshelves on the left wall, and three metal lateral filing cabinets against the right one. Behind her desk were windows. But all she could see through them was the blank concrete wall of the adjacent building and a narrow alley below, so she rarely opened the blinds. She had hurriedly nailed a couple of framed folk art prints depicting farm scenes on the wall across from her desk when she had set up her office. She had been just too busy in her first year to do any serious decorating.

There were two things she always put on her desk, however. Near the phone on her left was a photo of her parents in the Utah desert shortly after they were married, standing in front of a set of spectacular reddish cliffs. To her right and filled with paper clips was a small, almost rectangular carved rainbow fluorite bowl with irregular blue and purple streaks running through the otherwise clear polished crystal. The bowl had been a gift from her father, given to her when she was 12 after he returned from a trip to China.

She sat down at her desk and immediately did a search on her computer to find information about the peak oil conference Julia Hilliard had mentioned. It was being held at George Washington University not too far away. She scrolled through the schedule and decided to take a late lunch break and go to the 1:30 session on world oil reserves.

≈

When it was closing in on 1:30, Cassie ducked out of the building. As she walked down 19th Street, a light mist was falling, but not enough to require an umbrella. Charming row houses, now mainly offices and restaurants, soon gave way to tall modern structures that had obviously displaced houses like the ones she had just passed. A shame, she thought. She turned right on K Street, made her way over to 21st and soon she was in the Marvin Center where the conference was being held.

As she entered, she saw people filing into an auditorium. To her right was a registration table, but nobody was manning it just then. Several nametags lay on the table unclaimed, and Cassie decided to take one and pin it to her jacket so as not to look like a freeloader.

She went into the auditorium and found a seat at the back. A few moments later the speaker was introduced. He was a retired oil geologist she'd never heard of. The man had thinning gray hair combed back and was wearing a camel colored sport coat with black suede yokes on the shoulders. His string tie was fastened with a silver metal clasp in what looked like the form of a longhorn. When he started to talk, the sound system howled with feedback, and he had to stop a moment while the volume was adjusted on the sound equipment.

Then he began his presentation about the problems of estimating world oil reserves. Well, Cassie could already speak volumes concerning such problems herself. The speaker particularly emphasized that OPEC members had increased their reported oil reserves by 50 to 100 percent in the mid-1980s. He claimed this was not due to any new discoveries, but rather a response to new rules which linked oil export quotas to the size of a country's reserves; the larger a country's reserves, the larger the export quota. So naturally nearly every country in OPEC increased its reported reserves so it could have a bigger export quota.

Cassie had heard all of this before, but she was confident that even if it were true, the oil almost surely was there. Middle Eastern members of the cartel had so much unexplored area and such good prospects for expanding output that the whole presentation seemed completely off base.

The speaker said that the Kingdom of Ammar, the world's biggest exporter, would likely be unable to increase its output much from here. If that turns out to be the case, he said, the world was nearing its all-time peak in production. Ammar was the key, he insisted. He speculated that we might see a plateau in worldwide oil production for many years and then an irreversible decline starting in a decade or so.

Toward the end of his presentation he was interrupted by someone who announced that oil had just traded over $110 a barrel in New York for the first time ever. But there were no cheers or applause as Cassie had expected. She thought this group of dedicated doomsters might have been happy to receive some validation. On the contrary, the audience sat hushed and even awestruck as if they were witnessing the unfolding of some terrible event foretold by the gods but which no one had the power to avert.

The presenter concluded by saying that if you feel you can trust what the secretive, authoritarian regimes which now control most of the world's oil say about their own reserves, then you can relax. But if you don't, if you think they might be exaggerating for their own purposes, then you must prepare for the likely consequences of that view, namely a peak sooner rather than later.

Cassie got up when the presentation was finished and quietly exited the auditorium. On her way out she was approached by some conference goers who thanked her for her excellent writing on peak oil issues. She just smiled at them and then remembered that she was wearing someone else's nametag. When she approached the registration table, she removed the tag and placed it so it would be in alphabetical order along with the other unclaimed ones. She took a sampling of the pamphlets on the table, stuck them in a side pocket of her shoulder bag and left.

≈

When she got back to her office, she realized she had forgotten to stop at the sandwich shop across the street to get something for lunch. She put her bag down on one of the chairs in front of her desk, pulled some money out of her wallet and went to get something to eat.

When she returned, Larry Hilliard was standing in her office next to the chair upon which she had laid her bag. She noticed that some of the peak oil pamphlets were visible in a pocket she had left unzipped. She swooped in to pick up the bag and moved it behind her desk.

"Cassie," Hilliard said as she slid by him. "I wanted to talk to you about a few things on your Breckenridge Oil rewrite."

"Is there a problem?" she asked.

"No, nothing major," Hilliard replied. "I just wanted to go over some minor changes I'd like you to make." He took a seat.

Cassie put her sandwich on her desk and sat down.

"Please, don't let me keep you from eating something," Hilliard said. "You obviously haven't had a chance to get lunch."

Cassie's stomach sank. Suddenly, she didn't have any appetite. What did Hilliard mean that she "obviously" hadn't had a chance to get lunch? Had he seen the peak oil material? Did he know she had visited the conference? Did he think she was taking it seriously? Now she was in a small panic, and this was no time to panic with the big boss sitting on the other side of her desk.

"Go ahead," Hilliard insisted. "I don't mind if you eat while we talk."

"That's okay," she replied. "Let's just cover what you need to cover first, and then I'll eat."

Hilliard was right. The things he went over were truly minor. They could have been covered in an email. Cassie began to wonder whether that was really the purpose of his visit.

"About the other day," Hilliard said after they had finished discussing the revisions. "I hope you understand that none of what Evan and I said to you was personal."

"Of course," Cassie replied. "I understand."

"It's my job to look out for the entire firm," Hilliard continued. *But apparently not for the other clients, Cassie thought.* "And in the end it's really our job to tell our clients what to think. They don't have the time or the background to evaluate our analysis. They look to us to get that analysis right." He paused for moment. "I'm really a hands-off manager." *Hands off until you see that telling the truth might upset some people.* "You'll see that as we go along." *Yeah, go along and get along, that now seems to be the program.*

"Thanks for an excellent report," Hilliard said. "I'm really glad that Evan brought you to us. You have a bright future here." A broad smile grew across his face.

With that Hilliard got up and left. As Cassie straightened up her desk, she found her appointment calendar open. She hadn't left it that way. At least, she thought it had been closed when she left for the conference. There was nothing that Hilliard could have seen in it that was important anyway. But the fact that he might have been spying on her unhinged her slightly. This was an aspect of Larry Hilliard she had never seen, and she didn't know what to make of it.

≈

Cassie worked late that evening and when she came to a stopping point, she began thinking about what the speaker at the conference had said about Middle East oil reserves. She decided to access the EAI database on Ammari oil reserves. All she could find was the official Ammari estimate of total reserves for all of its fields. She knew the firm had to have done a field-by-field breakdown, but where was it?

Cassie had her door open, and she thought she could hear Bob Ulrich in the next office. She got up and looked in. The light was on, but he wasn't there. Then she was startled by a voice coming from behind her. She turned around. It was Ulrich who was carrying a cup of coffee in his hand.

"Are you looking for me?" he asked.

"Yes, Bob," Cassie said. "I'm looking for field data for Royal Sovoco." Royal Sovoco was shorthand in the industry for the Royal Sovereign Oil Company of Ammar, the government-owned company that controlled all oil and gas development and production in the Kingdom of Ammar.

"You cover North American oil and gas. Why do you need that?"

Cassie had to think of something to say and quickly. "I'm, ah, I'm doing an imports study, and thought it might be useful to have."

"Our group has already done that," he replied. "I can email that right over to you."

"Thanks, Bob," Cassie said. "I appreciate that. But our field-by-field analysis, what is it based on?"

"It's based on the only thing we have, the Royal Sovoco reserve statistics. We work back from them to each field based on what we can glean from technical papers and our usual sources of intelligence."

"So, you believe the Royal Sovoco reserve numbers?"

"Yeah, don't you?"

"Doesn't it give you pause that there's no independent audit of their numbers?"

"No, it doesn't give me pause," Ulrich replied. "There's so much oil under that desert they could give me a number that's twice what they currently claim, and I'd believe them." He stopped for a moment, looking at Cassie more intently than before. "What exactly are you getting at?"

"I'm not getting at anything."

"Oh, I get it," Ulrich said. "Did Hilliard put you up to this?"

"No." This last question made the day seem even stranger.

"Sure…sure." Ulrich was nodding, but he had a disbelieving smile on his face.

"You think Hilliard put me up to this?" Cassie asked.

"No, of course, he didn't; of course, he didn't." Ulrich was shaking his head and had a faux dismissive frown on his face.

≈ chapter 9 ≈

The next morning on her way to work Cassie was crossing Connecticut Avenue on the outer edge of Dupont Circle when she saw Dhanesh, the firm's IT manager, emerging from the Metro station escalator amid a throng of commuters. She wondered if he might be able to get the firm's Ammari field data for her, not just the imports study which Ulrich had sent her. She ran to catch up with him, weaving her way through the other pedestrians who were walking in various directions. A siren somewhere near the circle was gradually getting louder.

Dhanesh was waiting at the curb for traffic to clear on 19th Street when Cassie reached him. "Dhanesh," she called out as she approached him from behind.

He turned around. "Cassie, what is it? Are you okay?" he asked. By then, a fire truck with its earsplitting siren was upon them, lights flashing and horn blaring. The two of them covered their ears as the truck turned off Dupont Circle and sped down 19th.

When the truck had progressed far enough, both of them uncovered their ears.

"I'm fine, Dhanesh," Cassie finally responded. "I just need a favor."

"Sure," he said, "Anything for you, beautiful."

"You know, you could get into a lot of trouble talking to women in the office that way."

"I know," he replied. "That's why I only do it with you because I know you won't turn me in, and because, of course, you're in love with me." He wore a playful grin as he spoke.

People were passing on either side of them now as they stood at the curb.

"Let's go sit down," Cassie suggested. They walked a few steps to a table in front of the sandwich shop and sat down.

"Dhanesh, do we have field data for Royal Sovoco?" Cassie asked.

"Field data for Royal Sovoco is an Ammari state secret," he said. "Surely, you know that."

"Yes, but our firm must have its own estimates," she said.

"Yes, somewhere," he said. "But why would you need that? You're North American oil and gas."

"Yes, yes, I know," Cassie said with a slight note of exasperation. "But I'd really like to see that information."

"Well, I could get it for you, but I don't know what good it would be. I've seen it, and it just adds up to the official numbers that Royal Sovoco publishes. Unless…"

"Unless what?" Cassie leaned forward in her seat.

"Unless somebody had different estimates, say, that they might have put in their encrypted directory," Dhanesh said.

"What encrypted directory?"

"Everyone has one."

"Well, I don't."

"I'll set one up for you today."

"Great, but that's not what I'm after," Cassie said. "You indicated that there might be other different estimates in somebody's encrypted directory." She paused. "Wait a minute. Don't you encrypt everything we do on our servers?"

"Yes, we do. Most everything," Dhanesh said. "But there's a folder that you can encrypt yourself that no one, not even me, can decrypt. The passphrases are not on the server, just in people's heads if they've been careful."

"Okay…I see," Cassie said nodding. "But why would they encrypt these estimates?"

"If you had a private estimate that was different from what

the firm was putting out for the firm's largest client, would you make it easy to get to?"

"No, I guess not," Cassie responded. "But who in the organization might have their own set of private Royal Sovoco estimates, you know, that might differ from the official estimates?"

"I'd start with Hilliard and work my way down," Dhanesh said.

"Hilliard?" Cassie asked. Hilliard, yes, of course! she thought.

"If there's anybody that knows the Ammari oil scene, it's Hilliard," Dhanesh continued. "But even if there is such an estimate, you'll never be able to decrypt it unless you have the passphrase."

"I'll bet *you* could get it."

"Not even for you, beautiful," he said. "Like I told you, they're just in people's heads."

"You won't tell anybody I asked you about this, will you?"

"My lips are sealed," he said. He pulled an imaginary zipper shut across his mouth.

"Thanks, Dhanesh."

"Don't mention it," he said. "I mean literally don't mention it."

Cassie smiled as they both rose and crossed the street, completing their morning journey to work.

≈

Around noon Cassie was working in her office when Bob Ulrich stuck his head in her open door.

"Want to get some lunch?"

Cassie looked up. "Hi, Bob."

"How about it?"

"I don't know," she replied. "I've got so much to do I'm thinking about skipping lunch."

"Come on," he insisted. "We'll go to that Vietnamese place you're always raving about."

She twisted her mouth a bit as she thought about the offer.

"I'll even spring for lunch," Ulrich said.

"You don't have to do that," Cassie said. "But let's go."

She and Ulrich rode down on the elevator to ground level and soon they were outside in what was turning out to be another steamy Washington summer day. At first Ulrich walked so fast that Cassie practically had to run to keep up with him.

"Bob, could you slow down just a tad?" Cassie asked.

"Oh, sorry," he said. "I'm always in a hurry."

The restaurant was on P Street only a few blocks from the circle, and they reached the one-story yellow brick storefront in less than 10 minutes. Several people were eating outside on the patio beneath large umbrellas, but Cassie wanted to get out of the humidity.

Once inside, they sat down in one of the window bays, and a waiter immediately descended on them with menus and glasses of water. As they both focused on their menus, the faint fragrance of garlic, oyster sauce and ginger drifted from a nearby table. The waiter returned a minute later, took their orders, and then pivoted back toward the kitchen, which Cassie could see into behind the lunch counter.

Ulrich took a sip of his water. "You made quite a stir with your deepwater gulf report," he said.

"Quite a stir?" Cassie said staying cool in response to Ulrich's provocation.

"I can't believe you had the guts to call out Breckenridge Oil," he added.

"Did Hilliard put you up to this?" she asked.

"No," Ulrich responded. "I'm just talking here. Between us."

"Okay, then," Cassie said. "I wasn't trying to call out anybody. I was just calling it as I see it."

"Always the idealist, aren't you?"

"Bob, I'm not sure why I came to lunch with you today."

"Cassie, you're hurting yourself," he said.

"I'm not feeling any pain, Bob."

" 'Given current technology, we should expect the URR to be nearer to the low side of the Breckenridge estimate.' " He made quote marks in the air as he recited the sentence from her report.

"We *are* analysts, aren't we?" Cassie asked.

"Yeah, but we're analysts *for* somebody, not in a vacuum," Ulrich responded.

"So, I'm supposed to prostitute myself for Breckenridge Oil because it's a client of the firm."

Ulrich pulled back slightly. "I wouldn't put it that way."

"I think we need to be open to multiple perspectives at the firm." She looked out onto the patio for a moment to ease her discomfort.

"Don't be naïve, Cassie. There's only one perspective at the firm."

She turned back to face Ulrich.

"It's Larry Hilliard's perspective," Ulrich added. "There's lots more oil where that came from. Technology always gives us what we need, proving the doomsayers wrong again and again." Ulrich put his hands in the air to make quote marks again. " 'Whenever there's been a temporary shortage, people say we're running out of oil. But every shortage has turned into a glut.' "

Cassie stared at him slightly dumbfounded. "So, you and I, we're not about getting it right no matter where the facts lead?"

"But the facts lead to Larry Hilliard's conclusions," Ulrich insisted. "It's a happy coincidence. This is the firm's view, this is Larry Hilliard's view, and this is my view."

"And this is your view because it's Larry Hilliard's view?"

"Look, no one knows what the truth is with absolute

certainty. But this is what most analysts believe."

Cassie was growing increasingly miffed. "So, we should simply say what most analysts believe—even if it's wrong?"

"Cassie, you're never going to get ahead at the firm with an attitude like that," Ulrich retorted. "You can't tell people things that are way out of the box and work for a firm like EAI."

"Bob, do you think I don't know what you're talking about?" Cassie asked. "I changed that report against my better judgment to fit into that box." By this time her head was throbbing. Lunch no longer seemed that appetizing. She took her shoulder bag in hand and got up from the table.

"Where are you going?" Ulrich asked.

"I'm just not hungry anymore," she replied. She pulled some bills out of her wallet and laid them on the table. "Here's some money for my lunch. I have to go."

"Cassie, don't go," Ulrich said. He rotated in his seat watching her as she moved toward the door.

≈

By the time she returned to her office, the throbbing in her head had stopped. She discovered that Victor had called and quickly called him back.

"Victor, what's up?" Cassie asked.

"I have something to tell you," he said.

"Well, go ahead and tell me."

"Not over the phone."

"What's so sensitive that you can't tell me over the phone?"

"You can never be sure people aren't listening in."

"Don't be so paranoid, Victor."

"I'd rather tell you in person."

"Okay, how about after work tonight?"

"Can't do it," Victor replied. "I've got a gig in College Park, and I've got to be up there by six to set up. Could we meet tomorrow?"

"I'm going to a concert with Paul," she said. "But I could meet you afterwards."

"You're just going to ditch Paul?"

"Well, I wouldn't put it that way," Cassie said. "I'll make the necessary excuses and meet you at the café at Kramerbooks, say, about 10:30. Is that okay?"

"All right. I'll meet you there."

≈

The next evening as Cassie sat through a jazz concert with Paul, all she could think about was her meeting with Victor. What could he possibly have to tell her that was so delicate it couldn't be handled over the phone? Was it something about her? Was it something about somebody at the firm? She really hardly knew Victor, and this made it difficult to gauge what he might have to say.

When the concert concluded, Cassie told Paul she had to get back home. Paul offered to drive her.

"You don't need to do that," Cassie replied.

"But I want to," Paul said.

"I can just take the Metro back to Dupont Circle. You live out here in Rockville, and it's only 25 minutes on the Metro. Faster than driving really."

"There's something you're not telling me."

"No, there isn't."

He put his arm around her. "I want to stay with you tonight."

"Not tonight, Paul," she said. "I'm too tired, and I've got a big day tomorrow."

His disappointment was palpable, but he dropped her at the Metro station. He got out, walked over to her side of the Land Cruiser and gave Cassie a long, intense kiss before saying goodbye.

She climbed the stairs to the aboveground station, tapped

her Smartrip card on the fare gate and passed through. The yellowish glow of the station lights revealed an empty plat-form — that is, until a man in a green work uniform entered and walked past her, leaving behind a trail of smoke from his cigarette.

As she waited for the train, Cassie found herself feeling a little bad about lying to Paul. She hated secrets. But she didn't feel comfortable telling him that she would be meeting another man at 10:30 at night at a café. It's not that she had any designs on a romantic relationship with Victor. It's just that her meeting would have required a lot of explanation, and even she didn't know exactly what Victor wanted to see her about.

The truth is, she would have liked to have spent the night with Paul. Their schedules were such that it was turning out to be a rarer occurrence than either of them wanted it to be. If Paul had told her when they had made their plans that he wanted to stay the night, she would have scheduled her meeting with Victor on a different day. But now she was committed.

The Metro ride into Dupont Circle was uneventful. As she stepped off the station escalator at Q Street, she was ac-costed by a man holding a large Styrofoam cup asking for change. She reached into her pocket, pulled out some coins and deposited what she had into the cup. The man thanked her saying, "May the Lord bless you, and have a nice eve-ning."

She made her way across Connecticut and could see that the sidewalk was teeming with people, as it often was on clear summer nights. She continued to 19th where she turned toward Kramerbooks. When she spied the red awning of the open-air café, she looked for Victor near the entrance but couldn't see anyone waiting there. As she got closer, she spot-ted him already seated near the back away from the street. A smattering of people occupied tables here and there, a lull before the late evening rush. She passed through the entrance, and he rose to greet her as she approached.

"How was the concert?" he asked.

"They're not as good as you, but then it was jazz," Cassie answered as she seated herself at the small, square gray table.

"I like jazz," Victor said as he sat back down. The overhead spotlight shining down on the table made everything else in the café seem dark by comparison.

"I didn't take you for a jazz man," Cassie responded.

"Things are not always what they seem," Victor replied. "Which brings us to tonight's topic."

"Which is?"

Victor leaned forward and said in a hushed tone, "Lawrence Hilliard."

"So, what's the word on Hilliard?" Cassie asked in a quiet voice.

"You remember that I talked to the landscaper when we went to the open house?"

"Yes," Cassie said.

"A company called Century Associates was paying for Hilliard's landscaping."

"Yes, I remember."

The waiter arrived to take their order. Victor ordered the crab cake appetizer, and Cassie agreed to eat part of it. They each got a glass of pinot grigio.

After the waiter departed, Victor continued with his story. "I looked up Century Associates in the state corporation records of Maryland, Virginia and the District of Columbia."

"And?"

"And there were six listings. Five of the companies are now defunct. Only one is still operating, and its address is in Washington."

"Okay."

"There was no phone number. So, I figured I would go to that address and see what was there. It was a storefront operation with postal boxes. I went back the next morning to see if anyone would pick up mail from that box. No one did. Then I tried again the next day, and someone came and got the mail.

"I followed this woman every which way." Victor was moving both index fingers in various directions. "She went down into the Metro, came back up near Dupont Circle. Did some errands. Went back down, and I almost lost her. But I found her just as the train arrived. I hurried down the platform and squeezed into her car. I trailed her when she got off at Farragut North. Are you seeing what I'm saying?"

The waiter placed glasses of wine before both of them and then left.

"Farragut North," Cassie repeated, trying to understand.

"That's the K Street stop. All the lobbyists and lawyers are there," Victor noted as he took a sip of wine.

"Yes, of course."

"Well, I followed her to an office building and then up the elevator. And when she got off, she went into the law offices of Kerrigan, Forrester and Light," Victor said. "That's what I bring to you. Do you know anything about this law firm? I couldn't find much."

"Victor," Cassie said. "That's the law firm that represents Royal Sovoco and the Ammari government in the United States."

"What do you think this means?"

"Why would the law firm for the Ammari government pay for Larry Hilliard's landscaping?"

"But they didn't just pay for the landscaping."

"What?"

"I got information from the building permit. I called the general contractor who filed it, and I asked if they could confirm that they had gotten their last payment from Century Associates."

Cassie's eyes were widening by the second. As Victor continued, she inadvertently took a large gulp of her wine.

"The receptionist switched me over to accounting, and they confirmed they got the last payment of $623,000 and something—from Century Associates," he said.

"Let me see if I have this straight," Cassie began. "The law firm for the largest state-owned oil company in the world and its government is paying—correction, has paid for—a 12,000-square-foot Federal-style brick mansion for the chairman of what is arguably the most influential energy consulting firm in the country. Now, why would they do that?"

"Perhaps their client wants to reward Larry Hilliard for his excellent work," Victor said.

"They could have done that by simply paying the firm," Cassie said.

"But then the partners would get some of the money."

"Or they could have signed him up to a separate consulting contract—a conflict of interest with the firm, of course—but it happens all the time. Then, they could pay him directly."

"But they didn't do that either," Victor said.

"He could be trying to avoid taxes," Cassie said. "But the Ammaris have so much money they could just give him enough for a big fat bonus and then add more on top of that so that he could pay the taxes and still keep whatever millions they intended him to keep."

"So, the question is: Why does he wish to hide this from the firm and the tax authorities?" Victor asked.

As Cassie thought for a moment, the crab cakes appeared. They each took one and had a bite. "Victor, you said you had worked on computers before, right?" Cassie asked.

"Yes, I did that before becoming a trader."

"If you were trying to break into someone's account, how would you do it?"

"It's fairly easy to break into an account," he answered. "What are you planning on doing?"

"And, once in the account, how would you go about accessing encrypted information?"

"Well, it depends on the type of encryption, of course. But the best way is to go in through the front door. If you can find or figure out the passphrase, then you go straight in just like the user himself," he explained. "So, now you have to tell me whose account you are trying to break into."

"Larry Hilliard's."

"And what do you think you will find there?"

"I'm not sure," Cassie answered. "But if he has numbers for the oil reserves in Ammar, that is, field-by-field estimates, seeing those might tell me something."

"Ammari field-by-field numbers are a state secret," Victor responded. "How could even Larry Hilliard gain access to them?"

"If anybody has access to them, it would be Larry Hilliard."

"And what would he do with them if he had those numbers?"

"I don't know," Cassie responded. "But if those estimates exist, I want to see them. Victor, will you help me?"

"Yes, of course."

"By the way, why did you go to all the trouble of making those calls and following that woman to the law firm?"

"I detest fakes like Larry Hilliard and their smug certainty about things which they obviously know little about."

Just then Cassie caught a glimpse of a man near the entrance who seemed somehow familiar.

"What are you looking at?" Victor asked.

"I thought I recognized someone, but I can't place him," Cassie said.

"Where?"

"Near the entrance."

Victor twisted around, but by that time the man had disappeared.

"Which one?"

"He's gone now. Well, maybe it will come to me," Cassie

said. "Anyway, back to where we were. So, how do we start?"

"Like I said, the front door is always the best way to get in. Now, what is Hilliard's background?"

"What do you mean?"

"What did he study in school?"

"Let me think." Cassie pondered the question for a few moments. "It was political science. He's a political scientist by training."

"Good, excellent. He probably knows next to nothing about computers," Victor said. "So, here is what we can expect. Your IT guy will have told him that he needs to change his password every so often. Being a complete computer security idiot, he will have several passwords written down in the vicinity of his desk that he will use over and over. We have to get those passwords."

"You want me to go into his office and steal them?"

"No," Victor said in mock outrage. "We are just going to borrow them for a while." He put on a devilish smile. "Then, we are going to have to figure out his passphrase. Now the computer guy will have told him never to write down his passphrase. Since he understands this, but needs to choose a passphrase that his tiny little brain can remember, he will choose something that we can find in his biography.

"So, this is your assignment," he continued. "Try to get his passwords, and also research his life. The names of his children, of his grandchildren, of his pets. The kind of car he drives. The places he goes on vacation. His date of birth. His anniversary. The names of his father, mother, sisters and brothers, and so on. Now, he will think he has made himself invincible by mixing one of his numbers with one of these names, just like the IT guy told him. But he will actually have made himself more vulnerable since we have more names in our biography than numbers. So, we only need to make combinations of the few numbers with the many names. It's still a little tedious. But I have found that it works quite well, and it makes it much more difficult to detect any break-in because everything looks normal."

They both took a sip of wine.

"So, you think he is hiding embarrassing numbers in those files?" Victor asked.

"It doesn't make any sense to me," Cassie said.

"But you don't believe the Ammaris' official estimates?"

"Right now, I'm just curious to see if maybe Larry Hilliard has any information. You know, other than what's public," she said.

"What are you thinking?" Victor asked.

"I'd rather not say right now," Cassie replied. She was, however, thinking that those numbers, if they existed, might confirm that the Ammaris have plenty of oil. Hilliard had always been so positive about future oil supplies from Ammar that he might have numbers showing much greater reserves than the Ammaris had ever stated publicly. Information like that might depress oil prices, not an outcome the Ammaris really want. But if his private estimates were less than what the Ammaris were stating, the Ammaris would be all the more concerned that those estimates stay under wraps.

"Here's what *I'm* thinking," Victor said. "If the world becomes convinced that the Kingdom of Ammar cannot increase its oil production, fewer and fewer dignitaries will be kissing their rings in the future. Ammar will just become another country with declining oil. The interest and the money and the power will shift elsewhere to find new supplies."

"I'm not sure that's going to happen anytime soon," Cassie said.

"Let's see if you say that after you see those numbers."

"You mean, *if* I see those numbers, and *if* they even exist."

≈ chapter 10 ≈

The next morning Cassie came in especially early. As an excuse to get into Hilliard's office she had settled on the subterfuge of delivering the final version of her report on Breckenridge Oil in person. When she approached Hilliard's office, his assistant, Cecilia, was already at her desk. Cecilia was in her early sixties and had medium-length platinum hair which framed her delicate, pale face. Today, she was wearing a black pants suit and a purple top. Her reading glasses were perched on her nose as she arranged some papers on her desk.

"Is Larry in?" Cassie inquired.

"No, he hasn't arrived yet," Cecilia replied as she took off her glasses and let them dangle from the chain around her neck. "What do you need?"

Cassie displayed a large envelope in which she had placed her report. "Can I just put this on his desk? I want him to see it right away." Cassie *had* to get into that office.

"Okay," Cecilia said. "But don't move anything on his desk. He's very particular about that."

"Of course," Cassie replied.

She walked past Cecilia's desk and into Hilliard's capacious office. It had dark paneling from floor to ceiling. Couches and a table were positioned in front of a bank of windows which looked out onto 19th Street. Hilliard's desk was straight ahead, a monstrous, antique oval-shaped mahogany affair. Behind it was a long, mahogany credenza. The wood floor was covered with a large Persian rug.

She quickly made her way to his desk and started looking for any sign of passwords. She dared to pull out a few drawers, but found nothing. Then she pulled out an extender panel, the kind that people used to put typewriters on, and there they were on an index card taped to the panel. Cassie pulled an index card of her own out of the envelope she was carrying, laid the envelope on Hilliard's desk and then grabbed the first pen she could find. She had written five of the six combinations down when she heard Hilliard's voice. She looked at the sixth combination and recited it in her head as she closed the extender. She dashed to the other side of the desk and was seated just in time for Hilliard's entrance.

She turned and greeted him even as she was writing down the last password. "Larry, I just put the final Breckenridge report on your desk."

"Great," he said as he walked around behind his desk and put his briefcase down. "What were you writing?"

"Oh, I just remembered something and wanted to write it down," she answered. She got up and placed the pen back in the holder on the desk. "I think that's it."

"What's it?" Hilliard said eyeing various papers strewn across his desk.

"The report. I think I've gotten it the way you want it. It's right there."

"Oh, I see," Hilliard said as he located it on his desk. Then he looked up. "Was there anything else?"

"No, no," Cassie said. "I'll go now."

Cassie folded the card on which she had written the passwords and gripped it tightly in her hand as she made her way down the hall to her office. She passed by Bob Ulrich's office on the way and could see he was in. After she had ducked into her office and put the card safely into her shoulder bag, she got a notebook from her desk, went back to Ulrich's office, and knocked on the open door.

Ulrich was concentrating on something on his desk and

appeared startled by Cassie's knock.

"I didn't notice you there," Ulrich said as he rose from his chair.

"Don't get up," Cassie said. Ulrich sat back down and looked away from her for a moment with his hand under his chin. "What are you thinking about?" she asked.

He looked at her again. "I'm really sorry about lunch Tuesday," he said. "Sometimes when I try to help people, I go at it all wrong."

"You're absolved," Cassie said. "I know you were trying to help me. But now you can."

"Sure."

"Tell me everything you know about Larry Hilliard."

"Are you taking my advice, maybe just a teensy-weensy bit?" Ulrich held his index finger and thumb just barely apart as he spoke.

"Yes, maybe just a teensy-weensy bit," Cassie responded as she sat down.

She quizzed him about Hilliard for more than half an hour, but was careful to steer the conversation so he wouldn't be aware of what she was really after. She took copious notes as if she were listening to a college lecture. But it was names and numbers she was really interested in, and she ended up with a surprising collection of them.

≈

That evening Paul came to stay with Cassie for the night. But she was far too preoccupied with her research on Hilliard to pay much attention to him. She had closed the French doors leading to her den just off the living room and was busy surfing the Internet for stories and even personal information about Hilliard. Around 9:30 Paul opened the door and peeked in.

"You can't work 24/7, Cass," Paul said. "Why don't you

come out here and sit with me on the couch for a while?"

"I can't right now, Paul," Cassie replied. "I need to finish this."

"You can finish it tomorrow," Paul said.

Cassie swiveled her chair toward him. "Look, Paul, I said you could come over and stay, but I *am* going to finish this."

"Okay, I get it," he said. "I'll just turn on a baseball game. But you're going to miss a really good romantic comedy that's on television right now."

"Out, out," she said as she shooed him away with her hands. He closed the door and retreated back onto the couch.

That night she stayed up past 2 a.m. taking all the key words and numbers and trying different combinations. There were so many. Then she hit upon prioritizing them. Which ones, she asked, would be easiest to remember and most likely to be chosen? His wife's name, perhaps. His home telephone number, maybe. The names of his children and his parents. His birthday. His wife's birthday. His wedding anniversary. The model year of his car.

Once she had prioritized the words and numbers, she started making combinations again. She came up with close to 100 that she put into the likely category.

When she was done, she walked out into the living room and found Paul asleep on the couch. She went over to the window and gently slid it open. The night air was cool, and 16th Street was quiet. She moved across the living room, turned off the air conditioning, and then proceeded around the black granite counter and into the kitchen where she rinsed a few dishes, leaving them in the sink to wash later.

She paused for a few moments reflecting on the evening's activities. What was she really doing? And why was she doing it? If she got caught, she would lose her job. And that would mean foregoing a lucrative partnership and maybe a substantial windfall if the merger Evan had told her about went through. But worse than any of this, she might lose the trust of Evan Grant who had put so much faith in her.

She would talk it over with Victor some more to see if they really could get into Hilliard's account without being detected. And if there turned out to be nothing interesting in Hilliard's encrypted files, then that would be the end of it. She wouldn't be making her way down any list of people at the firm as Dhanesh had suggested.

As she contemplated her plan of action, she suddenly realized what Dhanesh had been trying to tell her. He knew something, but either wouldn't or couldn't say for sure that the information she wanted existed. *He* brought up the idea of encrypted files. *He* mentioned only Hilliard's name and no one else's. Dhanesh wasn't going to help her in any way that would get him into trouble. But he had given her a road map for finding what she wanted. And he was probably guessing that she would seek some help. Now she was frightened because she knew that she was almost certain to go through with her plan. She had to know what was in Hilliard's files.

≈

Over the weekend Cassie kept playing with various combinations of words and numbers that might make up Hilliard's passphrase. She called Victor twice and left a message, but he never called back.

On Sunday Cassie's mother called in the early afternoon concerned that she hadn't heard from her for several weeks. "I know you're busy, and I try not to bother you," her mother, Barbara, said.

"I'm sorry, Mom," Cassie said. "I've just been swamped and traveling a lot. But it's not a good excuse."

"Are you getting enough to eat?"

"More than enough, I'm afraid. I should try to cook at home more often."

"Is everything all right at work?"

"What do you mean?"

"You're not going to lose your job, are you?"

"What on earth would make you say that?"

"I don't know," Barbara said. "A mother never stops worrying about her children."

"I'm the one who's supposed to be worrying about *you*."

"Is Evan, okay?"

"Evan's fine, Mom."

"You know, I was thinking a few days ago about when you graduated from Stanford Business School. I was so proud of you. And look at you now. You've got this fabulous job in Washington, and you've made a great life for yourself." She stopped abruptly.

"Are you still there?"

"Yes, I'm still here. Look, Cass, I've got Maureen at the door. I didn't expect her so soon. Can I call you back later?"

"That would be fine."

After Cassie hung up, she decided to take her own advice and get something she could make for dinner that evening. She grabbed her cloth bag and walked down to street level. It was a clear, hot day. All was quiet now next door as she strolled past the vaulted entrance and gray stone tower of the Foundry Methodist Church. Every Sunday morning its bells would toll so loudly that Cassie would close any open windows for the duration.

She reached the end of the church building, crossed P, and then crossed 16th. She glanced down 16th toward the White House which was barely visible behind Winfield Scott's statue in Scott Circle. When she reached the other side, she saw a heavy-set man in shorts and a T-shirt having a cigarette as he stood along the semicircular drive just outside the Carnegie Institution.

A jogger brushed by her as she made her way toward the Whole Foods in the next block. She crossed 15th and passed the paint store that on weekdays served as a pick-up point for immigrant day laborers. Some would lean up against the white brick wall of the store, smoking and talking. Others would stand near the corner, hoping to increase their chances of getting chosen.

She reached Whole Foods and went in. She got the makings for pasta and red sauce, a salad to go from the salad bar, some yogurt and bananas for the next morning, and some hummus and pita bread for snacking.

She wanted to have a little wine with dinner and walked over to the wine aisle to see if the store had anything in small bottles. As she moved down the aisle surveying the selection, she had the strange feeling that she was being watched. She stopped, looked right and then left, but only saw an elderly woman bending down to grab a bottle of wine on the bottom shelf. Cassie resumed her search and settled on a four-pack of small bottles of merlot.

After paying, she walked out the door and started back home on P Street. Her cloth bag was bulging with groceries. As she crossed 15th, she again had the nagging feeling that she was under observation. She stopped this time, pretending to look in her bag and then swirled around to survey the streetscape behind her. Three children were riding skateboards on the other side of P Street. A young couple who had been walking behind her now passed by. A cyclist in a helmet and sunglasses was pedaling furiously on the street in her direction. Nothing seemed out of the ordinary. Probably just her imagination, she thought.

After she returned home, she fixed dinner and then curled up on the couch to continue reading the mystery novel she had started, it seemed, weeks ago.

≈

On Monday Cassie called Victor again and got no answer. She called once more on Tuesday, and still she got no call back.

On Wednesday morning Victor finally called Cassie at work. She told him she would step out of the office and call him back on her cellphone. She dialed him as soon as she cleared the front entrance, and Victor picked up after one ring.

"Where have you been?" Cassie asked as she walked down 19th away from Dupont Circle.

"Sorry," he said. "I was at a friend's cabin. No landline and out of range for my cellphone. What is so important that I should rate four messages?"

"I've finished my homework," Cassie answered. "Can we get together tonight?"

"I have a practice session until 6:30. Can you come by my house around 7 o'clock?" he asked.

"Yes, that'll be fine," Cassie said. As she was speaking, she caught a glimpse of the man she thought she had seen in the café at Kramerbooks the week before.

"There he is," she said into the phone.

"There who is?" Victor asked.

"Now I lost him."

"You lost who?"

"Remember the man I thought I recognized in Kramerbooks last week?"

"Yes."

"Well, I thought I just saw him across the street. But now he's gone." Cassie stopped for a moment.

"Are you still there?" Victor asked.

"It probably wasn't him. I didn't get a good look," Cassie replied. "Anyway, we're all set for 7 o'clock."

"Right. I'll see you then."

Cassie flipped her phone shut and started back toward the building entrance. Her cellphone rang. It was Paul.

"Paul," Cassie said. "Are you calling from the conference?"

"No, I had to come home this morning to deal with a crisis in the office," he replied.

"Is everything okay?"

"Now it is," he said. "But I sure would like to see you tonight."

"Ohhh," Cassie said. "Tonight's not good."

"What's happening?"

"I'll tell you later."

"Why not tell me now?"

"I said I'd tell you later." Sometimes Paul could be such a child, she thought.

"Fine," Paul said. "Later then." She could hear in his voice that he wasn't happy. "Now I want to make sure we're still on for the Fourth of July. Are we?"

"Yes, we are," Cassie said. "Don't be upset."

"I'm not upset," Paul replied. "I just miss you."

"I miss you, too," she said. "Maybe we can get together tomorrow?"

She could hear Paul breathe in.

"I'm out of town again," he said. "Look, we'll have the whole day together on the fourth."

They said their goodbyes, and she flipped her phone shut. Cassie knew she loved Paul. But he infuriated her at times. Yes, it was frustrating for both of them being so busy. But she wished he could be an adult about it and not act like a lovesick child half the time. On the other hand, it was clear he was crazy about her, and what woman doesn't like that? And he was handsome and fun to boot. Did she really think she could do better?

She returned to the building and ascended in the elevator to her floor. She once again tried to picture the man she saw — or at least thought she saw — on the street outside and compare him to the one at Kramerbooks. Was it really the same man? If so, why did he seem familiar?

≈

After work Cassie walked home and had some leftovers to eat. About ten to seven she got into her car and started toward Victor's, turning north on Connecticut out of Dupont Circle. But traffic soon became hopelessly snarled. She saw red flashers ahead and what she thought was an ambulance. Everything came to a complete halt, and she found herself penned in on both sides, unable to turn off Connecticut. She would have been better off taking the Metro and walking from the station to Victor's, she told herself. Finally, she reached Victor's house around quarter after seven and parked on the street.

As she approached his gray bungalow, he was standing on the porch between the A-shaped columns of flagstones that held up the roof. "I thought maybe you weren't coming," he said.

"Big traffic tie-up on Connecticut. Big accident," she said as she mounted the steps.

"Well, at least you're here."

When she reached the porch, she noticed open boxes of produce strewn about the floor. Inside were green cabbages, Swiss chard, salad greens in plastic bags, tomatoes and zucchini.

"What's all this?" she asked.

"Oh, that," he said. "I'm a drop-off point for a CSA."

"CSA?"

"Community Supported Agriculture. You pay a local farmer up front, and you get part of the harvest for the growing season."

She stared for a moment longer, spying what she thought were some cherries, and then followed Victor through the door.

The foyer opened immediately into a spacious living room with a fireplace against the far wall. The room was jammed with keyboard instruments of all imaginable types. Some were small. Others had long keyboards and all sorts of dials and switches above. One looked like a guitar with a keyboard.

Another keyboard was literally a sheet of some material rolled up on the only piece of furniture in the room, a red couch. Toward the far end of the room was a grand piano, and opposite that was what Cassie thought was a harpsichord. She pointed to it.

"Is that what I think it is?" she asked.

"Yes," Victor replied. "I'm just learning to play it. It's a whole different feel."

"And this. What is this?" Cassie was pointing to an instrument shaped like a trapezoid with strings drawn tightly across it.

"It's a hammer dulcimer," he replied. "Kind of like a piano in a drawer. You hit the strings with these." He picked up what looked like two sticks with slight curves at the end and began to plunk out a tune that sounded faintly familiar.

"That's fantastic," Cassie said when he had finished. "What's it called?"

"'Rakes of Kildare,'" Victor replied. "Well…welcome to my home. It's a little too musical for some tastes."

"Not at all," Cassie said as she walked around and drew her fingers across some of the various keyboards.

"Perhaps we should have a look at your homework," Victor said.

"Yes, of course," Cassie replied.

"Let's go into the dining room."

As Cassie entered the dining room, she pulled several sheets of paper out of her shoulder bag. Victor adjusted a rheostat on the wall to brighten the chandelier. Cassie sat down at the round oak table, and Victor pulled up a chair beside her.

She laid the sheets on the table. The top sheet had Hilliard's username and passwords on it, the ones she had copied from his desk that day, and the other sheets had her passphrase guesses. Victor spread them out and surveyed them briefly.

"Beautiful work," he said. "Let's give them a try."

He gathered up the pages and then walked through a doorway at the back of the dining room. He motioned for Cassie to follow him. Once inside Cassie saw Victor sit down at a desk with three computer screens on it.

"Oh, sorry," he said. "Let me get you a chair."

"No," Cassie replied. "I'll get it."

"What's the address for your firm's site?" Victor asked as she exited into the dining room.

Cassie gave him the web address as she carried a chair from the dining room into Victor's office. He was already trying to log into Hilliard's account by the time she sat down. But he ran through every password without success.

"You're sure you got these right?" Victor asked.

"As sure as I can be under the circumstances," Cassie responded.

"Let me check something. What's your username and password?"

Cassie told him, and Victor easily logged into her account. "Maybe we can't log into Hilliard's account remotely," he said. "We might have better luck going to your office."

"Victor, you can't just come there tomorrow and log into Larry Hilliard's account," Cassie said.

"I know," Victor said. "That's why we are going tonight."

With that he closed the browser page he had been working on and the screen returned to what Cassie quickly realized was a trading program for commodities.

"I thought you gave all this up," she said.

"I gave up doing it for other people," Victor responded. "And, you see, by playing at George Mason that night and then slyly making your acquaintance I was trying to get inside information for my trading."

She realized he was joking but went along with his joke. "So, what do you mean by inside information?"

"Well, you let me know what every imbecile of an oil analyst is thinking so I can do the opposite."

Cassie was hurt at being lumped in with people Victor considered imbeciles.

"Oh, I'm so thoughtless," Victor said. "I didn't mean *you*."

"But you said that all oil analysts were imbeciles," she replied. "So, do you think *my* work is worthless?"

"Absolutely not," he said. Victor paused for a few moments and then took a deep breath and let it out. "May I ask you a question?"

"Only if you think I'm not too much of an imbecile to answer it."

"Do you think you could forgive a silly Russian with a careless mouth?" He had an exceedingly contrite look on his face.

"All right, I forgive you."

"Good. Now let's go to your office."

Victor handed the sheets to Cassie, and she put them into her shoulder bag. Soon they were out the front door and getting into her car. Within 15 minutes they were walking up to the lobby of her office building. It was already past eight. Cassie realized they would both have to sign in if they entered the building. She halted and put her arm in front of Victor to stop him. She told Victor to walk around to the back and buzz one of the residences until he could get someone to allow him into the foyer. He would then use her key card to let himself in a side door that connects the foyer with the offices.

"What about security cameras?" Victor asked.

"Oh damn," Cassie replied. She thought for a moment. "How about this? Call me on your cellphone when you're in the foyer. That's when I'll approach the guard and try to distract him until you can get on the elevator which is right there. Get off at the fourth floor, and I'll meet you there."

"Okay," Victor said. "Now, when you get to the guard's desk, find the monitor. Since the monitor cycles through all the cameras, watch for the one on the foyer. After it flashes off, end our call and that'll be my signal to enter."

Victor took off and a few minutes later he called Cassie.

She answered and kept talking as she walked into the lobby and approached the guard's desk. He was an African-American in his sixties probably, and he wore a gray shirt with black epaulets and a black cap with a silver insignia on the front like a policeman's. To the guard's left was a monitor with a split screen showing four video feeds from the security cameras. Each feed was flickering as it switched from one camera to another. She kept making small talk on the phone with Victor until she saw the foyer entrance flash on the screen and then off. She ended the call abruptly and engaged the guard in conversation. After talking to him for a couple of minutes, she signed in, walked down the hall, turned into the elevator bank, and saw an elevator waiting with its doors open.

When she arrived on the fourth floor, she found Victor against a corner in the hallway just off the elevator and right under the security camera. He nodded to her. She proceeded to the entrance of EAI's suite and opened the door, whereupon he hurriedly followed her in.

The suite appeared to be deserted when they arrived. Even so Cassie and Victor moved quietly toward her office, and once inside locked the door to prevent anyone from getting in. Using Cassie's computer, Victor found he was able to log into Hilliard's account with ease. Cassie looked around to see what was readily available in Hilliard's unencrypted files. There was nothing that looked like it would contain information on Ammari oil reserves. Victor loaded a program onto her machine which he said would allow him to try out various passphrases more easily. He hit the encrypted folder, and it asked for the passphrase. The first three combinations on Cassie's list didn't work.

"What happened?" Cassie asked keeping her voice down so as not to be heard outside her office.

"It's going to log me off his account after every three unsuccessful attempts at decrypting," Victor replied. "This could be slow going."

"Won't all this show up in some log somewhere?" Cassie asked.

"No," Victor said as he continued to work.

"Why not?" she asked.

"Because I'm going to erase the log."

It was slow going as Victor had predicted. Cassie had a list of more than 500 possible passphrases. Fortunately, she had brought along a flash drive with the passphrases on it. Victor copied the entire list into his special program. The main task was logging back into Hilliard's account after every three tries. The system prevented Victor from automating this task. The two of them alternated every half hour or so putting in passphrases. At one point Cassie got them some coffee after she was sure no one was around anymore. After several hours, Victor, rubbing his eyes and yawning broadly, turned to Cassie.

"We need to rethink this," he said.

Cassie looked at her watch. It was nearly 3 a.m. "What should we do?"

"All right, it's not any of the obvious combinations, or even the not-so-obvious ones. So, our man Hilliard is not as much of a pea brain as I imagined." Victor put his hands together and moved them up to his lips. The office was silent except for the hum of the computer. Finally, he put his hands down.

"What were some of the least likely words and numbers?" he asked.

"Well, I thought maybe the birth dates of his grandparents would be least likely," Cassie said. "And, oh yes, he was married once before. The name of his ex-wife seemed like an unlikely choice." Cassie handed him some sheets from her shoulder bag that listed the sources for the passphrase combinations they were trying.

Victor turned back to the terminal and tried the first name of the ex-wife and Hilliard's grandfather's birth date. Nothing. He tried the grandmother's birth date. Nothing. "What other numbers do you have which you consider unlikely?"

"I was able to find his student number when he was at Princeton," Cassie said.

Victor found the number on the listing and used it in combination with the first name of Hilliard's ex-wife. Finally, miraculously, they were in.

He let Cassie take over her chair. She looked through the folders. There were perhaps 50 or 60 of them. She found one labeled Sovoco. She opened it up and inside was a single file. She opened that file, and she almost couldn't believe it: field-by-field estimates for Royal Sovoco. But where did they come from? She scanned one of the pages carefully and found a notation at the bottom which read: "Royal Sovereign Oil Company of Ammar – Confidential." Just below were the words: "For Internal Review Only." It looked like the real thing. In any case, she wanted copies.

"Can we copy this file?"

"Try it," Victor said.

She tried it without success. "It won't work," Cassie said.

"I might be able to get around it with enough time, but I'd say our best bet is to print the whole thing out. Try sending it to your printer."

That didn't work, either.

"Let me try printing from the screen," Victor said. She got up, and he slid into her seat. He pushed the necessary keys, but nothing happened.

"Maybe we can print it on a different printer," he said. Cassie watched as he searched the system for available printers. He found a listing including a printer labeled "Hilliard." He did some typing and pressed the enter key.

"Wait," Cassie cried out.

"Oh, damn," Victor yelped.

"What did you do?"

"Well, logically, you shouldn't be prohibited from printing to your own printer, right?"

"And?"

"Well, I thought I'd test printing it to Hilliard's printer. Only I wasn't thinking."

"You mean you printed it out on *his* printer! His office is locked!" Cassie cried.

"Let's not panic," Victor said. "First, it will have been printed from his account. But he won't recall printing it. It will seem suspicious, but where will the suspicion lie?"

"We've got to get those pages out of there, plain and simple," Cassie said.

"How exactly?"

"I've got to get in there first thing tomorrow morning and take them."

Victor was nodding. "Yes, I think you're right."

Victor said he would now erase any incriminating logs and remove the program he had loaded. It took him a few minutes, and then he shut down Cassie's computer.

Cassie gathered the various papers they had been referencing, and then the two of them left the office and rode down the elevator. They proceeded out into the lobby without thinking. Cassie realized their mistake when the security guard called out to them saying, "Now, don't forget to sign out." He was pointing to a binder on his desk.

Cassie froze. She looked at Victor. He motioned with his head that she should move toward the desk. She did and then signed out. She consciously put a smile on her face as she looked up at the guard.

"Thank you," the guard said.

Then Victor looked at the list. Cassie's heart was beating fast because she didn't know what Victor was up to. He leaned down over the binder containing the sign-in sheets and then wrote something on the page. The guard thanked him, and he and Cassie made their way out onto the street.

"What did you do?" Cassie asked as soon as they were outside.

"I found somebody who looked like a salesperson, someone not located in this building who forgot to sign out, and I signed out as him."

"You're lucky the guard didn't know this guy."

"Yes, I was lucky."

Cassie took Victor home and then drove back to her condo. Once inside, she quickly climbed into bed. But she had a hard time sleeping as she thought about what was ahead. In just a couple of hours she would have to get up, go in early and try to get the Royal Sovoco report out of Larry Hilliard's office before he arrived.

≈

The alarm clock woke Cassie at 6 a.m. She showered, dressed hurriedly, gulped down some yogurt and then headed out the door. As she walked along P Street toward Dupont Circle, she saw the first rays of sunlight peeking through the trees. A lone cab passed by as she crossed 17th. In the next block the low hiss of automatic sprinklers filled the air as they watered the small gardens and clumps of bushes in front of the town houses lining the street. Newspapers covered in orange plastic lay near the entryways. Up ahead she spied a rat roaming on the sidewalk. It ducked into the bushes as she approached.

It was still cool, but a heavy, humid breeze foretold another miserable summer day. When she arrived at the circle, it was nearly devoid of traffic. As she looked into the park inside the circle, she could see a few sleeping bodies through the slats of the long benches that ringed the area. And with the sun now brightening, birds were chirping in the tall trees that dotted the park. Despite her mission, she managed to enjoy the unusually quiet walk along her daily route.

As she approached her building, she saw that only a couple of the windows facing the street were lit. To the left of the doorway a man was sleeping on a small, empty patch of concrete next to the canopy. Once she entered, she had to sign in before riding up the elevator.

"Burning the candle at both ends," the guard remarked.

"What?" Cassie said.

"You were here last night, right?"

Cassie realized it was the same guard. "Oh, right," Cassie said. "Lots of work to do."

She got on the elevator, and soon she was opening the main door to the EAI offices. She realized that she must have been the first person there. She walked to her office, unlocked the door, put down her shoulder bag, and then just sat, waiting. She couldn't concentrate enough to do any work. She had left her door open so she might hear Cecilia when she arrived. Cassie knew that Cecilia almost always arrived before Hilliard, and today simply had to be one of those days, Cassie told herself.

Half an hour passed, and Cassie was surfing aimlessly on the web. She kept looking up at every little noise, hoping it was Cecilia. Cassie realized she didn't have any genuine business with Hilliard, so she would have to invent some. She decided to stuff some empty sheets of paper into a large envelope and pretend she was delivering something. She would insist that she had to put it on Hilliard's desk herself.

At around quarter to eight, more than an hour after Cassie had arrived, she caught sight of Cecilia passing her door. Cassie was worried that Hilliard could arrive at any moment. She gave Cecilia just two minutes to settle in, timing it with her watch. Then Cassie got up and walked down to the end of the hall and entered Cecilia's office.

"Good morning," Cassie said.

"Good morning," Cecilia replied. "I don't usually see you here this early."

"I have some things I have to get done this morning," Cassie responded. "Is he in?"

"No, not yet, thank god. I'm not ready for him," Cecilia said. "I'm usually here earlier than this. But too many things were happening at home this morning. What can I do for you?"

"I just need to lay this on his desk if I could." Cassie was tapping the envelope she carried lightly on the palm of her hand as she spoke.

"Oh, yes, of course," Cecilia said. "Let me open his office." She took out a key, unlocked her desk, and then opened a drawer from which she withdrew another key. The whole process seemed like it was in slow motion, but Cassie knew it had only taken a few moments. All she could think was that Hilliard might come strolling in any minute.

Then the phone rang, and Cecilia answered it, dangling Hilliard's office key with her other hand. She motioned indicating she would just be a minute. But a minute turned into two and then three as the clock ticked down toward 8 a.m., the time around which Cassie knew Hilliard usually arrived. Cecilia was clearly doing her best to end the call, but the caller seemed to want to know every possible time Hilliard might be available the following week. Cassie tried to get Cecilia's attention in order to get the keys from her. When Cecilia noticed, she once again motioned indicating she would be off the phone shortly. And then, finally, she was.

"Sorry about that," Cecilia said as she rose from her desk and moved toward Hilliard's office door.

"That's okay," Cassie replied.

As the door swung open, Cassie nearly collided with Cecilia brushing past her on the way in. After checking to make sure Cecilia had returned to her desk, Cassie immediately scanned the office for the printer. She found it on the credenza behind Hilliard's desk. She went over, pulled a large sheaf of paper off the printer tray, and looked at it. It was indeed the report they had printed out the night before. She tried to stuff it into the envelope she had with her. But it was too thick to fit with all the paper that she had already put into the envelope. She laid down the Royal Sovoco printout and pulled out some sheets from the envelope. At that point, she heard Hilliard's voice outside the door. She shoved the Royal Sovoco printout into her envelope, and it went in easily this time. She put the extra blank sheets on top of the envelope, quickly scooted around to the front of Hilliard's desk, and turned to face him as he walked in.

"Larry, I, uh—" she started.

"Hi, Cassie," Larry said. He continued to march straight toward his desk and then circled around behind it.

"Larry, I was wanting to talk—"

"No time to talk right now," he responded. "I've got prospects coming any minute for a meeting." He had opened his briefcase and was sifting through it for something. Once he found it, he put it on his desk and then looked up at her. "Whatever it is, it'll have to wait."

"Right," Cassie said. "I'll go, and we'll talk later."

"Great," Hilliard said as he gave her a big smile.

As Cassie turned to make her exit, out of the corner of her eye she saw what she thought was a stray page in the printer tray. Her heart rate skyrocketed. The page had to be from the Royal Sovoco report. She would have to figure out how to get back into Hilliard's office to retrieve it.

As she passed by Cecilia, Cecilia said something, but Cassie didn't quite hear her.

Cassie stopped and turned toward her. "What did you say?"

"Aren't you forgetting something?" Cecilia was pointing to the envelope Cassie was holding. Then Cassie remembered that she had said she was going to put it on Hilliard's desk.

"Oh, this," Cassie finally replied looking down at the envelope with a sheaf of blank pages sitting on top. "Larry said he couldn't talk to me about it right now. Too busy. Something about new clients."

Cecilia seemed to be nodding in agreement. "I have to go," Cassie said.

When Cassie got back to her office, she put the envelope containing the purloined papers onto her desk, sat down, and then pulled them out. Then she thought it might be wise to shut her door. She got up, closed the door and returned to her desk.

She hurriedly went through the report, looking at the page numbers to make sure they were sequential. She got to the last page and that appeared to be the end of the report. Maybe what she saw on Hilliard's printer was just a plain sheet of paper after all. Then again, there could be an additional page to the Royal Sovoco report, maybe just an end page with nothing significant on it. But even so, it might still give away that the document had been printed.

Hilliard had people due any minute. She couldn't just march back in there. She agonized over what to do. Finally, she decided to wait in her office—all day if that's what it took—until she could somehow get back into Hilliard's.

She nervously thumbed through the document now in front of her. It was not obvious from what she knew offhand about Ammari reserves that these numbers would add up to something different from the total the Ammaris were publicly acknowledging. It would take some time to examine the entire document carefully. She slipped the report back into the envelope, opened one of her file drawers and shoved it into an empty file folder. Then she closed her desk and for good measure locked it.

She got up and opened her door so she could see Cecilia pass by. Then she sat and waited and worried. She pulled out some work from her shoulder bag, but she couldn't concentrate. She sat back in her chair and fidgeted and rocked, hoping desperately for an opening.

At about 9:30 her phone rang. She picked it up, keeping her eyes peeled on the door in case Cecilia passed by. It was Victor.

"Did you get it?" he asked.

"Victor, we're talking on a company line," she said in a hushed voice.

"Now who's paranoid?" he retorted.

"Not now, Victor," Cassie said. "I'll call you back later." She could hear him still speaking as she hung up the phone. Just then Cecilia walked by, probably on her way to the copy room, Cassie thought.

Cassie got up and went to Cecilia's door. She looked both ways and saw no one in the hall. She proceeded quickly and on tiptoe so as not to make any noise. When she got to Hilliard's office, she heard nothing coming from inside and stuck her head in. It was empty. He and his guests must have gone into the conference room, she thought.

She walked straight toward the printer. But the sheet of paper was gone. Now she was in a panic. She looked on the floor to make sure it hadn't fallen. It simply wasn't there. Then she heard footsteps. She ran and hid behind Hilliard's open office door.

Since no one entered Hilliard's office, it had to have been Cecilia returning. Cassie peeked around the edge of the door and saw Cecilia standing in front of her desk. She was looking intently at some papers in her hands. She shook her head and then went back out into the hallway.

Cassie waited a few seconds, then moved quietly past Cecilia's desk. She leaned into the hall and saw Cecilia entering the copy room. With that Cassie darted out and moved as quickly as she could back to her office. She unlocked her desk, pulled the report out, stuffed it in her shoulder bag, and left the building.

Cassie started walking down 19th trying to remember where she had seen a copy shop. She knew instinctively she ought to have a second copy of the document she was now carrying. And she ought to get that copy made as soon as possible. Exactly what she would do with it, she didn't yet know. As she walked, beads of sweat formed on her forehead and dripped down her face. She wiped them off with her hand. By the time she reached M Street, she was starting to sweat through her clothes. She now remembered a shop just three blocks away on M and turned left.

When she reached the copy shop, she pushed the door open and was greeted by a blast of ice-cold air. It felt good against her heated face and body. She bought a copy card from a card dispenser and went to work. The total number of pages turned out to be 128. She got a clear plastic bag to put them in, placed them in her shoulder bag, and exited the shop.

She went straight to her condo. There she turned on the air conditioning, took off her wet clothes, hung them to dry, and then put on some shorts and a T-shirt. She pulled a bottle of sparkling water out of the refrigerator, opened it and took a big gulp. The gas bubbles seared her throat and filled her nose, stinging on the way through. She slowed down and drank the rest of the bottle at a more moderate pace. She now felt extremely tired. She lay down on the sofa, and there she fell asleep and dozed until her cellphone woke her up. It was Victor.

"Cassie," Victor said. "You never called me back."

"Oh, sorry, Victor," she replied. "What time is it?"

"It's about 3:30," he said.

"Good god, I can't believe I slept that long."

"Did you get it?"

"Yes, I did," Cassie responded. "But not without a game of cat and mouse."

"Okay, that's great," Victor said. "You will tell me if there's anything in there worth knowing?"

"I might tell a lot more people than you, Victor."

Victor said he would be gone to a festival all Fourth of July weekend, but would check with her when he got back. Cassie said it would take time to analyze all the information anyway. They both said goodbye, and she folded her phone shut. Then she reopened it and called Paul.

"How are you?" he said when he picked up.

"I'm fine. A little groggy right now, but fine," she said. "Look, Paul, are you going to be around this evening?"

"Cass, I won't be back in town until maybe 9 o'clock."

"Would you mind coming over and staying with me?" she asked. "I'm really feeling like I want someone to stay here with me tonight."

"You know I will," Paul said. "I'll be over as soon as I can after I get back."

Paul had to take another call, but reiterated his promise to stay over that night. Cassie closed her phone and lay back down. She wasn't up to examining the Royal Sovoco documents today. They would have to wait.

≈

Late that evening Cassie was lying on the couch half asleep with Paul next to her watching television when his voice suddenly rose above the murmuring on the set.

"What?" Cassie said sleepily as she opened her eyes.

"Isn't that your boss?" he asked. "Right there." He was pointing directly at the TV. "That's your boss, isn't it?"

Cassie finally focused on the television. There he was, Larry Hilliard with his big friendly smile. Opposite him was someone named Nigel Lake. He was identified as an energy investment banker. By this time Cassie was upright.

"Turn it up for a second," she said.

Paul increased the volume.

"If the Kingdom of Ammar has peaked, then the world has peaked," said Lake in an unmistakable British accent.

"So you don't think Ammar has as much oil as they are claiming?" the anchorman asked.

"No, I don't," Lake said. "When we look at the amount of reserves they reported more than two decades ago—the last publicly audited figures—and you look at how much they've pumped since then, it just doesn't add up."

"What do you think, Lawrence Hilliard?" The anchor's face and Hilliard's were now in boxes side by side.

"Our estimates show that the Kingdom of Ammar can pump for another 75 years at current rates," Hilliard said.

"What do you say to Nigel Lake who points out that Ammari oil reserves have been exactly the same for years?" the anchorman asked. "Doesn't that strike you as a little bit odd?"

"Not at all," Hilliard replied. "The Ammaris have a very active drilling program, and they gauge their drilling to match their production. They drill whatever they need in order to replenish their reserves."

"They can gauge things that well?" the anchorman asked. "Even when it comes to something as imprecise as drilling for oil?"

"Remember, we're rounding to billions of barrels, so it's pretty easy to hit the mark," Hilliard replied.

The screen changed, and the anchorman appeared alone. "That was earlier today. And crude oil in New York closed at $116.57, down more than two dollars from yesterday's record high."

"He is so smooth," Cassie said. "But what a load of shit!"

"Cassie," Paul said. "I never hear you talk like that."

"Well, I was brought up not to talk like that. But being around men in the energy business all day has had an effect on my locution."

"What was a load of shit?" Paul asked.

"It's not just drilling. Hilliard knows that the Ammaris simply manipulate their recovery factor each year until they get the reserve number they want. In other words, they manage that number. But what's really a load of shit is to talk about 75 years *at current rates* when the whole point is for them to ramp up production dramatically to meet demand."

"What are you saying, Cass?"

"Oh, don't worry about it, Paul," Cassie replied. "It's not important. Not tonight, not this weekend."

"If you say so."

≈ **chapter 11** ≈

The following day was the Fourth of July. Cassie got up late and felt well rested for the first time in a week. She and Paul went to Rock Creek Park for a bike ride. Though she knew it wasn't exactly his favorite activity, he was a good sport and rented a bike so they could both go.

It was considerably cooler than the day before, and the air invigorated her as they rode alongside the creek. When they finished, they returned Paul's bike to the bike rental and put hers in the back of his Land Cruiser. They drove to Dupont Circle to have crepes for breakfast at a place on P Street. They sat down outside at a black metal table for two that was still shielded from the sun by the building. After they got settled and decided what to have, Paul went inside to place their orders.

Several minutes later a server brought out their food: a chocolate and raspberry crepe for Cassie and Nutella and banana for Paul with lattes to drink. Cassie liked to say that she and Paul were charter members of the "dessert first coalition" because you never know what the future will bring. And this meal was really like having dessert for breakfast, Cassie thought. She and Paul sat and ate in silence, just enjoying the food. That was one of the things she liked about him. Sometimes he could just sit. He didn't have to talk all the time to fill the void like so many people do.

After they had finished eating, they walked over to the farmers' market on 20th and Massachusetts and browsed stalls covered with white canopies. Cassie could smell sausages cooking on a grill but couldn't see them. The narrow walkways were mobbed with people, and Cassie and Paul had to slide sideways occasionally to move through the crowd. In one stall several fleshy, orange melons lay cracked open, and thin slices were neatly arranged on plates as samples. Paul was no fan of melons, but Cassie ate a slice that turned out to be soft and sweet and full of flavor. In another stall, red raspberries in pint containers covered an entire table. Cassie couldn't resist and bought four pints. Farther on she sampled some locally made goat cheese and decided to buy a pound of it and a loaf of sourdough bread as well.

Afterward she and Paul walked back to his SUV and drove to her condo. There they washed up and dressed in fresh clothes. Cassie sat down on the couch to read the mystery novel she had been working on, while Paul watched an old movie on television. It was one of those rare midsummer days in Washington when it was worth having your windows open. A pleasant breeze drifted over them as they snacked on goat cheese, sourdough bread and fresh red raspberries.

"Why oil?" Paul asked.

"Why oil what?" Cassie replied as she finished chewing on a piece of bread and cheese.

"Why did you become an oil analyst? Why not a pharmaceutical analyst, for example? Why not an airline analyst? Now that's sexy."

"Oil, my dear Paul, is *the* essential liquid in the modern world," Cassie said.

"And all this time I thought it was Scotch."

"Very funny."

"At least I carry around drug samples to show people. I don't exactly see any oil lying around here." Paul was teasing her a bit.

"Au contraire, mon frère. This apartment is filled with oil, drenched in it, in fact." Cassie pointed to the flat-screen TV that sat on a wide mantle above the gas fireplace. "The casing of that television is plastic made from petrochemicals," she said. She reached over to the coffee table in front of her. "The remote here, also plastic." Cassie paused and turned to lift a pen from the side table. "This pen—"

"Okay, I get it," Paul replied. "Anything plastic is made from oil."

"I'm talking about the ink inside," she responded. "And if it's not oil-based, then it's soy-based, and soybeans are grown with pesticides and herbicides made from oil."

Cassie nodded toward the kitchen. "All the food in there is dependent on oil, not only for running the farm machinery and making the farm chemicals, but also for transport."

"Okay, okay, I see your point," Paul said, raising one hand to indicate he had heard enough.

"I'm not done yet," Cassie said. "This rug was made in Pakistan." She was pointing to the burgundy and gold colored rug with an elaborate floral design that spanned much of the hardwood floor in the living room. "It's made from polypropylene, which comes from propylene, which comes from petroleum. And because it's made in Pakistan where a lot of the electricity is generated by burning oil, some of the electricity that made this carpet probably came from oil.

"Some of my clothes, some of my blankets, maybe even the damask cloth on this couch were made using synthetic fibers derived from oil." Cassie scanned the room. "The paint on the walls, the varnish on the floors, the adhesives and caulks, just about everything used to construct this condo has oil in it, or oil was used to manufacture it or transport it.

"And, of course, out there virtually everything that has a motor on the road, on the sea, on the rails, in the air, runs on oil. Modern civilization couldn't function for a day without it."

"I thought we were just going to stick with your condo," Paul said.

"All right," Cassie said. "Well, while we're on the subject, why do you sell drugs?"

"Pharmaceuticals," Paul said. "And the answer to your question is, 'It's a living.'"

"You believe in them, don't you?" Cassie asked.

"You mean, do I believe prescription drugs work or do I believe that people want them?"

"Both."

"I believe that people want them to work."

"That's a strange answer."

"Haven't you wished for something to work and when it works, you say to yourself, 'I knew that would work,' when what really happened was your belief made it work."

"So, are you telling me sugar pills would work just as well?"

"On the contrary, if we didn't dress them up and put exotic stuff in those pills and give them inscrutable names — well, nobody would believe that they would work. That's the genius of it."

"You are really a cynic."

"I'm not a cynic. People are helped everyday by the drugs I sell —"

"Pharmaceuticals," Cassie interjected.

"Why should I care how they work?" He shrugged his shoulders. "Anyway, it pays the mortgage."

"But you rent. You don't have a mortgage."

"But if I did, this job would pay it."

"Good enough," Cassie said.

"Look, I'm not going to be pitching pills to physicians the rest of my life," Paul explained. "Right now I'm talking to our government relations office."

"Here in D.C.?"

"Yeah, here in D.C."

"That's not exactly your field."

"It's all salesmanship. I can either pitch one doctor at a time or I can pitch the whole U.S. Congress and the American people," Paul said. "I was meant for this."

"You really want to become a lobbyist?"

"Isn't that what you are?"

"I'm an analyst."

"No, you lobby for oil. You may not call it that, but that's what you do," Paul said with a self-satisfied smile. "You spoke so movingly a few minutes ago about the essential liquid of modern society that I thought I was going to cry."

"But you held back your tears."

Paul put on a sad face rubbing just below one eye with his index finger. "Maybe my eyes watered up just a little bit." He paused, staring out into space and then looked back at Cassie. "You know, you and I are alike. We want to persuade the world. Just give us something to persuade them of."

≈

Later that evening Paul took Cassie to an event at the Custis-Lee Mansion above Arlington Cemetery. Paul's boss had invited his salespeople to come for a reception and brief historical lecture on the events of the summer of 1776. During the lecture Cassie's thoughts drifted back to that lone sheet of paper in Hilliard's printer tray that she'd left behind when she retrieved the Royal Sovoco report. It worried her; but there was nothing she could do about it now. And maybe it really was just a blank sheet. That idea helped her let go of her fear and focus on enjoying the rest of the evening with Paul.

After the lecture most people moved outside, milling around under the portico among the beige columns, columns that looked as if they had caramel swirls in them. The group was waiting for the fireworks to begin on the Mall across the Potomac. Through the tops of the trees Cassie spotted the glow of the Lincoln Memorial against the darkening sky. The Washington Monument now looked like a milky quartz crystal standing on end with two small glowing red rubies for its warning lights at the top. To the right, the Capitol dome displayed a muted incandescence as did the Jefferson Memorial. Then suddenly, the first flares were in the sky, and Cassie could hear the distant pops and explosions echo across the river. Pink, red and blue streaking halos of light filled the night sky. Paul put his arm around Cassie. She turned to look at him, and he initiated a long kiss. As their tongues met, Cassie imagined the night of lovemaking ahead.

When the fireworks were done, Paul and Cassie drove back to her condo. They were barely in the door when Paul embraced her and started kissing her all over her face and neck. His scent filled her nostrils—not cologne, which he never wore—but his own natural scent which she always liked. She began unbuttoning his shirt, and he reciprocated by unbuttoning hers. When Paul's shirt was open she ran her hands up and down his hairy chest and stomach. Then she put her arms around him and held him tightly.

She released her embrace and took Paul by the hand, leading him through the living room and into the bedroom. Both of them sat down and finished removing their clothes. As Cassie sat on the edge of the bed, Paul knelt behind her, reaching around and caressing her breasts while kissing the back of her neck. She reached back and started stroking him. He moved his hands to rub her stomach and then down again to the inside of her thighs which he began to stroke slowly and gently. Then he started brushing his hair against hers and letting out short, quiet moans as she continued to stroke him. Finally, Cassie turned, kissed Paul deeply, and pulled him down onto the bed. They simultaneously pushed the covers out from underneath them and continued their lovemaking.

Afterwards Paul quickly drifted off to sleep. But Cassie lay awake thinking about her and Paul. No one had ever made love to her the way he did. He was attentive, gentle, and never seemed to be in a hurry. He could make a lovemaking session last for an entire afternoon—not that they had had that many opportunities to spend the whole afternoon in bed. And yet, now she found herself thinking about whether it was enough. Sex was by no means the entirety of their relationship, but maybe it was a bigger part than she had realized. Still, what woman wouldn't be happy with such a mate? Enough, she told herself. She had a tendency to overthink things anyway. Why not just enjoy herself with this beautiful, sexy man and see how things develop?

≈

The next morning Paul wanted to stay, but Cassie was anxious to dig into the Royal Sovoco report. She talked Paul into giving her the day alone, promising to meet him in Rockville for dinner and stay the night.

Paul gave her a long kiss on his way out. Then she went into her study and plunged into the documents. She retrieved the estimates that Dhanesh had sent her on email, the ones the firm used to calculate the field-by-field breakdown of Royal Sovoco's oil reserves. Then she read through the report that she and Victor had printed out from Hilliard's encrypted folder. It was clear that there was no way to make a side-by-side comparison since each report had grouped reservoirs in a different way. She would have to take the internal Royal Sovoco estimates and translate those into something she could compare to EAI's estimates. And that would take some time. But she undertook a preliminary tally of the internal estimates from Hilliard's file, and it showed that Royal Sovoco had about 150 billion fewer barrels of oil than it was claiming publicly.

She wanted to tell Victor right away, so she called him on his cellphone. He didn't pick up, but he called her back a few minutes later.

"Cassie, you called," Victor said.

"Victor, I've done some more homework on the project we were working on." She didn't dare say outright what she had found over an insecure cellphone connection.

"And you found out that things are not as they seem," he said. "Cassie, I think it would be wise for us to wait and talk about this face to face when I get back."

"You're probably right, Victor," she said. "I didn't have anyone else to tell so I called you."

"I understand. But we should wait until next week to talk about it."

"Okay, Victor. We'll get together when you get back."

She hung up and tried to return to the tedious work of recalculating the Royal Sovoco oil reserve data. But the weight of what she had discovered already lay heavily upon her. Was Victor right? Was Nigel Lake—the man she saw on television the other night opposite her firm's chairman—was Lake right that if Ammari oil production had peaked, then the world had peaked? Had the Ammaris been deceiving everyone about the country's oil reserves for years? Was the world really approaching *the* turning point in the history of oil, when there would be less and less of it every year from now on no matter what? And what would the consequences be if that moment were about to arrive? She couldn't imagine it. It was too immense a problem for her to contemplate sitting all alone at home on a morning during the Fourth of July weekend.

She needed some air and went out for a walk. As she walked down P Street toward Dupont Circle, the imposing red brick town houses with their turrets and pediments seemed somehow vulnerable for the first time. As she approached the circle, she stopped momentarily to look at the Iraqi Embassy. Though she walked by it nearly every day, she had never taken time just to look at this unremarkable, brownish three-story brick building with an archway marking its entrance. Today, it seemed to have special significance since it represented the country reputed to have the second or third largest oil reserves in the world, depending upon whom you asked.

She crossed over the circle and entered the tree-dotted park it circumscribed. To her right groups of men were standing around permanent chessboards, watching the players compete. A portable CD player sat in the grass facing the tables. But Cassie could detect no sound coming from it.

Nearby two young men reclined side by side on a shaded patch of grass. On her left two women were doing the same, though one appeared to be fiddling with a camera. On the benches that lined the perimeter of the park, a man sat strumming a guitar. A little ways away another was napping, using his backpack as a pillow. Farther down, a woman was working on a laptop computer, and a man next to her was on his cellphone. A woman walking her poodle was circling the fountain in the center of the park as a helmeted bicycle rider standing up on his pedals drifted by. Two men sitting on a bench nearby shared a bottle of something hidden in a brown paper bag. In short, life in Dupont Circle appeared entirely normal, except perhaps a little more subdued because it was a holiday weekend.

Cassie sat down for a moment on a bench near the round, double-tiered white marble fountain. Pigeons were pecking at the sidewalk, making occasional noises as if they were commenting on the cuisine. The water in the small top tier of the fountain fell gently through three widely spaced spouts into a large pool underneath, passing by three classical figures chiseled out of the central column. She had learned that they signified the wind, the stars and the sea, all of which may have seemed slightly alien to these urbanites who lived and worked in air-conditioned quarters and were blind to the night sky because of the city lights. But Cassie associated these with camping and rock hunting with her father when she was growing up. She could remember being scared on some of the steep slopes and cliffs that she and her father had encountered. It was clear what to be afraid of, namely falling. That fear was concrete and transitory.

But this — this fear that she now felt — was deep down and undefined, and it made her shudder inside. And, unlike the fear of falling, which had an obvious cause and remedy, this fear had no clearly understandable consequences and no clear remedy. She felt she needed to warn the people on the circle. But how would she start? What would she say? And, more important, what exactly were they supposed to do about it? No answers came immediately to mind.

She remained as if in a trance for maybe half an hour. She was aware of the people around her — sitting on the benches, reclining on the grass, circulating in the park. But she felt completely detached from them. She understood something they didn't, and for now it separated her from them.

Finally, she got up. She walked over to the café at Kramerbooks, got a latte to go and sugared it heavily. She was sipping on it as she walked back home along P Street, and the sweetness of the drink eventually unlocked her brain. She was free of the trance.

When she returned to her condo, she worked for a few hours crunching numbers and comparing the two reports. Each comparison was confirming her first calculations that showed the Ammaris had a lot less oil than they were letting on.

She was due at Paul's that evening. But she wondered what she would say to him. Probably nothing, she thought. She was having a hard enough time digesting the news herself. And, after all, what would she tell Paul about how she came to this conclusion — well, not exactly a conclusion, but more a sense of dread? No, for now she wasn't going to tell anyone except Victor anything until she'd thought about it for a good long time.

≈

Cassie spent the night at Paul's condo in Rockville, and it turned out to be a relief not to think about oil or work or

Royal Sovoco. She decided to take Sunday off as well and leave the rest of the number crunching and comparisons for later. She was pretty sure what that analysis would show anyway. It would just confirm what she now believed was true. All of modern society was approaching a turning point, and nobody was really prepared for it.

She decided to stay over at Paul's Sunday evening and catch an early Metro back to Dupont Circle the next morning. She was in the bathroom getting ready for bed and was looking for some cotton balls to apply cleansing solution to her face. She worked her way down the drawers next to the sink until she got to the bottom one. The drawer was full of blister packs containing pills. Some of the blister packs had been opened and the pills removed. She grabbed a handful and laid them out on the bathroom counter. They were pharmaceutical samples, and she recognized some of the drugs. They included stimulants, anti-anxiety drugs, mood enhancers, and sedatives. She sensed right away what was happening.

She gathered them up and took them into the bedroom where Paul was sitting on the bed undressing. She threw them onto the bedspread, and he turned to look at her.

"Are you self-medicating?" she asked.

Paul ran his hand through the packages. "Where did you get these?"

"Let me rephrase that," she said. "Are you self-medicating?"

"Come on, Cass." Paul had a pained look on his face. "This is what I do for living, and it's very stressful. So, I take a few pills now and then to get through the day."

"A few!" She was furious. "I saw how many packages were in there. This is completely stupid, and you of all people should know why."

"Look, I don't need any lectures from you on the dangers of pharmaceuticals. I know the warnings on each of these drugs by heart."

"Which makes me wonder about your judgment."

145

"*My* judgment!" Paul shot back. "Who's doing the judging here?"

"This is unbelievable."

"You're acting like I'm doing something wrong," Paul said. He got up and came over to her and tried to put his arms around her. But she turned and walked away and found herself facing the wall.

"What am I supposed to do?" Paul said. His voice was cracking now. "I can't take it when you're mad at me like this." She heard him slump down on the bed and turned to find him sitting with his head in his hands.

She sat down beside him and instinctively began rubbing his back with one hand. With that he began to weep, emitting barely audible cries. He was obviously in some kind of terrible pain that she knew nothing about. She now realized that the pills he was taking had allowed Paul never to *appear* very stressed by an occupation which was clearly very demanding.

After several minutes, he raised his head. His eyes were red, and he looked forlorn. Cassie got up, retrieved some tissues from the table next to the bed and brought them to him. After he had finished wiping his eyes and nose, she leaned down and kissed him lightly on the forehead. "Let's get some sleep," she said. He nodded, and soon they were both under the covers.

Paul fell asleep almost immediately. But Cassie lay in bed with her eyes open wondering about Paul, about her future, about the future of the world. Finally, her confusion and sense of dread overwhelmed her. She got up and quietly made her way to the living room. She stood at the window for a minute looking out onto the deserted, rain-slicked street below and listening to the drip, drip, drip of water onto the exterior sill. As she stared into the blackness, soundless tears came rolling down her cheeks.

≈ **chapter 12** ≈

Monday morning arrived sooner than Cassie had wanted it to. She left Paul's while he was still asleep, caught an early Metro and was back in her condo by seven. She cleaned up, got into a burgundy business suit and then walked to work. Outside, it was overcast and muggy. When she got to Dupont Circle, the rush of people moving along the circle's edge and the traffic jamming the lanes were no longer reassuring. This was the world that oil built. But how much longer would it last?

Late that morning she received a call from Marta Nilsen, one of the few women she had made friends with since coming to Washington. Marta had come from Norway to take a faculty position in comparative literature at Georgetown many years ago. She and Cassie had gotten together periodically ever since they'd met at a reception at the Norwegian embassy.

"How are you, my dear?" Marta inquired. "I haven't talked to you in weeks. I trust everything is okay?"

"Everything is fine, Marta," Cassie said. "It's good to hear from you."

"I know this is short notice," Marta continued, "but I was hoping you could go with me to a play at the Lansburgh Theater on Wednesday evening."

"I'd love to," Cassie replied. "What's playing?"

"It's called 'An Enemy of the People,' " Marta said. "It's by Norway's most famous playwright."

"I've never seen that play," Cassie said.

"It isn't done here in the United States very often, but in Norway you can't grow up without seeing it at least once or twice."

"What time does the performance start?"

"It starts at 8 p.m., and I'm going to suggest that we meet at the theater and then go out afterwards," Marta said.

"Yes, let's do that."

"Okay, goodbye for now."

"See you Wednesday. Goodbye."

≈

When Cassie got home that evening, she continued her comparison of the internal Royal Sovoco field-by-field oil reserve estimates with those used by EAI. It was midnight before she stopped, and she still wasn't done. But for the fields she'd been able to compare, the Sovoco numbers were quite a bit lower than EAI's estimates.

When she got up the next day, she realized that she had no appointments and only one conference call that could just as easily be handled at home. She phoned her office to say that she would be working at home that day in case anyone wanted her. She then proceeded to finish her comparison of the two sets of oilfield data for Royal Sovoco. It was late afternoon when she completed her work, and the comparisons and calculations did indeed confirm her original totals. All the fields were accounted for, and there was a difference of about 150 billion barrels between the official public estimate and the one in the confidential internal documents. Even so, the Ammaris would still have the largest oil reserves on the globe, or nearly so.

But the world's nations were basing their energy policies on a much higher number. That could prove problematic if the Ammaris were not actually able to deliver the flows of oil expected. Perhaps the Ammaris believed they had a lot more oil to discover. If so, why hadn't they drilled those areas they deemed most likely to contain oil and established more proven reserves? Yes, it was costly, but they had the money, and then there would be no doubt.

Cassie began to question everything she'd been told about the future of oil. She thought about what Victor had said about the limits on production from the Canadian oil sands. She thought about the problems she had discovered with deepwater drilling in the Gulf of Mexico. When she added that to an apparent ongoing deception by the government of Ammar and its state oil company, what projection, what information from an official source, could really be trusted anymore when it came to oil?

Yes, there was a lot of talk about large new discoveries off the coast of Brazil, West Africa, and elsewhere. But without the gigantic oil reserves thought to be in the Middle East, even these new finds might not be enough. As people in the oil business often say, "Depletion never sleeps." The day a well starts producing is the day it starts depleting. Every year the world has to make up for the decline in production from existing wells first before it can add to supplies. She often likened it to climbing up a down escalator. And Cassie decided that if the extra reserves claimed by many Middle Eastern OPEC members in the mid-1980s were merely phantoms—as the presenter at the peak oil conference had suggested—then the peak in world oil production was probably a lot nearer than most experts suspected.

She picked up the phone and called Victor. She needed someone to talk to. He was home and agreed to meet her at Kramerbooks.

When Victor walked into the café, Cassie was already seated next to the railing near the sidewalk and working on a piece of walnut pie. He snaked his way past several empty tables to reach her.

"You've got a head start," Victor said as he sat down. He moved in closer on the pie. "Are you sure you don't need some help with that?"

"Dessert before conversation, right?"

"Always," he said with a smile.

"Go ahead," Cassie said. "Dig in."

Victor unrolled the silverware from his black cloth napkin, picked up the fork, and sank it into Cassie's pie. He levitated a small chunk into this mouth. "Mmm. This is good," he said as chewed on it. "I'll have to remember to get a piece next time I come." A waitress arrived a moment later, and he ordered a cappuccino.

"Okay, my dear Cassie, what details do you have for me?" Victor asked.

"Victor, those Royal Sovoco estimates…" She sank her fork into the final chunk of pie and suspended it in midair. "I thought at first I might be missing some pages. But it's all there. The Ammaris' internal estimates show that they have 150 billion barrels less than they are telling the world."

"You see, this comes as no surprise to me."

Cassie had put the final bit of pie into her mouth and put her finger in the air to signify that she needed a few more seconds to finish it. When she was ready, she started to speak again. "Well, I know that, Victor. But it's a big surprise to me, and the gap is so huge that it isn't just a rounding error. This has to be an intentional deception."

"What are you going to do?"

"Nothing right now. I mean I've got stolen documents that I am almost certain are authentic. What am I supposed to do?"

"Maybe you should start getting ready."

"Getting ready for what?"

"For peak oil, that's what."

"How does one 'get ready' for peak oil, Victor? None of us can do anything about it. It's too big. It's going to overwhelm us."

"Yes, you might be right," he replied. "But I prefer not to just sit around. That's why I'm growing my tomato plants in the front and my garden in the back. It's pathetic, I know. But it's a start."

"You think food supplies are going to be affected?"

"Probably not right away, but someday. You're an oil and gas analyst. You know how heavily agriculture depends on both of those. Reduce the amount of oil you have, and you get food shortages. Unless, of course, everyone has gardens. It's not a perfect solution, but it's something." At that point Victor's cappuccino arrived. As soon as the waitress set it down, he picked it up and took a sip.

"Do either of you want anything more?" the waitress asked. They both said no, and she turned away.

"What about transportation?" Cassie asked. "We can't just junk all the cars tomorrow and expect people to get anywhere."

"Oh, but I wish we could!" Victor said as he put one hand on his chin. "But you're right."

"Victor, I'm frightened, truly frightened, and I don't know what to do."

"Nobody knows what to do," he replied. "But people are trying things all over the place. When you're confronted with something this big, you just make a start. And well, you already have. You have a bike. You walk to work. It's a start."

"But if things get bad enough, will I even *have* work?"

"I don't know. It might take 25 years of slow grinding downward before things get really bad. Or, it might happen just like that." He snapped his fingers. "But pretending it isn't going to happen—well, it may make you happier today, but tomorrow you will be unprepared, confused and sad."

"You don't think we have much time?"

"I am an oil trader by profession. No one has ever seen this kind of move in oil. Yes, I know it's supposed to be speculators. And maybe that's some of it. But the peak is coming.

That's what people are sensing even if they don't know it. And it will change *everything*—everything you think you know."

"What are you going to do? Are you going to stay in Washington?" Cassie asked.

"For the moment I have to tend to my tomato plants," Victor said. "But in the long run, probably I will go some-place else. I'm not sure Washington will be the best place to be. After all, the only thing they grow here is government."

As Cassie and Victor sat quietly for a moment, the wait-ress placed the bill on the table.

"Victor, I don't feel like sitting. Let's get up and move around."

Victor took a last sip of his cappuccino, looked at the bill and put some money on the table.

"You don't have to do that," Cassie said.

"No, it's fine," Victor said with a wave of his hand.

"Let's walk up Connecticut," she said.

"Sure, why not?"

They got up, walked through the bookstore and then out onto Connecticut Avenue. As they strolled up Connecticut, Cassie, the oil analyst, was suddenly aware of oil in a way she had never been. She had always taken it as a given. The price of oil next month or next year wasn't even the critical piece of information. More important was how to transport the oil, where those pipelines should be built, and who would get the contracts to build the pipelines. It was about oil ports and refining capacity. It was about oil company exploration budgets and new technologies. It wasn't about how much oil there was, but about how much you wanted to get out of the earth at any given price. It was in a way all about logistical issues. Long-term oil supply had never really been a question. But now it was, and she tried to discern what that meant.

She thought about her conversation with Paul about why she had chosen to be an oil analyst. She had essentially bragged about all the things in her condo that were derived from oil.

At the time it was really nothing more than a parlor game, a mere exercise. But now everything she saw around her seemed at risk. The very sidewalk she was now walking on required workers to maintain it using machines powered by diesel and gasoline made from petroleum. The pavement of the streets she was crossing was made partly of oil and required the same workers and bigger machines to keep it in good repair. The buildings themselves needed constant maintenance using materials derived from oil and service by people riding in trucks powered by oil. And those buildings needed fuel to keep their furnaces going. In some cases that fuel was oil.

The products in the store windows she was passing had arrived by truck, train and ship. The camera shop, the electronics place, the women's clothing store, the pharmacy, and the video store she passed, none of them would be operating without oil. Many of the products and even their packaging were made using materials based on petrochemicals, materials like plastic and synthetic rubber. Even the perfume that was emanating from the woman walking in front of her was probably partly derived from oil. And the cars and trucks and buses coursing through the street beside her all ran on some form of oil.

The restaurants she passed—Italian, French, Thai, Mexican, Greek, the steakhouse, the hamburger joint—all of them seemed at risk. After all, modern agriculture was so heavily dependent on oil.

Suddenly for Cassie the whole world had now become one big manifestation of energy, much of it in the form of oil. Humans were not the builders any more. They were just the guiding hands for the flow of petroleum that came from deep underground and then went deep into the life of society. Petroleum, she knew, was doing the lion's share of work for the world.

Cassie had understood all this intellectually before. She even knew the energy industry was *the* key industry in society.

Nothing got done without energy. But she had never before understood it so concretely as she did today. She wondered if she could ever go back to looking at the fountain in Dupont Circle and not think of the energy needed to pump the water, or see a farm field and not think of the oil that goes into the tractors and the combines, or even enjoy simply reading a book without thinking about the energy used to cut the logs that were moved to the mill and made into pulp and then into paper that was then shipped to the printer and bound into books that were shipped to the bookstore.

All of these processes she understood. But now they had taken a place in the front of her mind in a sort of house-that-Jack-built fashion. Even more important, which of these processes could continue if oil supplies were declining—not some time in the distant future—but soon? There was really no ready substitute for oil, at least not on any scale that mattered. Above all, the world seemed oblivious to this oncoming danger.

Her mind was a jumble of impressions, questions and speculations. The future had been so neatly organized in her brain before this past week. Now it was a disorganized clatter of barely inchoate ideas for living in a world that had always been right in front of her, but with which she was only now getting acquainted.

It was a world in which energy was no longer an invisible and forgotten force, but suddenly central to her everyday calculations. She imagined that human society would slowly become like an emphysema patient who, with each passing day, has less and less ability to make it up the stairs or across the street and for whom every step has to be carefully calibrated so as not to get out of breath. She didn't like that image. But she wondered what might prevent something like it from becoming true.

"Victor," she said as they strolled back toward Dupont Circle, "is there any way out?"

"There's always a way out." He looked at her. "Finding it in time is the hard part; and then not complaining that it isn't what you hoped for, that's the next part."

Somehow she found that less-than-happy answer enough to stop obsessing about the energy embedded in everything she was walking on or by. She wrapped her arm in Victor's, and they continued their stroll in silence.

≈ chapter 13 ≈

On Wednesday night Cassie boarded the Metro at Dupont Circle to meet her friend Marta at the Lansburgh Theatre. After reaching her destination, she rode the escalator up out of the station into a world where the heat of the day had finally abated and a gentle breeze was buffeting the street. As she made her way down 7th Street, she spied the marquee of the Lansburgh with its semicircular ring of glowing incandescent bulbs hanging underneath. On the sidewalk she spotted a figure that she was sure was Marta and quickened her pace to reach her.

As she crossed 7th, she waved to Marta who had a tan cardigan sweater draped over a white blouse. Below that she wore tan slacks and dress sandals. Her ash blond hair curled slightly upwards from her shoulders. Although 52, Marta's creamy skin made her look years younger.

"Marta," Cassie called out as she closed in.

"You look stunning tonight," Marta said as she embraced Cassie.

Cassie had thrown on some white slacks and a yellow scoop top before coming — nothing special — and thought Marta was simply being generous with her praise.

"Thank you. You look beautiful as always," Cassie said.

"For a middle-aged spinster," Marta quickly added. "Let's go in and find our seats."

They made their way through the lobby and then into the theater. An usher handed each of them a program and led them almost to the front of the orchestra. They sat down on the right side in what were essentially box seats stationed along a semicircular aisle that ran behind the main seating area.

"These are marvelous seats, Marta," Cassie remarked.

"I got them several months ago. I've been to this theater many times before, so I've figured out which ones to get," Marta replied.

"This theater is smaller than I expected," Cassie remarked.

"Who has time to go to the theater in this town?"

"You're probably right," Cassie said. "This is *my* first time since moving here, and I'm only here because of you."

Cassie looked at her watch and then quickly scanned her program. "An Enemy of the People" had been written in 1882 and was about a certain Thomas Stockmann, a medical doctor, who discovered that the town's baths, which attracted many tourists, were contaminated and required extensive repairs. That's as far as she got before the lights dimmed and the curtain rose.

The story line emerged as follows: At the beginning of the play Dr. Stockmann enjoys the support of many leaders in the community and of the local newspaper editor in his quest to rectify the problems at the baths. But soon all those who support him turn against him as the town's leaders conduct a campaign to discredit Stockmann. At the end of the play, the doctor loses his job as medical director of the baths and is vilified as "an enemy of the people." His opponents portray him as simply looking for a way to bring down the town's leadership. They also accuse him of profiting from the health scare. His father-in-law — unbeknownst to Stockmann — purchases all the depressed shares of the baths from the other owners. In the end Stockmann stands alone vowing to fight on.

When the play concluded, Marta suggested that they go to the tapas bar next to the theater. "It's such a pleasant night. We should sit outside," she said. They quickly found some seats on the sidewalk.

"I love going to the theater," Marta said. "I don't do it often enough."

"Too busy?" Cassie asked.

"Busy enough," Marta replied. "And I don't know many people who like going."

"Have you been seeing anyone?" Cassie inquired.

"Not for a long time," Marta said. "At Georgetown it is research and more research, and I don't mind it. I like to think of myself as a serious scholar."

"Maybe a bit too serious?" Cassie smiled as she spoke.

"Maybe," Marta replied. "How about you? How's Paul?"

"Paul's fine."

"You don't say that with much enthusiasm," Marta said. "Is there someone else, maybe?"

"Well, not exactly."

"Is it all right if I inquire about Mr. Not Exactly?"

Cassie laughed. "Well, he's Russian —"

"Oh, you must watch out for the Russians." Marta had a smirk on her face.

"Actually, he's been in the United States for 18 years."

At that point a waiter appeared. "And what would you ladies like?" he asked.

Cassie wanted something to eat and so did Marta. Since Marta had been to the restaurant before, Cassie agreed to let her choose some dishes to share which, as it turned out, included something with sliced apples, fennel and Manchego cheese and then another dish with sea urchins and peppers, and a third that included ham and cantaloupe. Then Marta ordered a glass of rosé, and Cassie, a glass of the house white.

"That all sounds wonderful, Marta," Cassie remarked as the waiter turned and left.

"Those are my favorites," Marta replied. "Now, back to your Russian friend. He has a name?"

"Victor."

"And you are dating this Victor?"

"Not exactly."

"There you go again with 'not exactly.'"

"Victor is helping me out on a project."

"What kind of project, if I may ask?"

"It's kind of confidential."

"Oh, I see." Marta took a sip of her water.

Cassie then remembered that she had been trying to find a safe place to put her second copy of the Royal Sovoco report.

"Marta, would you be willing to hang on to something for me for a while?" she asked.

"Well, yes, of course. What is it?"

"It's some documents."

"Confidential documents?"

"Yes, very."

"Cassie, are you in some kind of trouble?" Marta inquired.

"Not yet," Cassie answered. "At least I don't think so." At that point a waiter placed their glasses of wine on the table.

Cassie lifted her glass. "To you, Marta, for your friendship."

"And for yours," Marta said as they clinked their glasses together and each took a sip of wine.

As Cassie put her glass down, her eyes followed the waiter for a moment. He was placing drinks on another table a couple down from where she and Marta were sitting. Cassie spotted someone she thought was the man she had seen both in the café at Kramerbooks and on the street in front of her office. He was seated with his back to her, and she only caught glimpses of the side of his face.

"What do you see?" Marta asked as she took another sip of wine.

"It's someone I've seen before, but I can't place him."

"An old friend…a colleague, perhaps," Marta offered.

"No," Cassie responded. "I saw him recently in Kramerbooks when I was there with Victor. And then I saw him on the street in front of my office, but only for a moment."

"Do you think you are being followed maybe?"

"I don't know," Cassie said. "But I think I'm going to find out."

She got up and went over to the man and tapped him lightly on the shoulder. He turned around, but it wasn't the same man.

"Oh, I'm so sorry," Cassie said. "I thought you were somebody I know."

"Well, you know me now," the man said. "Hank Flaherty." He offered his hand, and Cassie took it, shaking it weakly.

"Would you like to sit down with us?" Flaherty asked. There were two others, a man and woman sitting with him.

"No, no thanks," Cassie replied. "Sorry to have disturbed you."

She returned to her table and sat down.

"So, it is somebody that you know?" Marta asked.

"No, it isn't." Cassie was increasingly troubled not by her faux pas, but by Marta's idea that she was being followed.

"Marta, if you knew something, something you thought the public ought to know, but releasing it would mean the end of your career, would you do it?" Cassie asked.

"My problem is that as a professor of comparative literature I know lots of things that the public has absolutely no interest in knowing," Marta said as she chuckled.

Cassie put her head down.

"So this is not a hypothetical question?" Marta continued.

Cassie looked back up and shook her head slightly.

"Do you think it will make a difference if you do?" Marta asked.

"I don't know," Cassie said.

"Remember our poor Dr. Stockmann in the play tonight. Despite everything, almost no one believed him. And in the end the baths were still open, and he was completely ruined personally."

160

"I guess no good deed goes unpunished," Cassie replied.

They were both silent for a few moments.

"Oh, here we are," Marta said. "Our meal at last." The waiter set down three plates of tapas and then retreated back inside. The wind came up suddenly and blew Cassie's napkin away. Marta reached over to an adjacent table, pilfered a place setting and unwrapped the napkin around it.

"There you are," Marta said as she gave the napkin to Cassie.

"Marta, you were still in Norway when the big oil discoveries were made in the North Sea, the ones that turned Norway into a major oil exporter, right?"

"Oh, yes, it was quite a time. Norway was already a wealthy country, but it became quite a bit wealthier."

"Did anyone speak out against the oil development?"

"A few people did, mostly environmentalists and a few marine scientists."

"And did anyone pay any attention to them?"

"Of course not," Marta replied. "The oil was too valuable. You know, our neighbor Sweden has decided they want to get off oil completely by 2020. Of course, they have no oil in Sweden to speak of. So, all that imported oil is a liability for them. However, in Norway if you were to talk like that, well, at first they would politely put up with you. But in the end they might very well label you, well...an enemy of the people."

Marta paused to take a bite from one of the dishes. She looked back up at Cassie who had yet to touch a thing in front of her. "Cassie, I'm not telling you what to do. I'm telling you to be very careful."

Cassie nodded.

"Now please...have something to eat," Marta said.

"Okay," Cassie said. She took a bite of what she thought was the sea urchin. It was wonderful.

"Marta," Cassie said, "I'm going to send a package with

the documents I told you about to your Georgetown office. Just put them in some out-of-the-way place, will you?"

"The FBI isn't going to storm my office, is it?" Marta asked.

"No," Cassie said, "it's not that kind of information."

"Well, you never know," Marta said. "After all, this is Washington."

≈ chapter 14 ≈

The following morning Cassie put her extra copy of the internal Royal Sovoco oil reserves report into a large envelope and slipped it into her shoulder bag. She made her way to Dupont Circle on foot as usual. The July heat was stifling, even for this early in the morning. She could feel a dew of perspiration forming on her face. The crush of people in the circle made her feel even hotter.

She was glad when she was finally inside her air-conditioned office. Her first order of business was to prepare the Royal Sovoco envelope for delivery to Marta by the firm's messenger service. She put it inside a large Tyvek envelope to make sure nothing would happen to it in transit. When she had finished filling out the necessary form, she waited until just before the scheduled pick-up time and took the package out to the reception area to watch for the messenger. She expected him to show up shortly. But she had to sit out in the reception area for almost 15 minutes, pleasantly saying hello to everyone from the firm who passed by while she held the equivalent of informational nitroglycerin in her hands. Peggy, the receptionist, told Cassie more than once that she could just leave it with the other outgoing packages for the messenger. Each time Cassie had to insist that she really wanted to give the package to the messenger herself.

Finally, the messenger arrived, and Cassie handed him the package and the form. He tore off the yellow receipt and gave it to her, taking the pink one for himself.

"I'll take the receipt," Peggy said.

Cassie handed it over, went back to her office and sat down in her chair. She felt exhausted. She leaned her head forward and nodded off until her phone rang.

She picked it up, and a female voice began to speak.

"Ms. Cassandra Young?" the voice said.

"Yes, this is she," Cassie said.

"His excellency, the Royal Ambassador of Ammar, Mr. Al-Jamil, wishes to speak with you."

Cassie was suddenly wide awake. "Yes, please put him through."

"Ms. Young, I am so happy you took my call," said the ambassador.

"How could I refuse the Royal Ambassador of Ammar?"

"Well now, I will be brief. I know you are a busy woman. I wish you to dine with me at the ambassadorial residence this coming Monday, if you are available."

"Would this be a reception of some kind?"

"It will be a private affair, just you and me," the ambassador said. "I have a proposition to discuss with you."

"Could we discuss it over the phone?"

"I'd rather do it in person."

"Mr. Ambassador, I can hardly refuse your invitation," Cassie said. "But could we meet perhaps at a nearby restaurant?"

"I anticipated your request," the ambassador said. "May I suggest that we dine at Citronelle?"

He surprised Cassie with his quick response. She was getting a little paranoid. Why would the Ambassador of Ammar be calling her? Was he trying to add her to his harem? Or was it something else?

"Ms. Young, are you still there?"

"Yes, Mr. Ambassador."

"It will, of course, be my pleasure to buy you dinner," he said. "Will you meet with me?"

"Mr. Ambassador, since Royal Sovoco and the Kingdom of Ammar are both clients of my firm, I think it would be best if I cleared this with Larry Hilliard first."

"Oh, I would be very much obliged if you didn't mention this to anyone," the ambassador said.

"I'm a little confused, Mr. Ambassador."

"I promise you we will discuss nothing that involves your firm, only you. Now, will you meet me for dinner?"

A restaurant full of people, she thought. She could leave anytime. She would be fine. "Yes, Mr. Ambassador. What time?"

"Shall we say 7 o'clock?"

"Yes, that will be fine."

"I will send a car around for you at 6:45 then."

"Oh, that won't be necessary."

"No, I insist," he said. "You are my guest."

"All right. Let me give you my address."

"No, that's all taken care of. A driver will be by your home to pick you up on Monday then at 6:45."

Taken care of! She was growing more paranoid by the minute. "Yes, Mr. Ambassador, I'll see you at Citronelle."

"Goodbye now."

"Yes, goodbye, Mr. Ambassador."

Cassie was immediately back on the phone calling Victor. But he didn't answer. She left him a message to call back saying it was urgent. Something was welling up in the pit of her stomach—a blind panic, starting out small and growing ever larger. She flipped the pages of her calendar trying to reconstruct her days and nights from the moment she met the ambassador to the present. She thought about the errant sheet that lay in Hilliard's printer that morning after she left his office with the printout of the Royal Sovoco report. Had Hilliard discovered that the report had been printed out and taken? Had he given that information to the Ammaris? Why would the ambassador from Ammar be contacting her if that were the case? Why hadn't Hilliard come down on her, demanded the report back, and fired her? She left messages for Victor three more times that day before she finally went to bed that night, a night during which she got precious little sleep.

It wasn't until the next afternoon that Victor called her back. She was in a meeting in the EAI conference room, but keeping a watchful eye on her cellphone. When the call from Victor came, she went out into the hall to take it.

"Victor, don't you pick up your messages?" she said in a hushed voice.

"Cassie, what's wrong?"

"I need to see you as soon as possible. I've been in a panic for the past day."

"All right, all right. When do you want to get together?"

"The meeting I'm in now is supposed to end at about four. How about we get together at Kramerbooks about 4:15?"

"Fine, I'll be there."

Cassie slipped back into the conference room, and when the meeting ended at four, she shot up and headed for the door. But Evan intercepted her.

"Cassie, where are you going in such a hurry?" he said.

"I've got to meet somebody in about 15 minutes, Evan, so, if you don't mind?"

"We were going to take the client for drinks and dinner, remember?"

Cassie slapped her forehead lightly. "Oh, damn," she said. "Look, Evan. Can I meet up with you later?"

"Well yes, of course," Evan replied. "Cassie, is there something wrong?"

"I'm not sure," she said. "I'll let you know."

"All right, then, off you go," he said shooing her away.

Cassie practically ran to her office, got her things and then bolted out the front entrance and onto the elevator. She had only to go across the circle, but she felt as if she needed to run, run away from something.

Victor was waiting for her at a table on the café patio. She slowed down so she could come in for a landing without toppling the chairs she had to weave past.

Victor got up and held out his arms. She embraced him and tears began rolling down her cheeks. A few people looked up but quickly returned their attention back to their own tables.

"It will be all right, dear one," Victor said. "Whatever it is, it will be all right."

Cassie pulled back from her embrace. Victor held her head and lightly wiped her tears away with his thumbs. "Come now, let's sit down, and you can tell me all about it."

Cassie composed herself. She pulled out a handkerchief and wiped her eyes and nose. "Victor, I think I'm in terrible trouble," she said.

"Really?"

"I've been in a panic since yesterday," she explained in a hushed tone. "The ambassador of Ammar called me and asked me to go to dinner with him."

"But why would this make you panic?" Victor responded keeping his voice low.

"When I went to Hilliard's office the morning after we printed out the Royal Sovoco report," she said, "I missed one sheet."

"You never told me this."

"I was hoping the sheet was blank. When nothing happened afterwards, when there was no indication from Larry or Cecilia, his assistant, that there was anything wrong, I thought I was home free."

"And now you think that maybe they saw this one sheet, and it had something on it?"

"Well, I'm worried. But nothing adds up," she said. "If Hilliard knew, and he knew it was me, he would have demanded the documents back. And then he would be within his rights to fire me on the spot."

"None of this has happened, but yet you are in a panic," Victor said.

Cassie leaned forward. "Why would the Ammari ambassador call *me* and ask *me* to dinner unless something was up?"

"Wasn't he making a pass at you at Hilliard's open house?"

"Well, maybe."

"So, you see he just likes beautiful women, and he wants to take them to dinner."

"But he said he had a proposition to discuss with me."

"All men have propositions to discuss with women," Victor replied.

"No, Victor," Cassie said dismissively. "A business proposition."

"So you see, you said it yourself. The ambassador wants to discuss a business proposition — you are meeting him in a public place, right?"

Cassie nodded.

Victor continued. "So, there is no mention of documents. No threats. No skulking in the night. Just dinner with the ambassador." Victor reached across the table and clasped Cassie's hands.

"I guess you're right," Cassie said. "I let my mind run away from me. But there's one more thing that's been bothering me, Victor."

"What's that?" They let go of each other's hands.

"The other night I was out with my friend, Marta, having dinner, and I mentioned the man I saw when you and I were here last. And then I saw him again — or at least I think I did — on 19th Street in front of our offices — when I was on the phone with you, remember?"

"Vaguely, I remember this."

"Marta said that maybe I was being followed. It came up because the night I was dining with her I thought I saw the man at our restaurant, and I went up to him to confront him. But when I tapped on his shoulder and he turned around, I could see it wasn't him."

"You see, there again, you are frightening yourself for no reason," Victor said. "Who knows about the report?"

"Just you and I as far as I can tell," Cassie replied. "And I gave a copy to my friend, Marta."

"Because you want her to read it?" Victor looked puzzled.

"No, just for safekeeping. So that if something happens to my copy, then I'll have another one."

"Do you think your friend — Marta, is it?" Victor asked. Cassie nodded. "Do you actually think she told someone about the documents? Or perhaps she is a spy for the Ammari government?"

Cassie could see he wasn't serious. "No, of course not," she answered. "Victor, usually you're the paranoid one."

"Yes, I know," he said. "But today we must switch roles, and I must help you see as clearly as you can. Do you plan to do anything with the report?"

"You mean release it?"

"That would stir up a hornet's nest."

"I don't know what I'm going to do. But right now, I have to go, Victor," Cassie said. "I've got to meet Evan and some clients. We promised them drinks and dinner. I'm sorry. I hate to cry and run."

Cassie now had a bit of a smile on her face. She got up, leaned over and gave Victor a kiss on the forehead. "Thank you," she said.

"You're very welcome."

≈ **chapter 15** ≈

The weekend took its usual path. Bike rides in Rock Creek Park and evenings with Paul. Cassie did puzzle over what kind of business proposition the ambassador might have in mind. But he was a consular official. What kind of work could he offer her for which she was qualified? And why would he be interested in hiring an American whose only claim to foreign language expertise was two years of college French? It had to be related to her current work. But that didn't make any sense either. If someone from the oil ministry or Royal Sovoco wanted to hire her, why would the ambassador be speaking to her? That would be way below his pay grade.

On Sunday morning Victor called and asked Cassie if she would like to join the Washington, D.C. peak oil group which was getting together for drinks that afternoon. She agreed to meet Victor in front of the Brickskeller at four. She realized she must have passed the place a hundred times, but never really noticed it.

Around 3:30 Cassie left her condo and started walking to the Brickskeller. It was just off P Street near Rock Creek Park, and when she finally turned onto 22nd, she saw Victor up ahead tethering his bicycle to a small, wave-shaped rack. He was in his black-and-white checked top and black biking shorts. He straightened up, saw Cassie, and waited for her to approach.

When she reached him, she dispensed with any greeting. "Victor, your friends will think I'm from the dark side, so please don't tell these people where I work," she said.

"I won't tell them, but they may ask," he replied. The two of them turned toward the Brickskeller's canopied entrance. They stepped onto the dingy burgundy carpet on the stairway which was flanked by black wrought iron railings, and they made their way up to and then through the entrance. Once inside, Victor pulled open a heavy wooden door on his right, and Cassie followed him down a steep flight of stairs that emerged into a bar.

A line of round red vinyl barstools stood empty in front of a battered wooden bar. Behind the bar was an entire wall of coolers with glass doors—the kind one sees in the supermarket. All of the coolers were jammed with bottles of beer, but none looked familiar to Cassie. Victor then led her through a short passageway that emerged into a dark dining room with exposed red brick walls. Narrow, lighted display cases containing single rows of beer bottles and cans were mounted near the black ceiling. Below the cases hung framed posters and what looked like wooden barrel tops with names like Heineken and Dinkelacker carved into them.

The two of them found the group sitting in a particularly dark corner away from the windows in the otherwise deserted dining room.

"Alexander Nevsky," a man in the group called out to Victor as he and Cassie approached.

Cassie leaned into Victor as they moved toward the group. "Why is he calling you Alexander Nevsky?"

"That's Chuck. He's been calling me that ever since I lent him my copy of the Eisenstein film. It's about a medieval Russian prince who drives out the Germans," Victor responded.

"And you must be his princess," said Chuck, a short, youthful, muscular, and full-haired blond, who rose to greet them. He introduced himself to Cassie and shook hands with the two of them. Chuck then handed Victor a DVD case. Victor looked at it for a few seconds, turning it over to glance at the back.

"I thought you'd like to see the latest peak oil document-ary," Chuck said. "Especially since the music is by Philip Glass." Victor thanked him and everybody took their seats at the group of tables that had been moved together. Beer bottles, some half-empty, were standing next to glasses holding various levels of fluid colored amber or brown or, in Chuck's case, almost black.

Victor introduced Cassie only by name, not occupation, as she had asked.

"I'm Kevin," said a slight man with short, graying hair sitting at the end of the table on Cassie's left.

"He's our Department of Energy representative," Chuck said.

Kevin nodded to Cassie and then responded to her quizzical look. "I work in an area where I'm allowed to have my own opinions," he said.

"I'm Jay," said the man across from her.

"And I'm Harold," said the man sitting beside Jay. Harold put his arm around Jay. "We're together," Harold added.

Jay looked like he was in his mid-thirties, had on a red, button-down collar shirt and wore his brown hair in a pony-tail. Harold, who looked a little older, had a heavy build under the faded blue T-shirt he wore. His round face was framed by a head of thick black hair which seemed to defy gravity.

Harold turned to the woman next to him. "This is Lydia."

"Hello," she said with a shy smile. Lydia wore round gold wire-rimmed glasses. Her straight blond hair had gray streaks here and there. The lines in her face told Cassie that she was probably in her early sixties.

"Where's Phil and Mary?" Victor asked.

"Phil's sister is getting married this weekend in Maine," Chuck replied. "Cassie," he continued, "Jay and Harold here were the organizers of the recent peak oil conference in Washington."

"Did you by any chance go?" Harold asked Cassie.

"Yes, I did," Cassie replied.

"What did you think?"

"Don't put her on the spot, Harold," Jay piped in.

"That's all right," Cassie replied. "I only had time to duck into the session on global reserves."

"Pretty bad, wasn't it?" Harold said.

"I thought the presentation was fine," Cassie replied.

"No, I mean the situation," Harold continued. "When I saw his slides, I thought, 'We are in even deeper doo-doo than I realized.' And I already thought we were in deep doo-doo."

"Did anyone see that piece in the New York Tribune about oil shale?" Kevin said.

"Yeah, I read that," Chuck said.

"I saw it," Lydia replied.

"I thought I was going to throw up," Kevin said. He turned his attention to Cassie. "I work on unconventional oil at DOE. The reporter made it sound like the U.S. is going to go back to being an oil *exporter*. And the sources for his story were all industry sources. Of course, *they* think it's all going to work out just fine."

"And naturally, they had the obligatory quote from Larry Hilliard," Chuck added. "Can't they give this guy a rest? I mean he's been wrong every year this century about the direction of oil prices, and still they quote him like he knows something."

"Apparently, that's how you become an expert in the oil markets," Jay said. "You have to get it wrong *every year*." Jay turned to Kevin. "Say, Kevin, how come *you* don't talk to the New York Tribune?"

"I'm allowed to have my own opinions, but not allowed to broadcast them in the media," Kevin replied.

Cassie looked at Kevin and said, "I want to hear more about oil shale."

"The problems are huge," he continued. "Where do they get the water to process this stuff on the Colorado plateau?

That area is practically bone dry after the long drought that started at the beginning of this decade. And then the heat they need to extract it and process it? They'll have to use natural gas in huge quantities. Where's that going to come from? And why not just use the natural gas to make liquid fuels if that's what you need? You know, the Energy Information Administration projects that we might get 140,000 barrels a day from oil shale by 2030. That's something like six-tenths of one percent of the country's projected oil use. Who are these guys kidding?"

"What about Shell?" Cassie asked. "Aren't they using heaters in wells to melt the kerogen underground and then turn it into oil before extracting it?"

"You didn't tell us you had an oil expert, Victor," Chuck said.

At that point a waitress wandered into the dining room and came over to the table. Victor and Cassie both ordered beers. And Chuck ordered a second bottle of the sludgy porter he was drinking.

Kevin started in again. "Right now, I believe they're expending almost as much energy to extract the stuff as they get back. That's not much of an energy source; it's closer to an energy sink."

"Why not just pour gasoline on the ground and burn it?" Harold piped in. "It would be a better use of energy than what Shell's doing in Colorado."

"I'm doubtful they'll get very far with this," Kevin continued. "I'm not saying it can't be done. I just don't think it'll be economical on any scale that would make a big dent in the supply problem. I mean they'd have to build nuclear power plants all over the plateau to do it. And where's the water for *those* plants going to come from?"

"So, do you think we're in 'deep doo-doo' like Harold says?" Cassie asked.

Kevin smiled and snorted as he looked over at Harold.

"Harold's a bit of a doomer."

"Hey, if you want a genuine doomer, it's Chuck," Harold said pointing to the end of the table where Chuck was sitting.

"Yeah, but I'm the *happy* doomer," Chuck said with a big smile. He looked at Cassie. "You can read my website, 'The Happy Doomer.' It's all there. The fate of humanity is sealed. It's just a question of accepting the inevitable."

"Yeah," said Jay. "Solar flares, EMP, a well-placed asteroid, supervolcanoes, and, of course, peak oil. Chuck lays it all out for the uninitiated."

"Boy, you guys think of everything," Cassie remarked.

"Yeah, but I just happen to think that peak oil is going to get us first," Chuck said as he lifted his glass and finished it off.

At that point the waitress brought the beers ordered by Cassie, Victor and Chuck. Once the waitress had departed, Harold and Lydia started to speak at the same time.

"Let the woman talk," Jay said to Harold.

Lydia started again. "Have you read a book called 'The Challenge of Man's Future?'"

"No," Cassie replied.

"It's not in print any more, but you can find it in the library," Lydia explained. "Well, it was written in 1954, and it pretty much predicts everything we're going through now." She paused. "But the main thing that struck me was how vulnerable our complex machine culture is. I mean he talks about what would happen if a significant part of the machine infrastructure just stopped working or was destroyed for whatever reason. Everything is so interdependent that our whole society could just collapse."

"So, you think this is going to happen?" Cassie asked.

"No, not in that way," Lydia responded. "But declining fuel supplies could sure put us on that road. We've got to relocalize everything."

"Relocalize?" Cassie asked. "What exactly do you mean?"

"Well, everyone else can just cover their ears because they've heard me say this a thousand times, but for Cassie's benefit: We've got to produce everything closer to where we live: food, furniture, clothing, everything. We import cut flowers from Colombia to my grocery store. Does that make any sense when we have greenhouses right here? We ship strawberries from California to Washington, D.C. year round to my supermarket, even when strawberries are in season here. We've sent most of our manufacturing for household items to China. So, now we export wood grown in the United States to China which they make into furniture and ship back to us. All that back and forth is based entirely on cheap transportation and cheap fuel."

"That's the point," Cassie said. "It's a lot cheaper to have that furniture made in China."

"But what are we going to do when it stops being cheap?" Lydia asked. "When that cheap fuel goes away, we're not going to be able to afford this very energy-intensive global system. We're going to have to do things locally and regionally. Except we've gutted every manufacturing industry in America because we believe that this cheap, Chinese extravaganza can go on forever. It can't. Not with the situation we face with oil."

"I see things changing more gradually," Victor said, "but with occasional crises that people won't understand are really related to energy problems."

"What do you mean, Victor?" Lydia asked.

"It'll seem like the problem is financial," Victor replied. "But as I keep telling anyone who will listen: Money is nothing more than the ability to command energy to do what you want it to do. Whether that energy is in the form of a machine doing something for you or a person doing something for you. That means the first symptom of an energy problem will be a financial collapse. And our leaders will undoubtedly think that the solution will be financial. But like any misdiagnosis, that misdiagnosis could be deadly.

"You see, when the collapse comes to America, we'll find out just how fragile all our arrangements are. When the Soviet Union disintegrated, and the country went into a deep depression—far worse than the one in the 1930s—well, what happened? Because most everyone was living in state-owned housing, they just stayed in their apartments. And because very few people had private cars, everyone just kept riding buses and trains. And they kept going to their jobs because most businesses were state-owned and stayed open, at least for awhile. And there was a tradition of kitchen gardens. People knew how to grow food, and they just expanded their gardens, and they were able to survive.

"Of course, Russians never had the kind of life you see in the U.S.," Victor said. "It's hard to hurt yourself falling out of a ground floor window. But here in America, people live mostly in private homes with mortgages, and many of them will be thrown out of their homes. And most people, because of where they live, can only get around using their cars, which, if they can't afford the payments any more, will be repossessed. And, of course, almost all businesses here are private, and so they will react very quickly to lay people off when times are bad. They're thinking of their own survival, not the civil unrest that will follow. And as far as food is concerned, almost no one in America knows how to grow food any more."

"You know how to paint such a lovely picture, Victor," Chuck said.

"What we're facing," Harold added, "is a predicament. Problems have solutions. But if you are in a predicament, all you can do is cope."

"Can't we just transition to a natural gas-based economy?" Cassie asked looking at Kevin again.

"There's probably a lot of natural gas out there," Kevin said. "But is there enough to replace most of the things we do with oil in, say, the next 30 years? I doubt it. It doesn't mean natural gas won't help cushion the blow, but it's not even close to the whole solution."

"What a minute, Kevin," Harold said. "You're not thinking this through. I don't believe we have 30 years to make the transition. It's important not only to ask how long it will take to make the transition. It's important to ask how long we *have*. We're going to face declining oil supplies soon. I mean look at oil prices; they are well over $100 now. That's one indication that we're close if not already at the peak.

"This is the classic rate-of-conversion problem," Harold continued. "We're going to have declining energy supplies just when we need to build a whole new energy infrastructure. Remember, we had *expanding* energy supplies when we were building the oil infrastructure we have today. But people who've been hit by the big economic calamity Victor sees coming, just how eager are they going to be to pay far higher utility rates and far higher taxes to subsidize our conversion to natural gas or any other alternative?" Harold spoke with increasing animation. "How eager are they going to be to fund all this when their incomes are going down or disappearing altogether? And then how fast can we do it? It took a couple of generations to build the oil infrastructure we have today. Now we've got to build a whole new natural gas fueling infrastructure to run our cars. Who is going to build all the natural gas filling stations and extra pipelines? And who is going to move first, the filling station owners or the car manufacturers? If the car companies produce natural gas vehicles that can't get fuel—well, they just won't do it. In which case the filling station owners won't build any natural gas fueling stations. It's a chicken and egg problem. And then we're expected to do all this quickly under circumstances that are going to be really nasty if Victor is right."

"But natural gas is going to peak, too, Harold," Lydia interjected. "And much sooner if we start using a lot more of it. We really need to get away from all fossil fuels."

"Lydia's right, of course," Harold added.

Kevin shook his head. "I think you're all being too pessimistic. I know part of what Harold is basing his thinking on is the Hirsch Report which DOE commissioned in 2005. But I think once people understand the problem, things will move very quickly. There's going to be a lot of pain, I agree. It's not going to be pretty. But I think we can still address the problem of peak oil."

"But people are never *going* to understand the problem," Chuck said. "All the pundits, the so-called experts, the politicians, the media—they're all telling the public that everything's fine, that there's nothing to worry about because we have everything taken care of. That's why we're all doomed."

"You're making me hungry, Chuck," Jay said, chuckling a bit.

"Well, every condemned man deserves to get what he wants for his last meal," Chuck replied.

With that they summoned the waitress. Jay, Chuck, Harold and Lydia all ordered something to eat. Cassie ordered another beer. She thought she could use it to help her recover from what she'd just been listening to.

After the waitress had gone, Jay asked Cassie where she worked. This was the question she did not want to answer, so she just said she worked for a consulting firm. But Jay kept probing politely.

"I think these guys will still like you if you tell them," Victor said to Cassie.

"Okay," Cassie said. She drew in a big breath and let it out. "I work for Energy Advisers International."

The table was silent and eyes were widening everywhere.

"Really?" Harold said.

"Yes, really," Cassie said.

Harold and Jay looked incredulously at Victor. Then so did everyone else.

"Really," said Victor nodding.

"Wow," Harold said. He maintained his look of amazement as he turned his gaze back to Cassie. "You are deep in enemy territory."

"Maybe I'm not in enemy territory anymore," Cassie said under her breath.

"What?" Harold said.

"Forget it," she said. Cassie got up. "I think I'll be going."

"But Cassie," Victor said, "you've got another beer coming."

"Why don't you just drink it, Victor?" Cassie said. "I really need to go."

Cassie thanked everyone for the lively conversation and made her exit. When she reached the street, she felt as if she could breathe again. But it would only be a short reprieve, she realized. She had to get her mind focused on her meeting with the Ammari ambassador the next day.

≈

On Monday evening she was already waiting in front of her building when a black Lincoln Town Car appeared promptly outside at 6:45. The driver opened the door for her and she got in. Traffic was hopelessly jammed on 16th, and when the car finally advanced far enough, the driver turned right on P rather than try to continue to Scott Circle. He quickly made it to Dupont Circle. But once he got into the circle, traffic came to a halt. An accident had occurred, and a police car appeared shortly on the periphery but was unable to penetrate the thick phalanx of vehicles now sitting motionless.

A few cars started inching toward the outlets and a policewoman managed to direct several cars off the circle. Finally, the limo was moving again slowly. The streets everywhere were jammed, particularly with trucks, which seemed odd to Cassie.

She arrived at Citronelle about 15 minutes late, and she reflected that she might have done better just taking the

Metro. The driver got the car door for her and then said that he needed to speak to the ambassador and so would accompany her into the restaurant. She said she had never been inside, and so he led the way. He opened the door into the lobby of the Latham Hotel and motioned for her to step through. He then led her to the restaurant entrance which opened into a lounge. The driver walked only a short distance, turned and led the way down a flight of stairs. Cassie thought it odd that this restaurant, which she knew was rated one of the best in the country, should be essentially underground.

At the bottom of the stairs the maître d' greeted them and promptly led them through a crowded dining area. The wall to the far left was glass. Behind it an extensively stocked wine cellar was visible. The right wall, much nearer, was flagstone. They proceeded down a few more steps and into a private dining room which nevertheless had a large, square lattice window that looked out into the main dining area. Without it, the room would have been a bit claustrophobic.

As they entered, the ambassador, who was dressed in a black suit and tie, rose to greet them.

"I am so glad that you are here, Ms. Young," he said as he shook her hand.

"A thousand pardons, ambassador," the driver said.

The ambassador looked over to him. "It's all right, Mohammed." And then he addressed both of them. "The American truckers are in Washington protesting high diesel prices, and they are snarling traffic everywhere." He turned back to the driver. "Thank you, Mohammed. You can go now."

As the driver turned to leave, the maître d' pulled Cassie's chair out, and she sat down. The ambassador sat down as well.

"I am sorry your little trip turned out to be so trying," he said as he placed his napkin onto his lap.

"Well, it wasn't trying for me," Cassie said. "I didn't have to drive."

"Yes, of course," he said. "I took the liberty of ordering some wine. Does this suit you?" A waiter, seemingly from nowhere, picked up the bottle on the table and displayed the label for her. It was a Château Lafite-Rothschild which she surmised from the name had to be an extremely expensive bottle of wine.

"I'm sure it will be fine," Cassie said. The ambassador nodded his head slightly, and the waiter poured a glass of the red wine for Cassie, refilled the ambassador's glass, and then disappeared.

The ambassador picked up his glass, and then gestured with it in Cassie's direction. "A toast," he said. "To new possibilities."

Cassie lifted her glass, touched hers to his, and then took a sip. "And what new possibilities might those be?" she asked.

"We must let them mature a bit longer," he said as he swirled the dark red liquid. "Like this wine which needs to breath a bit more." He placed his glass back on the table.

"Tell me about yourself, Ms. Young," the ambassador continued.

"Well, there's not much to tell," she replied.

"You needn't be shy."

At that point another waiter entered and presented them with menus.

"I can recommend the lamb," said the ambassador. "But, of course, everything is good here."

They both glanced at their menus for a bit, and then laid them down almost simultaneously. The ambassador sat back in his chair and looked at her intently. She discerned that he was waiting for her biography.

"Yes, of course," she said. "You want to know a little about me. Well, I grew up in the Chicago area. I went to Wellesley and studied economics. Then I got an MBA from Stanford. I worked for a regional brokerage out of Chicago as a broker and then as an energy analyst before coming to work for EAI."

"So, you are all work and no play?"

"I like to bicycle, go to concerts, eat gourmet food and read mystery novels."

"Very good," said the ambassador. "Have you solved to-night's mystery?"

"You didn't bring me here tonight to hire me to work at the embassy."

"So, we start with the process of elimination."

At that point the waiter approached and took their orders. Cassie ordered the asparagus vichyssoise and the duck. The ambassador ordered the lamb and some caviar to start.

"It's hard to get good caviar anymore," he remarked. "Here, they manage to get the best." He paused for a moment to take a sip from his wine glass. "Please continue."

"I am an oil analyst by trade, and the Kingdom of Ammar has a lot of oil to sell."

"Yes."

"So, it's possible that the Kingdom may have need of a few oil analysts to trace out the larger picture for them."

"Yes."

"But what's not clear is why the royal ambassador to the United States would be tasked with offering such a position to a relatively inexperienced oil analyst who focuses on North American oil and gas."

"Bra-*vo*," he said. "I will hardly have to do any of the talking this evening—except to clarify this last point. You see, I'm the one with the relationship."

Cassie stared down at the table for a moment, swallowed, and then looked back up at the ambassador. "With all due respect, Mr. Ambassador, we don't have a relationship."

"Perhaps I was a bit indelicate. Perhaps a better term would be that I am the...contact. Is that how you would say it?"

"Yes," Cassie replied. "I think that captures it exactly."

"So, let us not delay any further," the ambassador continued. "I am tasked, as you say, with discussing a possible position for you with Royal Sovoco as an analyst working right here in Washington."

"Well, I'm quite flattered I have to say, but—"

"But?"

"I'm happy where I am."

"Naturally, I don't expect you to accept a lateral move into another organization," the ambassador explained. "But this would not be a lateral move for three reasons. First, you would no longer be a North American oil and gas analyst. You would be a global analyst. Second, your pay would immediately double. And third, since you would be working in a foreign country—that is, foreign to us—you would get a generous housing allowance as well."

"Mr. Ambassador," Cassie replied. "I'd love to make twice what I do now. But really, how could you possibly know how much that is?"

"Oh, Ms. Young, I know exactly how much it is, down to the dollar."

"But how do you know this?"

"Please, Ms. Young, this is Washington."

"So, you know exactly how much I make?"

The ambassador retrieved a fountain pen from his jacket and opened it up. The waiter who had poured her wine appeared as if on cue, presented the ambassador with a blank card, and then withdrew. Cassie now realized that this waiter was attending only to their table, standing just outside in the hallway within sight of the ambassador but out of her view. The ambassador wrote something down on the card. As he was writing, Cassie could see that the pen he was using was studded with small diamonds in a ripple pattern. When he finished, he handed the card across the table to Cassie. Written on it were her base salary, her previous year's bonus, and then a notation below that read, "2X."

"Well, that would certainly be a lot of money," she said still staring at the card.

"We would guarantee it. No bonus to earn. You'd get a straight salary."

Cassie tried not to show her astonishment. She was making a very good living already. But this would be a huge leap. Still, she was suspicious of the whole offer. Did the Ammaris somehow know that she had the Royal Sovoco reserve estimates? Were they simply trying to buy her off? Or was the ambassador trying to bring her into his orbit, his harem, so to speak?

"Where would I work?" she inquired.

"Not at the embassy, if that's what you mean," he said. "Royal Sovoco has a small office out in McLean, Virginia. You would be working there."

"Yes, I am aware of it. But I'm not sure I'm ready for this."

"Oh, we think you are quite ready for this, and we hope you will choose to pursue further discussions with us."

"I really need some time to think about this."

"Of course. But you would be doing me a great service if you could reply by Monday next."

"Certainly, I could do that. Should I call you at the embassy?"

"Yes, by all means, please do. And make your response yes. Even a royal ambassador has superiors he must answer to."

"I'll think about it."

"And if you have questions, I'll put you in touch with our head man in the McLean office."

"Thank you, I appreciate that."

The ambassador then looked in the direction of the door and nodded his head slightly. A waiter appeared immediately and set the caviar and the vichyssoise on the table.

"Now it is time to abandon business for pleasure. Please enjoy," the ambassador said.

For the rest of the dinner, the ambassador was utterly charming, telling several stories about his boyhood in Ammar and his days at Cambridge. Cassie could hardly match the exotic tales he wove. But she did entertain him with a couple stories of her adventures in the wild with her geologist father. When they had finished what turned out to be an exquisite and no doubt very expensive meal, the ambassador got on his cellphone and summoned a car for Cassie.

"Thank you for a most enjoyable evening," the ambassador said as Cassie was preparing to leave.

"Thank you, Mr. Ambassador, for a lovely meal and such interesting stories," she responded.

"I look forward to hearing from you."

"Yes, Mr. Ambassador, by next Monday." With that she rose and shook his hand. The waiter who had attended to their every need during the dinner accompanied her all the way to the hotel lobby entrance and opened the main door. Her driver, a different one this time, opened the door of the limo and then closed it after her. Within 10 minutes she was back to her condo.

≈

The evening had actually been mildly exhilarating. It seemed like a brush with danger and high-stakes danger at that. But she had no intention of taking the job because it just didn't add up. She had merely stalled the ambassador, hoping to discover more information that might shed some light on this curiously timed and overly generous offer.

Now she needed to communicate with Victor and tell him about this latest development. When she called him, he said he was in the middle of a practice session and wouldn't be able to see her until midnight. They agreed to meet at Kramerbooks.

Victor showed up at the café shortly after midnight. Cassie had been nursing some tea while she waited. The late night crowd had petered out, and there were only a handful of tables still occupied.

"I'm sorry I'm late," he said. "Our session went longer than I anticipated."

"That's all right," Cassie said. "I'm just glad you came."

"What is it that is so important that it brings you out at the witching hour on a weekday?"

"I had dinner with the Ammari ambassador earlier this evening."

"Oh, that's right. I completely forgot."

"He dangled a job as an analyst for Royal Sovoco in front of me."

"This strikes you as unusual?"

"Coming from an ambassador, who offers to double my pay, and he does all this when I'm in possession of internal documents—very damning internal documents—belonging to the company he wants me to go to work for…"

"Dear god! He must know something. But how?"

"That's a good question."

"We have never spoken of these things over the phone."

"No, not explicitly. Only indirectly."

A waiter arrived. "Anything else here? Perhaps you'd like something, sir."

"Nothing for me," Victor said.

"Nothing else, thank you," Cassie added. With that the waiter thanked them and placed the check on the table.

Victor restarted their conversation. "We must assume now that Larry Hilliard knows something, too."

"I think so," Cassie said.

"But what we don't know is whether he knows that it was you."

"Well, the Ammaris know something."

"And they are trying to solve their problem with money. They are not offering a job," Victor surmised. "They are sending you a message."

"Which is?"

"They have not seen their reserve numbers in the newspapers. So, they believe those numbers are for sale," he explained. "They think you may have their information. They want it back. They are willing to pay. And they are waiting for your counteroffer."

"I don't get it, Victor."

"They are not sure *who* has the information. They are probably making similar offers to other people in your firm. And if you have the information, they want it back without a fuss; and, they are willing to pay a lot for it if there will be no fuss. This is what they hope to avoid."

"What do you mean by fuss?"

"They want that information destroyed without having to resort to harsher measures."

"Are you saying they may use violence?"

"They do not want to use violence. That is why they approached you and probably several others in this manner." Victor paused and put his hand on his chin. "You see, they do not want to tell people who were *not* involved that such documents exist. If they were certain that *you* were the one, they might have made a deal then and there."

He gestured with his index finger in her direction as he continued. "They are testing you and the others right now. They can simply terminate negotiations with each person as they eliminate them from suspicion. But they figure that the one who has the documents will come back with a counteroffer, a counteroffer to sell them the information."

"You're sure about this?"

"I am never sure about anything, so we must proceed with caution."

"And if I turn them down?"

"They may conclude that you do not have the documents. Or you could decide to sell the report back."

"Victor, you're not serious? I don't want to be involved with these people."

"But you *are* involved with them. And they will keep looking until they find their documents and destroy them. So, we must consider all options."

"I'll just give the report back to them, both copies."

"And what? Say you are sorry? It's all just a big misunderstanding?"

"What are you getting at, Victor?"

"They want to *know* that you can be *bought*. If you can be bought, they have the money to keep you silent for one hundred lifetimes. If you can't, then there will be only one way to keep you silent. But I do not think they want to go there."

"Oh my god." Cassie sank back into her seat. "But aren't you in danger, too, Victor?"

"I doubt it," he said. "They have no way to know that I helped you, and I'm just a silly musician whom no one will believe anyway. But you—you are an analyst for a respected energy consulting firm. So, it is a different matter."

"I need to remind you of something else," Cassie said.

"What?"

"I sent a copy to my friend, Marta, to her office at Georgetown, just so I'd have an extra one, in case I lost mine or there was a fire or something like that."

"But they do not know this."

"How could they know it if they aren't even sure that *I* have the documents?" Cassie said. "Maybe I should just destroy them."

"It would be wise to get rid of the copy in your condo. But I think you may want to leave the other with your friend in case you somehow need it for leverage. The game is moving too quickly for us to be sure exactly what to do. As for your copy, you will need to shred it. But as a precaution, you must do something the municipal sewage officials will not like me to tell you. You must flush it down the toilet."

"What?"

"You cannot put it in the trash. It is too easy for them to

find it there. You cannot carry the shredded paper somewhere else and dump it. They may be watching you. We do not know. You must dispose of these documents in your condo as I have suggested so there will be no trace, and they will never know that you had them." Victor paused for a moment and then continued. "Did you scan anything?" he asked.

"Scan anything?" Cassie responded.

"Did you scan the report into your computer? Into *any* computer?"

"No, I didn't," Cassie replied. "Do you think I should have?"

"It's better that you didn't. In case they take your hard drive, they will find no evidence that you ever had these documents."

"Okay."

"Now, when must you respond to the ambassador?" Victor asked.

"I have one week."

"Let us see how things develop. In the meantime, you must be cautious," Victor said. "Now, how did you get here?"

"I walked."

"I will walk with you back to your condo."

"Okay."

Cassie put some money on the table next to the bill and indicated to Victor that they should leave. They walked back to Cassie's along P Street. The blazing hot day had turned into a pleasant warm evening. A few cars trundled down P as they walked. The windows of the town houses were now mostly dark and that made the sidewalk especially difficult to see. Both Victor and Cassie stumbled on a section of concrete that had been thrust slightly upward. When they arrived at Cassie's building, Victor accompanied Cassie up to the door of her third-floor condo.

"Now, go inside and get some rest," he said standing at the door with her.

"Victor, would you stay tonight?"

"What will your boyfriend, Paul, think?"

"He won't even know."

Victor looked to the side as he thought about her request and then finally looked back and responded. "I will sleep on the couch."

"Yes, of course," Cassie agreed, though she found herself strangely conflicted.

After they entered the condo, Cassie set about shredding the Royal Sovoco report. Victor took the shreds and put them a little bit at a time into the toilet, flushing, it seemed, a hundred times before they were all safely down.

After that Cassie got Victor a blanket and a pillow for the couch. Then she went back into her bedroom and got ready for bed herself. Just as she was about to slip under the covers, she decided to check on Victor.

She peeked into the living room and could see the light coming in from the street glance off his still open eyes. She walked in and his head turned toward her. She knelt down next to the couch without saying a word. She began to stroke Victor's head and then slowly lowered hers and kissed him on the lips. No sooner had she finished than Victor moved up to kiss her, cupping her head in his hand. Then he lay back down and the two of them just stared at each other for a minute. Finally, Cassie decided she should leave it at that and said good night. Victor just smiled back at her.

≈ **chapter 16** ≈

Two days later Cassie found herself in Evan's office when Larry Hilliard came on the screen of one of Evan's four televisions. She asked him to turn up the sound.

Hilliard was testifying before the Senate energy committee, and it appeared that he had just sat down. Cassie recognized the committee chairman as Senator Phillips whom she had met at Hilliard's open house. And sitting at the table of witnesses was the congressman from Maryland, O'Connor, who had been talking with Phillips at the party. There were two other faces at the table that looked familiar. She recognized one as the SandOil executive, Harrison Cole, with whom she had spoken in Fort McMurray. The other was Clay Thompson, the company's government relations VP, with whom she had had a conversation on her flight back to D.C. aboard SandOil's corporate jet. Senator Phillips welcomed Hilliard to the hearing and then asked him to state his name and place of work for the record.

"My name is Dr. Lawrence Hilliard, and I am chairman of Energy Advisers International, an energy consulting firm, which is headquartered here in Washington," Hilliard said.

"Now, Dr. Hilliard," the senator continued, "just so the committee understands, you are here today as an independent expert, and you are not as such representing any particular corporation or government. Is that correct?"

"Well, senator, just so you and the other distinguished senators who are here today understand, Energy Advisers

International consults for corporations and governments throughout the world on a wide range of energy issues and projects that include the whole gamut from wind and solar, to nuclear, to oil, natural gas and coal," Hilliard explained. "But today I am not representing any particular client, but rather come to advise you based on my 28 years of experience in the energy field."

"Thank you for explaining that, Dr. Hilliard," Phillips said. "Now we will begin with your opening statement."

Hilliard started with the usual litany that the world has substantial reserves of oil and other fossil fuels, that any transition away from fossil fuels should be gradual and market-driven, and that the government's role should be to create a level playing field.

Then it hit Cassie. Hilliard must be shilling for the Ammaris. He was only pretending to give an evenhanded assessment of the world's energy future. In fact, he had been consistently pushing the notion in his public testimony that the world would have to continue to rely on oil for the largest share of its energy needs for decades to come. Now, that wouldn't have seemed shocking to most people, and even to most experts. But what if it were known, if it were provably true, that this assessment was not based on an understanding of the facts, but rather based on Larry Hilliard's status as a stealth lobbyist in the employ of the Ammari government?

That's what the payments to build Hilliard's new house had to be about, Cassie concluded. There simply couldn't be any other reasonable explanation. And she knew that beyond the possible tax evasion which the gift of the house amounted to, there was Hilliard's probable status as an unregistered foreign lobbyist or "foreign agent" as the law called those who lobby for foreign governments.

Though Cassie judged it unlikely, it was possible that Hilliard was declaring the house as a gift or a payment on his tax return and thus avoiding a problem with the IRS. But if he were actually a registered foreign lobbyist for the Ammari government, everyone in Washington would know that fact including Senator Phillips. It would only take a quick check of the registrations to know for sure. And if, as she suspected, Hilliard had failed to register as required by law, the worst of his problems would not be with the government. The Justice Department would only slap him on the wrist and tell him he had to register. No, the worst of his problems would be with EAI's clients. They would be raging mad at this man who was supposed to be giving objective counsel to many of the world's largest energy-related companies of all types and to the governments of countries that are both exporters and importers of energy. They would demand the resignation of this man who was really just a lobbyist for one country and its state-run oil company. Cassie figured Hilliard would be gone from EAI in 24 hours if the information ever got into the press.

She noticed on the crawler on CNBC that the oil price had hit another record that day at $127 a barrel. She was no longer as confident as Hilliard apparently was that oil would be considerably cheaper in the years ahead. Despite what Hilliard had to have known about the size of Ammari oil reserves, she knew he was a firm believer that technology would allow the world to vastly increase its oil supplies. Cassie was beginning to understand what Victor meant when he said that technology was treated as if it were some sort of fairy dust that solves all problems.

As she turned back around to face Evan, she thought about telling him that she suspected Hilliard of being a lobbyist for Ammar. Then she thought it might be better to probe Evan for information that would shed light on why Hilliard would do such a thing. She wouldn't do her probing right then. It might seem a little odd. She would ask Evan to lunch and slip her questions into casual conversation.

Cassie got Evan to agree to meet her for lunch the next

day. Then she hurried back to her computer and checked the Department of Justice's foreign agent registration database online. There was no Larry Hilliard to be found, and, of course, this didn't surprise her.

≈

The next day Cassie and Evan lunched at the Vietnamese restaurant on P Street that she frequented. Cassie let the conversation drift wherever it pleased until she saw her opening.

"The house that Larry just built, what do you think it's worth?" she asked.

Evan had just taken a bite of one of his rice rolls and begged her indulgence until he could speak. "Well, it must be worth at least 10 million, maybe more," he said in a somewhat garbled manner as he chewed his food. "Just the lot alone in Falls Church had to be worth five million." He wiped his mouth with his napkin.

"Larry must have a lot of money to throw around," Cassie remarked as she lifted a spoonful of her egg noodle soup toward her mouth.

"Not as much as he used to."

"Why is that?"

"Well, now this is just between you and me, all right?"

"Of course."

"I didn't get this directly from Larry. And I don't want to say who told me. But so confident was Larry in his view that oil prices would fall that he decided to short oil in the futures market last year, and he took on a big position," Evan said.

"He didn't get out in time, did he?"

"Apparently, he kept *increasing* his position even as prices rose," Evan explained. "Then he finally gave up and closed everything out, incurring millions in losses, maybe even up into the double digits. Now, Hilliard is a very wealthy man, but I'm told — and mind you, I don't know this for sure — that he lost half his wealth in that one transaction."

"Half?"

"I don't know for sure, but a big chunk." Evan hoisted some vermicelli onto his chopsticks, but paused just above his bowl. "You know the old joke about how to make a small fortune in the commodities markets?"

"Yeah, I know," Cassie replied. "Start with a big fortune."

"So, the man's not poor by any means if 10 or 12 million represented half his wealth; but I've got to believe it put a dent in his lifestyle. Which is why I can't figure out why he'd go into hock to build that thing in Falls Church," Evan said. "But look, he's going to get a huge windfall when this merger goes through with GCC. Maybe he figures he'll pay it off then, and pocket what's left."

"How about you, Evan, did you get burned?"

"Oh, love, I learned long ago that it's far more profitable to sell market advice than it is to take it." Evan had a self-satisfied smile on his face. "I'm a treasury bond man myself. I leave the speculating to others."

Well, finally she had the motive, the piece that was missing. But what should she do now that all the pieces had come together? She wondered whether this had anything to do with the Ammari ambassador's offer to her. But the only conversation she had had about any of this was with Victor who had found out *who* was paying for Hilliard's new mansion.

For now she was just going to sit on her newfound knowledge of the Ammaris' motive for giving Hilliard a brand new mansion. The situation was too volatile for her to know what to do with the information.

≈

On what turned out to be an exceptionally warm Sunday, she was riding her bicycle in Rock Creek Park when she saw Victor coming the other way near the old Pierce Mill Dam.

She waved to him, and he stopped.

"I'm sorry to say, dear Cassie, that you look like a wet dishrag today," Victor said with a smile.

"I know. The heat and the humidity are just brutal," Cassie replied. "But I had to get out and get some exercise. You're looking like you've just had a shower with your clothes on yourself."

Victor nodded in agreement.

"Look, I've got some news for you," Cassie continued. "Let's go over to the picnic table and sit down."

They walked their bikes off the paved trail and leaned them up against each end of a heavily shaded picnic table on the bank of the creek. The sound of the water crashing over the nearby dam surrounded them as they removed their helmets and backpacks and sat down across from one another. Cassie pulled a towel from her backpack and wiped off her face.

"So, what is the news you have for me?" Victor inquired.

"Are you ready for this?" Cassie began. "I am almost certain that Larry Hilliard is working as an unregistered lobbyist for the Ammari government."

"This is bad for him?"

"Pretty bad, I think."

"How do you know this is true?"

"Well, you're the one who figured out that someone else was paying for that mansion he built in Falls Church," Cassie said. "And I'm the one who figured out that it was the Ammaris who were paying him off the books so to speak. But what was missing was why."

"And you believe they are paying him to lobby the American government?"

"Yes, but the Ammaris don't want anyone to know that that's what he's doing," she explained. "He often presents himself as an independent expert who is speaking for no particular client or country. But he has been shading all his so-called expert testimony in the direction that the Ammaris want him to with the aim of keeping everybody dependent on Ammari oil for as long as possible. After all, even if their reserves are what their internal report shows, they probably still have more oil than anyone else in the world."

"What Hilliard is doing is somehow a surprise?"

"Well, remember, EAI has clients not just in oil and gas, but also in wind, solar and biomass. And we consult not just with countries that are oil exporters, but also with countries that are large *importers*."

"I am getting your drift," Victor said. "Many clients will not like what he has been doing."

"Exactly," Cassie said. "If I were a client, I'd drop the firm in a heartbeat."

"He is risking the whole firm for a mansion in Falls Church?" Victor was shaking his head.

"But he doesn't think he's risking anything of the sort. He thinks he can have his cake and eat it, too," Cassie said.

"So, are you going to blow the whistle on him?"

"What do you think I should do, Victor?"

Victor stroked his chin with one hand and twisted his mouth up temporarily. "I think you should drop the whole thing and forget it."

"I thought you hated this guy."

"I dislike him. I don't hate him."

"Then, why are you saying this?"

"You are thinking now that you will take him down with this."

"Don't you think he deserves it?"

"Yes, of course, he deserves it. But—"

"But what?"

"This is Washington. You start out thinking you are going to bring someone down. But it is *you* who ends up in the ditch. You are playing with fire. You do not know what this man is capable of."

"So, I should just let it go?"

"Why ruin your career and your life over this insignificant weasel of a man? You don't have enough trouble already?"

Cassie pondered what Victor was saying. She had no way of knowing how Hilliard might strike back if she released the information. And she still had to deal with the Ammari ambassador.

"But what if I just leaked it to the media on the condition that I would not be identified as the source?" she asked.

"This man has many friends in the press. You can see his smiling face on television and read his name in the news-papers almost every week," Victor said. "Do you know some-one in the Washington press corps whom you can trust absolutely? Who would not expose your identity to Larry Hilliard?"

"No, I don't."

"You see, dear Cassie, you are not prepared for this fight. Perhaps someone else is, but not you."

"I know you're right, Victor," Cassie said. "I just hate to see him get away with this."

Victor shrugged his shoulders with resignation. "We are better off just preparing for the future. Let someone else worry about Larry Hilliard."

They both sat for a minute without saying anything.

"Now...you must tell me how things go with the Ammari ambassador after you talk with him, and you must remain cautious in your daily routine," Victor said.

"I will," Cassie replied.

Then she got up, and Victor rose with her. As they were walking their bikes back to the path, Cassie said, "Victor, you are a true friend."

"It is the most important thing I can be."

She leaned toward him and kissed him on the cheek. He took one hand off his bicycle and ran it gently back and forth through her hair. And then he kissed her on the lips tenderly and for what seemed like minutes before he withdrew.

Cassie's brain was swirling with desire and confusion. "Victor," she started.

He touched his finger to her lips to quiet her. When he withdrew it, he kept his gaze on Cassie as he put on his helmet and mounted his bike without saying a word. Then he turned and rode away.

≈ **chapter 17** ≈

Cassie was dreading daylight as she lay awake in her bed in the early morning hours of Monday. Today was the day she would have to contact the Ammari ambassador and turn down the job offer with Royal Sovoco. Perhaps that would end everything. Or would it?

As she walked to work along P Street and then around Dupont Circle, the heat and humidity already seemed worse than the day before. And the forecast was for a record high. Beads of sweat formed on her forehead, and she wiped them away with a handkerchief. The morning sun seemed as intense as if it were midday.

When she entered her building, the lobby felt cold, icy cold. As she waited for the elevator, she contemplated the images on the brass doors. Recent events in her life had changed their significance altogether in her mind. Vulcan, the god of fire, now seemed like the agent of a Faustian bargain. Give humans the extraordinary power of fossil fuels for a century or two, and then watch as their foolish shortsightedness eventually crashes the civilization they build using those fuels. And across from Vulcan, Ceres, the goddess of grain, was now completely dependent on those fossil fuels for her bounty. Then there was the cornucopia, the horn of plenty, the supernatural horn that would give those who possessed it whatever they wanted. Behind that symbol today was not man's mastery of nature, but the one-time gift of oil, natural gas and coal, never to be repeated in the epoch of humans.

Once she got to her office, she worked until around 10 o'clock when she decided she should call the Ammari ambassador and give him the bad news. She looked up the embassy number on the Internet and wrote it down on a notecard. She picked up the receiver, but then she put it back down. She didn't feel right making the call from a company phone.

She went down to the street, crossed 19th and sat at an empty table in front of the sandwich shop. The heat actually felt good, warming her up from the comparative cold of her office. She pulled out her cellphone, took the notecard bearing the embassy number from her pocket, and entered the number into her phone. The embassy switchboard picked up, and she asked for the office of the ambassador.

"Good morning, Ms. Young, if a morning as hellishly hot and humid as this one can be called good," said the ambassador with a slight chuckle.

"Good morning, Mr. Ambassador."

"I hope you have some good news for me," he said.

"Well, I'm not sure you will regard it as good news."

"I am sorry to hear that."

"I have decided not to pursue your generous offer," Cassie said. "I'm truly honored that you thought me worthy of such a position. But I'm afraid I must refuse. I am very happy with where I am currently working."

"Well, of course, you are," the ambassador replied. "Larry Hilliard treats his people very well. And naturally, money cannot be the only consideration in one's life."

"Thank you again, Mr. Ambassador, and thank you for the lovely dinner."

"I hope that we will be able to have dinner again sometime."

"Perhaps we will."

"Well, I won't keep you. I know you have a very busy schedule as do I. Goodbye, Ms. Young."

"Goodbye, Mr. Ambassador."

There, now that was done. But would it make the whole mess go away? She could only hope that the Ammaris would hit a dead end in their search for the Royal Sovoco oil reserves report—if, in fact, they were looking for it. She called Victor and let him know that she had turned down the job, but otherwise had nothing to report.

The next 48 hours passed without anything untoward happening, and Cassie was hopeful that the whole matter had blown over.

On Wednesday morning Evan stuck his head through Cassie's office door.

"Do you have moment?" he asked.

"Sure, come on in," she replied.

He walked in closing the door behind him.

"Love, have you been approached by Royal Sovoco about a job?"

Cassie was immediately filled with fear. Where could Evan have gotten that information?

"Well, um, as a matter of fact, yes," she replied.

"So have a number of other people in this office. I'm not sure how many yet," Evan said. "But it looks like they are trying to raid our firm. Thing is, I can't figure out why. I mean they have access to these people through our consulting arrangement. And surely, they don't need all of them."

"I don't know what to say, Evan, except that I turned them down flat."

Evan managed a smile. "Well, good. I'm glad. It wouldn't have been a very good move for you anyhow. Now—"

"That's all right, Evan—"

"No, let me finish. I know that someday you may choose to leave this firm for a better job or to go in a different direction. And you know that I want the best for you. And you know I promised your father that I would do my best to keep you safe. Is there anything that I should be concerned about?"

Cassie's head was now spinning. Did Evan know about the Ammari report? Is that what he was getting at? If he were sure, he would have just come right out and said it. He would have confronted her, Cassie thought.

"No, nothing that I can think of." Cassie did her best to seem nonchalant.

"Good. I'm glad. And thanks for sticking with me here."

"You know I wouldn't just up and leave without consulting you."

"Of course, I do." He nodded, seeming to be comforted by what she said. "Well, I better let you get back to work."

≈

That night Paul came to stay with Cassie. And she was glad to have him. But long after Paul had drifted off to sleep, Cassie lay awake. She got up and went into the living room and looked out the window onto the street. As she did, she thought she caught a glimpse of somebody looking up at her. As soon as she stared directly at the person, he or she — Cassie couldn't tell which — turned and started walking away.

She heard Paul come into the living room.

"What's wrong?"

"Oh, I couldn't sleep, so I came out here. I was looking out onto the street and thought I saw someone looking up into the window."

Paul stepped in front of her and looked down.

"He — or she — is gone now," Cassie said.

"You seem tense. Is something wrong?"

"It's nothing. Just work," she said.

Cassie hadn't told Paul about the Royal Sovoco documents or the ambassador's offer or Larry Hilliard's extracurricular activities. So far, she had only trusted Victor in such matters. And she wasn't sure she wanted to discuss them with Paul. Since their spat over his "self-medication" as she had so judiciously put it, she found herself increasingly unwilling to share things with him. Partly this was because they hadn't really talked about his drug-taking since then. She neither understood the cause of his apparent distress nor knew whether he was doing anything to address it — other than taking more pharmaceuticals, that is.

"You've been like this for a while," Paul continued. "Are you sure you want to stay in this job?"

"I'm not sure of anything right now." Cassie looked out again onto the street.

Paul wrapped his arms around her from behind and gave her a light kiss on the neck. She reached back and stroked his head gently a few times and then brought her arm down again. They stood there that way for a minute or two looking out the window in silence.

Then Cassie turned toward Paul and gave him a kiss. As she pulled away, she said, "Let's both try to get some sleep."

Soon after they climbed back into bed, Paul was sound asleep. But Cassie just lay awake staring at the ceiling for what seemed like another hour before she finally drifted off.

She awoke before dawn from a violent dream. Paul was already awake calling her name.

"Cassie, Cassie, wake up. You're having a bad dream."

Her breathing was labored with fright. Paul held her and began rubbing her back gently. She squeezed him tightly.

Finally, when Cassie let go, they both sat up in the bed. "Was it a bad dream?" Paul asked.

"Yes, it was." Cassie said. "I was walking down a deserted street at night in my nightgown. I went to the various houses trying to get inside, but nobody would answer. A police car came by, just creeping along on the street as I was coming off the porch of one of the houses. I waved my arms, but he couldn't see me. So, I ran toward the street. But before I got there someone grabbed me from behind, and I couldn't get away."

She could feel herself breathing harder again. Cassie lay down, and Paul moved close to her putting his arms around her. He kissed her again on the cheek. After a few minutes she calmed down, and they both went back to sleep.

≈

When Cassie went to work that morning, she couldn't shake the feeling that someone was watching her. Maybe it was the bad dream from the night before. But she *did* see somebody on the street looking right up at her window, didn't she? She needed to talk with Victor. She sensed that things were not over, that the Ammaris were still looking for their documents, and that she needed a next move.

She arranged to see him at the Willard Hotel bar after work where Victor said he would be meeting with an old friend who had come to town. He said he would be done by 5:30, so Cassie caught a bus on Connecticut Avenue around 5 o'clock to meet him. She rode to Lafayette Square where a large band of protestors were holding up signs denouncing oil companies for high oil prices. Before leaving the office she had glanced at the oil futures price and noticed oil had hit a new all-time high above $134 that afternoon.

She got off the bus and snaked her way through the throng as they chanted, "Down with big oil!" If they only knew how fortunate it would be if the big international oil companies *could* control the price of oil, Cassie thought. In that case oil prices might be set by some regulatory agency, the way utility rates are. But nearly 80 percent of the world's reserves were now controlled by governments and their state-run oil companies which gave the major international firms little to work with these days.

Cassie emerged onto Pennsylvania Avenue in front of the White House where a considerable number of Capitol police officers were strolling on the now closed street. She walked past the short metal columns meant to prevent the passage of vehicles and then by police cars, more barriers and a guard-house near the 15th Street entrance to the area. From there it was only a couple of blocks to the Willard Hotel. As she walked down 15th beside the Treasury building, she wondered why this street hadn't been blocked off as well. She felt as if she could simply climb up, open one of the windows, and let her-self in—though she was sure it wouldn't be quite that easy.

Finally, she turned and crossed 15th, and soon she was mounting the steps of the canopied entrance to the Willard. Inside, tall caramel-colored marble columns dotted the lobby; and, large semicircular windows ringed the mezzanine above. Classical music was playing in the background, and Cassie could hear French voices among a group of smartly dressed black men whom she supposed were diplomats. She spotted Victor sitting in the back near the entrance to the bar. As she approached, she saw another man on an adjacent couch sip-ping a drink and talking to Victor.

Victor looked up and saw Cassie. "Please come and sit down," he said. "Cassie, this is Gregor, a friend of mine from New York." Gregor wore a cropped beard and had long, flow-ing black hair. He got up and shook Cassie's hand.

Then Gregor looked at his watch and excused himself, apologizing for having to run off. After he had gone, Cassie sat down in Gregor's spot.

"What is happening? You look worried," Victor said.

"Someone was watching the condo last night," she replied.

"You are certain of this?"

"I'm not certain of anything. All I know is that I get up in the middle of the night, and I look out my living room window, and there's somebody standing on the street looking up into my condo," she explained. "As soon as I look down at the person, he or she turns and walks away."

"Please now put a smile on your face," Victor said in a quiet voice.

"What?"

"We are having a good time as they *watch* us," Victor continued. "We are just two friends meeting."

"Oh, okay." Cassie finally put a smile on her face.

"If we are going to talk," Victor said maintaining his smile, "then we should get out of here. We'll go out for a walk, okay?"

"Sure, sure," Cassie responded nodding and keeping her smile intact.

Victor motioned to the waiter and paid his bill. Then they both got up and walked out onto the street. He led her in the direction of the Treasury building.

"Hold my hand as we walk," he said.

"What?"

"Do it."

Cassie grasped his hand. Soon, they reached 15th Street, crossed, and turned left toward a small square behind the Treasury building. In only a few steps they reached the edge of the square. In the middle stood a statute of someone on a horse; Cassie was too far away to read who it was. Once they were circling the sidewalk on the outer perimeter, Victor began to talk more freely.

"Keep smiling," he said. "We're having a good time. We are friends out for walk. That is all."

"You really think I'm being watched."

"Yes, and I spotted the man who was watching you almost as soon as you alerted me. He is about my height, straight brown hair, parted on the left. Long, thin face, not gaunt, but thin."

"Yes, that's the man I saw in Kramerbooks and, I think, on the street in front of my office."

"Keep smiling."

"Yes, of course," Cassie said.

"Now, tell me more."

"Victor, if it's the Ammaris, then they are still looking for their documents."

"They've probably gotten all their responses from people in your firm," Victor said.

"You were right. They did contact a number of people in our office to discuss job offers."

"But now they have come up empty, and they must narrow the field," he explained. "If they break into one apartment looking for their documents, it will be seen as a misfortune. Two break-ins happening to people from the same firm may be dismissed as a coincidence. But ten break-ins will smack of a conspiracy, and they do not want that kind of scrutiny from the police."

"What are you saying?"

"They are looking for signs," he replied. "Who are the ones who look most guilty? Where have they stashed the report? At home? In a safe deposit box, maybe? In a bus station locker? They do not want to solve this problem with a shotgun. They want to solve it with a rifle."

"You mean that figuratively, right?"

"But of course," Victor said.

"What about Marta?"

"Perhaps we should consider destroying her copy as well. But you cannot go to her office and lead them to it. You will need to see her in person and tell her to shred the documents and put them in the recycling so they will be totally destroyed. The Ammaris do not know yet to look in her office, so I think this will be okay."

"Look, maybe I should just release all this to the press," Cassie said. "Maybe that's the best way to protect myself. If the information becomes public, then it will be pointless for them to do anything."

"No, we have been over this with regard to another matter," Victor admonished her. "You do not have any contacts in the press you can trust. And even if you did, they would have to check out your story, verify if the figures are authentic. And how would they do that? And then, even if they could satisfy themselves, how long would it take? Weeks? Months? And what would you do in the meantime to protect yourself?"

"But the Ammaris will have no idea how the press got those documents," Cassie said.

"They are watching you," Victor said. "How can you be sure they won't see what you are doing? And even if you could get the documents to a reporter undetected, say, by email, you will need to talk to this reporter to substantiate the authenticity of these documents. He or she will have to be satisfied that you are who you say you are. Are you sure you will be able to hide such a meeting from the faithful watchman who is now following us?"

"I'll just go on the record then. Right now. And then it will be too late for them to do anything."

"Assuming they print the story, then you will lose your job. And the Ammaris will label you a disgruntled employee who cannot be trusted. They will say that you are mentally unstable and maybe that you are some kind of drug addict. You will never get another job as an analyst," Victor said.

"I am *not* a drug addict," Cassie replied forcefully.

"The truth will not matter. They will smear you any way they can."

"Okay, okay, you've convinced me," Cassie said.

"Now, let us try to play the happy couple again for our paid professional observer," Victor said. They both put on smiles as they began to work their way back to their starting point.

Victor continued. "We must take you home. We must not hurry. We are enjoying ourselves. We are going to your place where I will drop you off. We will embrace and kiss each other. All is well. Then you will go up to your condo and call Marta and arrange a meeting. Do not mention on the phone what this meeting is about."

When they reached the street, Victor hailed a cab. Within 10 minutes they arrived at Cassie's building, and they both got out while the cab waited. Victor detected that the "faithful watchman" as he called him had gotten a cab right behind them. Cassie did exactly as Victor directed, embracing him and then kissing. She then went up to her condo. But before Victor continued home, she waved to him through her living room window, a touch Victor added to their routine while they rode in the cab.

Once Victor was gone, Cassie closed the curtains and went to her phone. It showed that she had two messages. The first was her mother checking in and wanting to know if everything was all right. The second was from Marta asking her to call back as soon as she could.

Cassie immediately dialed Marta's home number, and Marta picked up.

"Cassie, I'm so glad you called," she said.

"What is it, Marta?"

"Well, you know that package you sent me?"

"Yes, could we get together and—"

"I know where I put it, but I cannot find it anywhere. I hope you have copies."

"What?"

"It's gone. I don't know what happened to it. You do have a copy, don't you?"

Cassie was numb. She didn't know how to respond.

"Cassie, are you still there?" Marta asked.

"Yes, yes, that's okay, Marta," Cassie said. "We'll talk about this later."

"Okay, if you say so."

"Yes, it's okay, Marta."

"All right, then, goodbye, my dear."

"Goodbye."

As she was putting down the receiver, Cassie realized something that shocked her to her bones. She realized that she and Victor were the only people who knew Marta had a copy of the Royal Sovoco report. She began to think the most horrible thoughts. She thought maybe Victor had wanted the documents all along and was conniving to get them, while misdirecting her attention toward the Ammaris. Maybe *he* was planning to sell them to the Ammaris. He talked about it, even suggested as much to Cassie. And he said the Ammaris would be willing to pay a lot.

On the other hand, he might just release the information to the media himself once he'd set up a trade in the oil markets that would make him a lot of money. Maybe he had discouraged her from doing the same because he wanted to do it himself and time the release for maximum profit.

Cassie sank down on the couch. Could there be any truth in these speculations? Could she have been completely duped by him? Now she didn't know whom to trust. She thought maybe she should talk to Paul about it. But even as she thought about that, she felt uneasy.

Maybe she should talk to Evan. But if she did that, he would surely be obliged to fire her, and she didn't want to put him in that position. She could even approach the Ammari ambassador and renew their discussion about a job at Royal Sovoco. In effect, she could let him know that she could be bought. But what good would it do if Victor still had a copy of the report and was about to release it? Then it occurred to her that if Victor was the one who took the report from Marta's office—and it had to be him, she thought—then there were no documents to be found by the Ammaris and perhaps she was completely off the hook. Neither the Ammaris nor apparently Larry Hilliard had so far been able to pinpoint who had taken the report and perhaps they never would. After all, it was printed from Larry Hilliard's account on *his* printer. And Victor had somehow erased the computer logs related to their caper that evening. So, even if Victor eventually released the report, it might seem perhaps as if Hilliard had given it to Victor. She couldn't be entirely sure of all this. But it gave her some hope that perhaps the worst had now passed.

≈

The weekend brought her some relief as she spent much of Saturday biking through Rock Creek Park and around the city. On Sunday she and Paul rented a canoe on the waterfront near Georgetown. It was a bright, sunny day, but not so hot as it had been. As they started out from the boat launch, a jet taking off from National roared overhead. The boardwalk along the riverbank was thick with people moving both ways. Cassie saw boaters drinking on yachts moored along a dock which paralleled the boardwalk. The motor on one of the yachts suddenly came alive, and the boat began to move into open water, gurgling the oily smell of marine exhaust in their direction.

They paddled all the way up to Key Bridge. Sailboats glided through the water on either side of them as light traffic moved across the bridge above. The wake from an occasional powerboat rocked their canoe. They decided to turn around and paddle along the Virginia side toward the channel between Virginia and Roosevelt Island. They could see that there would be much less boat traffic to deal with in that part of the river.

When they reached the channel, Cassie noticed a parking lot for visitors to Roosevelt Island behind the trees on the Virginia side. On the footbridge that spanned the river, two people were crossing from Virginia onto the densely wooded island.

As Cassie and Paul continued to paddle quietly in the middle of the channel, she decided to tell him about the events of the last several weeks. He was now the only person left whom she felt she could talk with about her ordeal. Her reluctance to bring her work problems into their relationship and her nagging concern over his nascent prescription drug problem melted away.

"Paul," she said, "you know I've been kind of tense for the last few weeks."

"Yes, I noticed that, but you didn't seem to want to talk about it."

"I'm going to tell you things that may seem hard to believe."

"Try me."

"A little over three weeks ago, I stole some documents from EAI, or more specifically, from Larry Hilliard's files."

"You did what?" He stopped paddling in the front of the canoe and twisted around to look at Cassie.

"Listen carefully. These are not just any papers. They are internal documents that detail the oil reserves of the world's largest oil company, the government-run oil company of Ammar."

"This is serious, isn't it?" Paul returned his gaze forward and started to paddle again.

"This is very serious. It's serious not so much because of what I did as what I found out."

"And what was that?" he asked. He stopped paddling waiting for her answer.

"I found out that those reserves are not nearly as big as is commonly believed," Cassie replied. She now lifted her paddle out of the water as well. "And that means we may be on the front edge of the biggest energy crisis the modern world has ever known."

"I don't understand," Paul said. "I thought we had plenty of oil for a long time to come." Paul turned around to face Cassie and placed his paddle across the canoe in front of him.

"We have a lot, but not as much as everyone will want. And from what I've seen, sooner rather than later we will have less and less each year. I don't even understand all the implications of this yet myself. But I am now convinced of it." With both of them ceasing to paddle, the canoe was now drifting slowly with the current.

"Why did you need to steal this information?" Paul asked.

"I did it because I wanted to prove to myself that what Victor Chernov — the musician I mentioned to you — that what he was saying was not true. Or maybe I thought he might be right. I'm not sure anymore what I was thinking."

"He put you up to this?"

"No," Cassie replied, "but, the only way I could get the information I wanted was essentially to break into Hilliard's files with some expert help from Victor."

"Good god."

"Well, now those documents have been stolen from *me*. And I don't know whether they were stolen by him or by the Ammari government or by someone else. All I know for sure is that they are gone."

"Well, I say good riddance!"

"Yes, except there's one problem."

"What's that?"

"The Ammari government may know that I've seen that information. I don't think so, but they may. And they may be concerned that I will spread it around. They don't want that to happen."

"What are you saying?"

"I may be in some danger. I'm just not sure."

"Cassie, how could you get yourself into this? I can't believe this. I was planning for us to have a life together."

"Did I hear you right?"

"How could you get involved with this man?"

"I'm not *involved* with him." Cassie felt a tweak of conscience as she spoke. She had, of course, been misleading Paul about her dealings with Victor. But now for the first time she realized just how strong her feelings for Victor were. "I have had some conversations with him, and he helped me get this information — which in retrospect I wish I had never gotten."

"Yes, but now you are in trouble."

"You're talking to me as if you're my father. As if I'd gotten in trouble at school or something."

"No, that's not it. It's just—how could you do this?"

Just then Cassie noticed a speedboat racing in their direction.

"Paul, I think that boat is headed right toward us," she said.

Paul turned to look. "No, we've got the right-of-way. He'll turn off before he gets here."

"I'm not so sure he can see us."

Paul looked again. "You know you may be right. Let's start paddling, and fast."

Paul quickly spun around so that he was looking forward again, and they both put their paddles in the water and stroked furiously. But as they headed toward the Roosevelt Island shoreline, the speedboat seemed to alter its course to intercept theirs.

"He's going to hit us, Paul," Cassie said. "We've got to jump now and swim away."

The boat was less than 50 yards away. They both flung themselves into the river and began to swim as fast as they could away from the canoe.

As they swam, Cassie could hear the engine of the boat move away from them, and then sirens. Soon, a Coast Guard boat pulled up next to them, and a crewman threw out life rings. Cassie and Paul grabbed onto the rings and were pulled to the side of the boat where they both climbed up onto the deck.

"You folks all right?" one of the crewmen asked as he handed them towels.

"Yes, I think so," Cassie said. "How about you, Paul?"

"I'm fine," he replied. "Who was that crazy bastard?"

"We're chasing him, and I think we're going to get him," the crewman said. "We'll get you folks to shore, and then retrieve the canoe. It's a rental, right?"

"Yes," Paul answered.

"Don't worry about it. We'll get it back to the rental place. We'll just need you to give us a statement after you've dried off, and then you can go home," the crewman explained.

Within half an hour they were on their way back to Cassie's in Paul's Land Cruiser. Cassie was over the fright of the errant speedboat, but she was brooding over the way Paul had reacted to what she had told him. She still couldn't believe it. She was possibly in mortal danger, and yet he spoke as if it was all about him, about his needs. Soon they were parked in front of her building.

"I'll come back after I clean up and stay the night," Paul said.

"No, I think I want to be alone," Cassie replied.

"Are you sure?"

"Yes, I'm sure."

"Are you going to be okay, Cass?"

"I just need some time."

"All right." Paul kissed her on the lips, but she merely let him without really reciprocating. Then she got out of the car and hurried to the front entrance.

That night Cassie mulled over what Paul had said in the boat. Yes, he knew how to be attentive and even sympathetic. He was a "nice" man. But was he really the man she wanted? And she pondered the boating incident. It seemed as if some crazy, probably drunk, boater was behind it. But was that really what happened? Perhaps in a few days the Coast Guard would know something.

She desperately needed to talk to someone she could trust. She thought about talking to Marta. But Cassie didn't want to involve her any further. So that left Evan. But if she told him, she would certainly lose her job. And he would be deeply hurt by what she had done. Still, she could make out no good alternative. She decided to tell him everything the next day at work and accept the consequences for her job and her relationship with him.

≈ **chapter 18** ≈

When she awoke that Monday morning, Cassie felt more rested than she had in some time. Yet, she was still a little shaky. She wondered if Evan could somehow find out what the Ammaris knew and what their intentions were with regard to her. She wondered whether he had enough influence to convince them she was no threat. That would certainly put her mind at ease regardless of what now happened with her job. And if she had to, she would point the Ammaris in Victor's direction if they weren't already headed there.

When she came out into the living room, she played the messages on her answering machine which she had neglected the night before. There were three, all from Victor. He wanted to talk to her. But she was afraid to talk to him. After a bite of breakfast, she headed to work.

As she walked along the edge of Dupont Circle toward 19th, she could see a figure that looked like Evan in front of her office building. He was talking to someone. As she got closer, she slowed down and then stopped. The man Evan was talking to was the man she had seen in Kramerbooks and that Victor had spotted in the lobby at the Willard. In fact, she now finally remembered where she had first seen this man. It was in the EAI offices, coming out of the conference room as she and others were filing in for a Monday morning meeting. And now Evan was talking to this man! A few seconds later the man walked away and got into a car that had pulled up.

By the time Cassie arrived at the entrance, the car was long gone, and Evan had retreated into the building.

Suddenly, Cassie had second thoughts, big second thoughts, about saying anything to Evan. She began to think that maybe Victor was not the one who had taken the report from Marta after all. Maybe Evan had figured out that Cassie had printed out the report and removed it from the firm. But how could Evan have known about Marta? And why hadn't he come to Cassie directly? Why hadn't he just asked her for the report? Now she was more confused than ever.

She tried to work that day, but she could think of nothing but the jumble she had now made of her job and her life. She went out for two long walks just to calm down. When she got back from the second one, she had another message from Victor. But she ignored it.

The next day she finally got focused, though she was so tired by late afternoon that she knocked off work early and went home. When she arrived, she found another message from Victor among the messages on her machine. She checked her cellphone and found a message from him there as well. The messages were basically all the same: *Call as soon as you get this message.* She turned on the air conditioning and decided to take a nap. When she awoke, it was already close to nine. She was surprised she had slept that long.

Now she was hungry, and there was little to eat in the condo. She decided to walk to a nearby café and get something to take out. Yes, it was starting to get dark already. And Victor had warned her to be cautious. But then, maybe it was Victor she needed to be cautious of. She wasn't going to be a prisoner in her own condo. Besides, the café was only four blocks away.

She made her way down to the street and out the front entrance. The streetlights were just flashing on. As she hit the sidewalk, someone behind her yelled out something.

Cassie jumped when she heard the voice. Then she looked back and saw Victor.

"Jesus!" she cried out. "You scared the living daylights out of me."

"How come you don't return my calls?" he asked as he approached her.

Cassie started walking down 16th away from him, and he followed.

"What are you doing?" he said as he caught up with her again.

"What are *you* doing, Victor?" She hastened her pace, and he continued to walk alongside her.

"I've been trying to get in touch with you."

"Don't you already have what you want?"

"What do you mean?"

"The report, don't you already have it?"

"I told you to destroy the other copy."

"Well, somebody took it from Marta. Maybe it was you."

"You think it was me?"

"I don't know what to think." Cassie stopped abruptly and turned toward him. "You were the only one besides me who knew that my friend Marta had a copy."

"Now, this is absurd! All this is making you crazy."

"That's the first thing you've said tonight that I agree with."

Cassie started walking again. She turned down P Street toward 17th.

Victor caught up with her again. "Cassie, someone bugged my house."

"What?"

"If they bugged my house, they probably did the same to you. This is what I was going to tell you."

"Why should I believe you."

"Cassie, what has gotten into you?"

She stopped again. She was now more furious than afraid. "Victor, I don't know who to believe right now. You say my condo is bugged. Well, it probably is. But by whom? You? Evan Grant? The Ammari government? The CIA?—I don't know."

"What has happened?"

"If I knew that, I wouldn't be this confused." Cassie started walking again. And Victor followed her.

"Let's just go back to your place, and I will show you where they planted these devices," Victor said.

"You're not going into my condo, Victor."

"But Cassie, you must believe me."

She kept on walking as Victor stayed glued to her for another response. Traffic on the street was nonexistent as they continued down the sidewalk. Then a black SUV pulled up along the curb just ahead of them. Someone opened the door, jumped out of the back seat and faced them. As Cassie and Victor came up to where the vehicle was parked, the man walked in front of them and flashed a gun.

"You will step into the car, please," he said. "Now."

Both of them hesitated. The man pointed the gun right at Cassie's chest. "You must get in."

Cassie's heart was beating like it had never beaten before. She was frozen with fear. But then her mind moved directly from fear to complete clarity. She decided she was never getting into that vehicle.

"I tell you for the last time, you must get in the car," the man said.

"Cassie," Victor said. "I think we should get in." In that instant she wondered if Victor had set this whole abduction in motion. He was, after all, waiting for her when she came out of her building. Victor began moving toward the car, but Cassie broke away and ran.

Almost instantly she collided with another man who pushed her back so hard she fell to the ground. Gunshots rang out. She looked toward Victor and saw him struggling on the ground with the man who had threatened them. She turned back to where the second man had been standing. But he was now lying flat on the sidewalk moaning. A woman appeared out of the twilight with a gun in her hand. She rushed up to the man on the ground and disarmed him. Then she turned back and looked in Victor's direction. By this time another man was helping Victor subdue the first perpetrator. Cassie could hear sirens, then screeching and then a crash.

Within seconds the scene was surrounded by police who had their weapons drawn.

"Lay down your gun," a voice barked. "And get on the ground!"

The woman slowly put her gun down and then lay face down on the ground. A police officer rushed in, handcuffed her and then helped her up. "I'm the one who called you," she said.

"And you are?" the officer asked.

"My ID is in my right pocket."

He fished out the ID and looked at it.

"Okay, I'm going to take these cuffs off. But don't go anywhere."

Cassie was being helped off the ground by another officer when the woman came over to her. "Ms. Young, are you all right?" she asked.

"Yes, I think so," Cassie replied. She then thanked the officer for helping her and assured him that she was fine. He turned to talk to another officer nearby.

"It's a good thing your man took down the other guy. I'm not sure things would have turned out so well if he hadn't," said the woman.

"Is Victor okay?"

"Have a look for yourself."

He was standing up, and the man he had tackled was being led away by police. But Victor was now conversing with someone who had a familiar face. It was the man who had been talking to Evan that morning, the man who had been following her all this time. And now, he and this woman had come to her rescue.

The man saw Cassie looking at him, and he came over to her.

"Ms. Young, I'm Ray Keene," he said in a Virginia accent as he extended his hand and she shook it. "I'm so sorry about all of this."

"Thank you, Mr. Keene," Cassie said as she turned to the woman. "And thank you Ms...."

"Becky Severn," the woman said.

"Your man, Victor," Keene said, "took a big chance, and it saved everyone—everyone except that poor fellow that Becky shot." Keene was pointing to the other perpetrator who was being taken away on a stretcher. Farther down the street Cassie now noticed that the SUV had crashed into two police cruisers that had pulled in front of it.

"Mr. Keene," Cassie asked. "Who hired you?"

"Well ma'am, that's a complicated story," he replied. "But I'm going to have Evan Grant explain it to you."

≈

Later after everyone had given their statements at the police precinct, Keene approached Cassie and Victor.

"Ms. Young, I think it would be wise to stay in a hotel this evening," Keene said. "I've been in touch with Evan, and he would like you to come to work tomorrow at about 2 p.m. but not before. He has a few things to work out. Now, if you'd like, Becky will escort you to a hotel."

"I'll take her," Victor said.

"Fine," Keene said. "Just make sure she gets there."

"Mr. Keene, do you know who those people were?" Cassie asked.

"I'm not sure, but I've got a pretty good idea," Keene replied. "I'm gonna be there tomorrow when Evan talks to you. I'll know more then."

"These people were trying to kidnap me," Cassie said. "I'd like to know who they were."

"My guess is that they export a lot of oil."

"I see," Cassie said.

"Two o'clock tomorrow and not before," Keene said.

"Right," Cassie replied. "And thank you for everything."

"You're welcome."

An officer approached Cassie and Victor and told them a police cruiser was waiting to take them. The officer escorted them out through a back entrance and put them into the car.

"Where would you two like me to take you?" the officer who was driving them asked.

"Drop us at the Willard," Victor said.

"Victor, I just need a place to rest my head for the night," Cassie said.

Victor put his finger up to her lips.

"Go ahead, take us there."

The officer dropped them at the Willard, and Victor walked with Cassie into the lobby.

"I am going to get you a room," Victor said.

"I can take care of it, Victor."

"But I want to do it," he replied. He marched up to the registration desk and within a few minutes he was back.

Victor handed Cassie the key card as he spoke. "Now, go get some rest, and we will talk in the morning."

"Victor, I am so sorry," Cassie said.

"There was no way for you to know," he said. "Now you must get some rest."

"Victor, would you stay with me tonight?"

"If you want me to."

"I mean *stay* with me."

He took a big breath, and then smiled. "Of course." He stroked her cheek, and she tilted her head against his hand. "You are such a lovely one. I couldn't bear the thought of losing you," he said.

Cassie could see his eyes welling up with tears. She put her arms around his neck and kissed him.

≈

That night she made love with Victor. It was stimulating, yes. But there was something more, something she didn't experience with Paul. She realized that sex with Paul was more like a game, a fun game to be sure. But the object of it seemed to be nothing more than to enhance each other's pleasure. There was nothing wrong with that. Still, sex with Victor was about something larger, a joining together of souls as well as bodies. Cassie had thought that's what she had with Paul. But now she could feel that it wasn't. Not even close. Victor had come into her life by chance, a chance meeting at a concert. Now he had changed her life irrevocably.

In the morning the two of them had no place to go, so Victor ordered room service. The cart rolled in by the attendant had croissants, muffins, fresh fruit, coffee, and orange juice. Victor tipped the man, and then he and Cassie sat in their robes at a small table and helped themselves to some food.

"Victor, do you think those men last night…" Cassie stopped to take a deep breath. "Do you think they were going to kill us?"

"I don't know," he said. He spread some butter on a muffin as he spoke. "Maybe they just wanted to scare you. And, of course, I was in the way."

"You're just trying to make me feel better, aren't you?"

"Was I that obvious?"

"No, but I think I already knew the answer to my own question." Cassie finally picked up a piece of pineapple with her fork and took a bite.

"We must wait to see what Ray Keene and your friend, Evan, have cooked up," Victor said. "Perhaps they will find some way to shield you from this danger."

"I hope so, Victor," Cassie replied. "I'm not frightened so much anymore as I am tired, worn out. I just want it to be over."

Victor rose from his seat and came around behind Cassie. He began massaging her shoulders. She closed her eyes and leaned her head back to enjoy a few moments of relaxation.

Late that morning she and Victor checked out. They took a cab to her condo so she could clean up and put on some fresh clothes. Then they waited together.

When it was getting close to 2 o'clock, Victor said, "We'll get a cab."

"We can just walk, Victor," Cassie responded.

"Not in this heat," he replied. "It's well over 100 degrees out there. The television says we're headed for a new record for today. You'll be a wet dishrag by the time we get you to your office."

When they went out the door of her building, a blast of the superheated air hit her body and she relented. Victor hailed a cab, and they climbed in for the short ride to her office. When they arrived, he paid the cab driver. Victor said he would wait in the sandwich shop across the street until Cassie had finished her meeting with Evan.

Cassie hurried up to her office—or rather what she now believed would be her former office by the end of the day. She sat in her chair for a few minutes trying to compose herself. She had never really gotten a chance to decorate the place. Everything was so hastily done when she started. Maybe she sensed from the beginning that her stay at EAI was going to be temporary. Now she was sure of it.

≈

She got up and walked over to Evan's office. When he saw her coming through the door, he moved toward her and gave her a hug.

"Oh, my dear Cassandra," Evan said. "Things have gotten so complicated." He held onto her tightly for a few more moments and then released her.

"Let's sit down," he said as he closed the door.

Cassie saw Ray Keene standing on the other side of Evan's desk.

"Good afternoon, ma'am," Keene said. "Are you feeling better?"

"Yes, thank you," she said. Cassie moved to the other side of the desk and then everyone took their seats.

"Cassie, you are as dear to me as a daughter," Evan said. "And you know that I will do everything in my power to help you. But there are things that are beyond my control." He stopped to gather himself. "You can't stay here at EAI. The partners won't have it. I'll help you get a job elsewhere, but you have to leave here."

Cassie knew this was coming. But now that she had officially been told by her boss, her mentor, that she was fired, she slumped in her seat feeling ashamed of the way she had conducted herself.

Evan rose from his chair and began to pace back and forth behind his desk. "What I am about to tell you must never leave this room. Agreed?"

Cassie nodded her head.

"Of course, Evan," Keene replied.

"Larry Hilliard is a brilliant but flawed man," Evan continued. "He trusted no one; and so, he eventually lost the trust of everyone. He routinely spied on associates who were being considered for partner. He said he didn't want any surprises."

"I'm sorry, ma'am," Keene said as he looked at Cassie.

"I couldn't stop the practice, and so I short-circuited it. I hired Raymond here on a separate retainer to report back to me first and allow me to edit what he told Hilliard. And I told him to take special care of you. Which turned out to be a very good thing, indeed. When Ray figured out that someone else was watching you besides him and his partner, Ms. Severn, we decided that we needed to find out who. Well, that wasn't the hard part. It was pretty easy to figure out that it was the Ammaris. What was hard was to figure out why.

"When Royal Sovoco started making overtures to every associate, we knew they were searching for something. We noticed that the one associate they didn't talk to was Bob Ulrich. We didn't know what to make of that until now. Ray did a little investigating and figured out that Ulrich has been reporting to the Ammaris on the activities of this office. And one of the things Ulrich somehow managed to catch wind of was that Larry Hilliard was in a panic over some pilfered records, Ammari records. Hilliard didn't reveal this to the rest of the firm for obvious reasons. At first, Ulrich apparently didn't know the precise nature of these documents, nor how sensitive they were. But the Ammari government seemed to know exactly what they were," Evan explained.

"Ulrich also figured out much later that the most likely candidate for the theft was you," he continued. "And Bob ultimately reported that to the Ammaris. At the beginning, however, they looked at all the associates and even a few of the junior partners." Evan paused for a moment and then looked at Cassie. "Just so you know. Bob Ulrich no longer works for this firm as of this morning. But he did one good thing. By rummaging through everyone's files, he satisfied the Ammaris that we have no printouts of their internal reserves report in this office.

"Now, the Ammaris, as you know, have their documents back, and I'm sure they've destroyed them by now," Evan added. "And they searched your condo thoroughly and then apparently copied your hard drive to see if you had scanned the documents into your computer and possibly emailed them somewhere. They seem satisfied that you did neither. They also had one of their people here today working with IT to make sure that report, even in its encrypted form, no longer exists on our servers. And I received word just before you came in that they are now satisfied about that, too.

"Tomorrow, Larry Hilliard will step down as chairman of EAI and resign from the firm. I will assume that post temporarily until the partners have a chance to vote on who will be the next chairman," Evan said. "Have you read today's paper?"

"Not yet," Cassie replied.

Evan picked up a newspaper from his desk, opened it to an inside page and handed it to Cassie. Below the fold was a story with a headline that read: "When is an energy analyst really a lobbyist?" Hilliard was being investigated for having acted as an unregistered lobbyist for the Kingdom of Ammar.

Evan continued. "I have been trying to ease Larry Hilliard out of this firm for six years. But your little piece of investigation was the thing that made it possible."

"Wait a minute," Cassie said. "How did you find out about this?"

"I confess that Ray and I were desperate to find out why the Ammaris were watching you. We were getting nothing from the telephone taps that Hilliard had ordered on all associates' and partners' phones. He did this after the Ammari report was taken. But he did not tell Ray why he was doing it at the time. So, I had Ray get someone to listen in on your conversations away from home using special bugs. When we heard the conversation in the park with your friend Victor, we knew we had a bombshell. We thought this might be what the Ammaris were concerned about. We didn't know about the Royal Sovoco reserve estimates at that point."

"I apologize, ma'am," Keene said sheepishly. "There was no other way."

"You could have just asked me, Evan," Cassie said.

"And you would have told me everything?" Evan replied. "You had gone on this long behind my back. For what reason should I have trusted you?"

Cassie looked down because she knew that Evan was right. She certainly wouldn't have told him everything.

"Later on we did learn there were documents involved," Evan said. "But we didn't know the nature of those documents until this morning when I met with the Ammari ambassador and the vice president of Royal Sovoco. Reading between the lines I have surmised that Hilliard had been hinting that he had such documents and was using them as leverage with the Ammaris — to insure that their business stayed with EAI and to ensure that they paid him generously for his lobbying." Evan paused. "Now what I want to know from you, Cassie, is what exactly you thought you were doing." He leaned down putting both hands on his desk and staring right at her.

"I'm not sure now," Cassie said. "I wanted to know the truth, and I thought I could find it by looking in Hilliard's files."

"And what were you going to do with that information once you had it?" Evan asked as he stood back up and folded his arms.

"I just wanted to see it," Cassie replied. "Then I was going to make a decision about what to do."

"Were you going to release it to the press?"

"I don't know. I thought I might."

"And then what? What was your plan when there was mass chaos, when the oil markets went crazy, when people started to riot maybe?"

"Oh, Evan, don't be so melodramatic," Cassie replied.

"Oh, so you have a plan for calming people's fears, do you?"

"I didn't think I needed a plan because I thought people would be able deal with it."

"And if they couldn't?" Evan asked. He paused for a moment then looked straight at Cassie. "This firm has no endgame for oil. This country has no endgame for oil. The world has no endgame for oil. And so it seems, *you* have no endgame for oil. You were just going to spring it on everyone and hope for the best, is that it?"

Cassie was silent. She felt overmatched.

"Well, you are *not* going to spring it on *anyone*," Evan said. His tone was sharp and angry.

"I'm long past that," Cassie said.

"I'm glad to hear it," Evan replied. "I have convinced the Ammaris that the best way to handle this is to have you sign a confidentiality agreement that specifically mentions Ammari reserve information that you've had access to and forbids you from ever discussing it with anyone. For that you will be paid a substantial severance from this firm."

"What about you, Evan? Aren't they worried about you and other people in the firm?"

"Only you, me, Dhanesh, Ray, Hilliard, Ulrich and your friend, Marta Nilsen, even know that report exists."

Cassie noticed that Evan had left out Victor and Paul. But her pulse jumped when he mentioned Marta's name.

"I'm telling you that that is the official line from Ammari intelligence," Evan said.

Now she understood him. Evan knew Victor and possibly Paul were aware of the report, but the Ammaris didn't.

"Ulrich found out about Nilsen by looking through the courier receipts," Evan continued. "You don't send that much by courier, love, so it was fairly easy for him. Hilliard may be leaving EAI, but you can be sure he'll be getting lucrative consulting contracts from Royal Sovoco as far as the eye can see in order to keep him on a leash. Besides, changing his story now would make him look like a fool. As for Marta Nilsen, they don't regard a professor of comparative literature without any documentary evidence as a real threat to the confidentiality of their reserve data. And as for Ulrich, he's their man, and they can deal with him in whatever way they see fit as far as I'm concerned."

"But what about you, Evan?" Cassie asked.

"Neither Raymond nor I nor Dhanesh have seen the documents," Evan said. "We don't know what's actually in them, and it's going to stay that way. As of today all of us are covered by confidentiality agreements with Royal Sovoco and bound not to disclose what little we know."

"But what about those people who were arrested last night? Won't all this come out at the trial?"

Keene turned in his seat toward Cassie. "They were Ammari nationals. I am certain they were sent here specifically for this task because the Ammaris couldn't chance it if something went wrong," he explained. "There will be no trial, and they will never talk. They will plead to whatever the prosecutor wants. And in exchange their families will be well taken care of by the Ammaris."

Evan put down a piece of paper in front of Cassie. On it he placed a pen and then a check made out to her from the firm for $2 million. The amount made her gasp. But Cassie now felt corrupted. The Ammaris were having their way. They were buying her silence, and she didn't like it. She sat motionless.

"Come on, love," Evan said. "It's the only way they'll ever leave you alone. You've got to sign. And then you've got to get out of this town. Get as far away as you can, and never talk about oil in public again."

Cassie picked up the agreement and scanned it. It was a standard agreement except for the specific words about Ammari reserves. She put it back down on Evan's desk, signed it and tore off her copy. She then folded the check and placed it in her pocket.

"Well, that's all, love," Evan said. "I'm going to miss you."

Cassie got up and gave Evan a hug and a kiss on the cheek. She said goodbye to Keene, and then left. She went down to street level and out of the building. It was as if she had stepped into an oven as she walked the short distance to the sandwich shop where Victor was waiting. Once inside it was cool again, and she found him sitting at a table reading a newspaper.

"Well, how did it go?" Victor asked as he set the paper down.

"I'm finished in the oil business," Cassie said.

"Well, the oil business is gradually winding down anyway."

Cassie snorted and managed a weak smile. She told Victor about the confidentiality agreement and the payment. He said it was the right thing to do. She said she had to deposit her check, and then return to clean out her office. But she suggested that they get together later.

≈

That evening Victor and Cassie met for dinner at a small bistro in Georgetown. Afterwards, they went across the river and up to the Custis-Lee Mansion from which they could see all of Washington. They sat on a blanket on the ground in front. It was still quite hot as the sun finally disappeared below the horizon. The city lights were already bright under the midnight blue sky that was slowly fading to black.

"Oil hit 147 today," Victor said.

"Where do you think it's going from here?" Cassie asked.

"Who knows? My guess, probably down."

"I thought you were a peak oil guy."

"Yes, but these high prices will crush the economy; and then oil demand will drop, and prices will crash."

"And then what?"

"I'm just guessing. We are now living in an uncharted future, and what we've seen so far is just the prelude. But I think after the price of oil crashes, it will rebound very quickly, and people will be surprised. Then it will crush the economy again, and oil will crash again. And we will go through this many times as we bump up against our limits."

Cassie looked out at the lights in the District. The glow of the Lincoln Memorial, the Washington Monument reaching up into the night sky, the muted light of the Capitol dome and the Jefferson Memorial, all stood out against the Washington skyline. Car lights streamed along the streets like red and white corpuscles through arteries. The city was dotted with lights everywhere. That so much of the night could be obliterated was a testament to how energy-rich modern society was.

"As the crisis deepens," Victor continued, "people will blame it on the oil companies. And they will blame it on the politicians. And then, they will blame it on the Arabs and the Russians, too. They will do everything but blame it on geology — because they don't know the most important thing there is to know: that geology is destiny. If you understand your destiny, there are things you can do. But if you don't, then you are hopelessly lost."

They both sat quietly for a moment. Cassie saw a shooting star, but wasn't fast enough to point it out to Victor.

"What do you think would have happened if the Ammari oil reserve figures had somehow made it into the press?" she asked.

"I think few people would have understood their significance, even people very high in government," he replied. "I think the Ammaris would have made every effort to discredit them. In any case, people would convince themselves that there is plenty of oil elsewhere and that it will be easy to find alternatives. I think in the long run there would hardly have been a ripple in the public's mind."

"Really?"

"Perhaps someday we will find out if I'm right. Just not today."

"What are you going to do, Victor? Are you going to stay in Washington?"

"I have some land near Vancouver. I think very soon I'm going to go there and try to grow more tomato plants…and other things, too."

Cassie looked down for a moment and then turned to Victor. "Victor, I'm going to end it with Paul."

"I see," he said. "What do you think you will do now?"

"I don't know," Cassie said. "Except perhaps...go live in Vancouver...on some land...where I could grow tomato plants."

Victor had a smile that was gradually expanding. "I think that is the best idea I have heard in a very long time."

He put his hand on the back of her head, gently pulled her toward him, and gave her a deep kiss. As they came out of it, another shooting star traversed the sky, and they both found themselves pointing it out to the other and laughing.

≈ epilogue ≈

Six months after leaving Washington for Vancouver with Victor, Cassie was in a café and discovered a recent copy of the New York Tribune sitting on a shelf of reading material. She picked it up and began to thumb through it, scanning the headlines quickly as she turned the pages. Deep in the interior of the paper, one headline stopped her cold: "Energy analyst speaks from the grave, or does he?"

She scanned the first paragraph and saw Hilliard's name. She went back and started at the beginning:

WASHINGTON—A top energy analyst recently emailed a seemingly shocking revelation to major news organizations throughout the country. The email claimed that the world's largest oil producer is running low on fuel and lying to the world about it. The curious part of the story is that the energy analyst, Lawrence Hilliard, is dead, killed in a car crash two months ago near his Virginia home.

Hilliard had previously been chairman of Energy Advisers International, a prominent Washington, D.C.-based energy consulting firm, before a scandal involving illegal lobbying led to his resignation.

The message included an attachment that appeared to be an eyes-only internal review of oil reserves at Royal Sovoco, the national oil company of the Kingdom of Ammar, the world's largest oil exporter. The review seems to indicate that Ammari oil reserves — thought to be the largest in the world — are only half those publicly claimed by the government.

But a spokesperson for Royal Sovoco said the emails were an obvious hoax. "Normally, dead people don't send email," said Ahmed Al-Dineri, the company's director of communications. "Clearly, the flimflam artist who sent this email forgot to check the obituaries."

Members of the Tribune's technical staff attempted to trace the origin of the email, but were unsuccessful in pinpointing its source.

A tiny minority of energy analysts has been claiming for years that Ammari reserves are overstated. But since the country allows no independent audit of its reserves and field-by-field reserves are not made available to the public, most analysts have been using the aggregate number published by the government.

Cassie thought she knew someone who could make it possible for dead people to send email — her old friend Dhanesh at EAI. Perhaps Hilliard had arranged for the emails to go out automatically if he were ever killed.

Cassie looked on the Internet later that day, but could find only the Tribune's story and several sites that linked to it. No other news organization ran anything about the reserves report. And in the months that passed after she had seen the story, she found no follow-up to it. It was just as Victor had predicted. The story didn't even make a ripple in the public's mind.

≈ ● ≈

Glossary

Alphabetical Listing (Chapter Number in Parentheses)
Definitions Provided Below by Chapter

Definitions By Chapter

Except for movie, book and article titles, all italicized words
in the definitions are defined elsewhere in the glossary.

Chapter 1

Aberdeen – A major oil city on Scotland's eastern coast servicing oil-fields in the North Sea.

aggregate – Crushed stone and sand often mixed with *bitumen* to make asphalt for paving.

Athabasca River – A major river in Alberta that flows through the oil sands mining area around *Fort McMurray*.

bitumen – A black, viscous mixture of hydrocarbons occurring naturally. It is the substance from which oil is derived in the oil sands.

caustic soda – Sodium hydroxide, also known as lye. A white substance that creates a strongly alkaline solution when dissolved in water and which is used to manufacture chemicals and refine petroleum.

deepwater – Water deeper than 600 feet.

Eurocopter – European manufacturer of helicopters headquartered in France.

Fort McMurray – A boomtown in northeastern Alberta which services those working in the Athabasca Oil Sands to its north. Population exceeded 70,000 in 2008.

law of receding horizons – This informal law describes the problem that rising energy costs pose for those exploiting unconventional energy resources. As the price of energy rises, so does the cost of exploiting expensive, hard-to-get energy resources precisely because they require so much energy to extract. Thus, energy projects which appear economical at high prices turn out to be marginal or even loss makers as the now high-cost energy used to build and run such projects makes them uneconomic. The phrase was coined by Canadian journalist Roel Mayer.

Rogers Centre – Toronto athletic stadium that holds approximately 46,000 spectators. The stadium has a retractable roof. When closed, the volume inside the stadium is 56 million cubic feet or 1.6 million cubic meters.

SAGD – Steam-Assisted Gravity Drainage. A method of petroleum extraction in which steam is pumped down a well to an area containing viscous hydrocarbons which, once melted, run downward toward a second well through which they are pumped to the surface.

sulfur – A yellowish element used in a variety of manufacturing processes. Most often recognized as the source of the distinct smell of a burning match. Sulfur occurs naturally in oil. In order to reduce sulfur emissions, which are the cause of acid rain, many governments now set maximum allowable sulfur levels in fuels such as gasoline and diesel. That means some sources of oil such as bitumen must have sulfur removed before they can be used to make vehicle fuels.

Super Puma – A particularly rugged helicopter made by *Eurocopter*, the largest version of which can carry 24 passengers plus a pilot. This helicopter is often preferred by offshore oil and gas operators in harsh environments such as the North Sea.

synthetic oil – Synthetic crude oil made from *bitumen* using various energy-intensive *upgrading* processes.

toe to heel air injection – A patented form of fireflood used to extract heavy oils such as *bitumen*. Steam is first injected to warm up the underground oil. Then a portion is ignited, and air is driven into a well to assist the combustion. The heat helps liquefy the heavy oil, and the pressure from the combustion gases pushes the liquefied oil up other wells to the surface.

upgrader, upgrading – Apparatus and processes respectively used to convert *bitumen* into a fluid that is suitable for refining by conventional petroleum refineries.

Chapter 2

Blue Ridge – A mountain range that runs from Georgia to Pennsylvania forming a distinct *geologic province* within the Appalachian Mountains.

coastal plain – Relatively flat land along a seacoast. The Atlantic coastal plain runs from New York to Florida.

geologic province – An area sharing common geologic traits.

Glass, Philip – American composer (born 1937) probably best known for his film scores including those for *Dracula*, *The Fog of War*, *The Hours*, *The Illusionist*, *Koyaanisqatsi*, *The Thin Blue Line*, and *The Truman Show*. Glass is also the composer of many operas, symphonies, concertos and solo works. He pioneered a style characterized by the use of simple musical structures woven into complex repetitive patterns. The style became known as minimalism, though Glass has distanced himself from this term.

Harper administration – The administration of Prime Minister Stephen Harper of the Conservative Party of Canada, which came into office in February 2006. Harper has championed free trade and integration with the United States. As prime minister and a member of parliament from Alberta he has been supportive of oil sands development.

Piedmont, the – A plateau on the eastern side of the Appalachian Mountains that runs from New Jersey to Alabama. The Atlantic coastal plain lies between it and the Atlantic Ocean.

radio telescope – A receiving dish designed to listen for radio waves from extraterrestrial sources such as stars. Often mistaken for a satellite dish.

Triassic lowland – Basins formed when North America and Africa began to separate during the Triassic period from 250 to 200 million years ago.

Chapter 4

aboveground factors – Factors not related to geology which affect the production of oil, natural gas and other underground resources. These include market prices, taxes, regulatory constraints, subsidies, available technology, ownership of and access to resources, physical infrastructure, workforce availability, and political and social stability in areas where production takes place.

Chapter 5

3-D seismic visualization room – A theater specifically designed to show three-dimensional visualizations of *seismic data.*

bends, the – Decompression sickness brought on by sudden changes in ambient pressure such as occurs when a diver surfaces quickly from depth. The change in pressure causes gas bubbles to form in the blood which may result in symptoms including joint pain, mental confusion, dizziness, shortness of breath and paralysis. Divers are routinely treated successfully using a *hyperbaric chamber.*

blowout – The uncontrolled flow of oil and/or natural gas from a well. Often initiated by an explosion related to the inability of a drilling crew to contain the pressures within the well.

casing pipe (sometimes just "casing") – Thick metal pipe used to reinforce a freshly drilled portion of an exploration well called the *openhole.*

cuttings – Rock fragments produced by a rotating *drill bit.* Cuttings are examined for characteristics that tell drillers the composition of the strata through which they are drilling.

delineation wells – Wells drilled after a successful exploration well demonstrates the presence of producible hydrocarbons. Delineation wells are drilled to help determine the full size and configuration of the *reservoir* or reservoirs. Sometimes called "appraisal wells."

drawworks – A powerful machine on a drilling rig that reels a strong, thick wire rope in or out as it operates the hoist on a drilling derrick used to handle various heavy pipes and apparatus over the *drill floor.*

drill bit – A specialized boring tool at the end of a *drillstring* which cuts away rock and other debris in order to create a passageway for oil or natural gas to reach the surface.

drill floor – The floor immediately beneath a drilling derrick through which the *drillstring* is inserted for drilling a well.

drilling mud – A heavy, specialized fluid, often a combination of water, clay and other chemicals, that circulates in the *wellbore*. Its purpose is to carry away *cuttings*, lubricate the *drill bit*, and contain pressures within the well in order to prevent a *blowout*.

drillstring – The entire apparatus spanning the *wellbore* including the drillpipe and *drill bit*. The drillstring is rotated to drill the well.

flow test – A test designed to gauge the pressure and flow rate of a *reservoir* discovered by an exploratory well. Often, oil or natural gas is allowed to flow up to the surface for a period of time in order to allow measurements to be taken.

hyperbaric chamber – A sealed chamber used to treat *the bends* by allowing ambient pressure to be reduced gradually, thereby preventing gas bubbles from forming in the blood.

motorman – The person assigned to keep all the engines on a drilling rig or an offshore platform in working order.

mudlogging cabin – Compartment, often a trailer, in which samples of the drilling mud taken from the well are analyzed. *Cuttings* are analyzed to determine the presence of hydrocarbons and to understand the underground strata. Especially important is detecting the level of natural gas in the mud, which can be an early warning sign of danger.

openhole – A portion of an exploratory well which has not yet had *casing pipe* inserted to support it.

pipe deck – The deck on an offshore platform on which various types of pipe needed for drilling and casing are stored.

power tongs – Large, powered wrenches used to grip and manipulate pipe on the *drill floor*.

reservoir – An underground deposit of oil and/or natural gas consisting of tiny droplets of oil infused in porous rock or rock impregnated with natural gas capped by a nonporous layer that keeps the oil and/or gas from migrating to the surface and escaping.

seismic data – Data obtained by creating sound waves at the surface of the earth or the ocean, sometimes using explosives, and recording reflections of those waves from underground layers. The data is fed into computer models to create a visual depiction of the layers. Usually this is done to help determine whether the layers could contain reservoirs of oil or natural gas. (See *3-D seismic visualization room*.)

semisubmersible – A floating offshore drilling platform that is designed to have part of its structure submerged to enhance stability. The platform is either tethered to the bottom of the sea by several large anchors or held in position by a computer-controlled propulsion system.

topside – The structure of an offshore platform that sits on top of the legs. The topside includes the derrick, power plant, oil and natural gas processing equipment, living quarters and helipad.

well test – Includes the *flow test* and other measurements of an exploration well.

wellbore – The entire length of a well including segments with *casing* and those without, if any. Sometimes called the "borehole."

wire line unit – A testing unit that deploys measurement devices on a wire line that is lowered into the *wellbore* during drilling. The tests reveal important information about the area traversed by the *wellbore* by measuring such characteristics as the electrical conductivity of the strata and nuclear radiation from naturally occurring radioactive elements.

Chapter 6

E&P companies – Exploration and production companies (as opposed to refining and marketing companies). Some large oil and natural gas companies, referred to as integrated oil companies, involve themselves in all four aspects of the business.

Lower Tertiary – Refers to a geologic era which ran from about 65 million years ago to 23 million years ago. In this case it is shorthand in the oil industry for a specific area of the Gulf of Mexico where *deepwater* drilling plunges into strata formed during the Lower Tertiary. Such wells can be in thousands of feet of water and extend up to 20,000 feet below the seabed.

original oil in place – The total amount of oil contained in a reservoir. Because of technological and geologic constraints, the worldwide average *recovery rate* has historically been between 35 and 40 percent of the original oil in place. This rate varies widely with the quality and location of the *reservoir*.

recovery rate – The fraction of the *original oil in place*, usually expressed as a percentage, that can be extracted from a *reservoir*.

reserves – Any underground fossil fuel that has been positively identified and can be extracted profitably using existing technology at current prices.

trend – a geologic feature; the direction of that feature.

URR – Ultimately recoverable resource. The absolute amount of a resource that can be extracted over the lifetime of a particular oil and gas field based on a set of assumptions about price, technology, and the quality of the oil and/or natural gas.

Chapter 7

magic pudding – A reference to a classic Australian children's book in which the title character is a pudding that continuously renews itself no matter how much of it people eat. The full title of the book which was first published in 1918 is *The Magic Pudding: Being The Adventures of Bunyip Bluegum and his friends Bill Barnacle and Sam Sawnoff.*

Peabody – The Peabody Institute. A music conservatory located at The Johns Hopkins University in Baltimore, Maryland.

Chapter 8

art deco – A style of design in the decorative arts and architecture popular in the 1920s and 1930s. Characterized in part by geometric forms and the use of newly available materials (at the time) such as aluminum, chrome and stainless steel.

OPEC – Organization of Petroleum Exporting Countries. A cartel of 12 major oil exporting countries which seek to influence world oil prices by managing their oil production, restricting supply to force prices up and increasing supply to bring them down.

Chapter 9

encryption – Encoding used to protect sensitive information.

passphrase – A set of numbers and/or letters which are used to encode or decode an encrypted message or file.

Chapter 10

at current rates (of production or consumption) – The quantity of world reserves of commonly used finite commodities is often expressed in terms of years of supply "at current rates of consumption." Examples of finite commodities include oil, copper, phosphorus and other minerals. The problem with this method is that neither production nor consumption remains constant over time. If consumption is rising swiftly and reserves are not, then supplies will not last nearly so long as estimates based on current rates of consumption would suggest.

recovery factor – See *recovery rate* under Chapter 6 definitions.

Chapter 12

depletion – The emptying out of an oil or natural gas *reservoir* or ore body of any kind as extraction proceeds.

Chapter 15

EMP – Electromagnetic pulse. An intense pulse of electrical energy, the chief danger of which is the destruction of electrical infrastructure, including computers and computer networks, through overloading. An exceedingly destructive form of the phenomenon can be produced by the high-altitude explosion of a nuclear weapon. Another source can be a severe solar storm.

energy sink – A process or product that absorbs energy. Some fuels which are touted as energy sources are actually energy sinks. Hydrogen is an example. It takes more energy to produce it than it provides when burned.

Hirsch Report – Informal name for a 2005 report commissioned by the U.S. Department of Energy. While projecting no particular date, the report said that the onset of world peak oil production would produce a very specific kind of energy crisis, one marked by a shortage of liquid fuels, which are critical in transportation and agriculture. The authors studied what measures could be taken to replace liquid fuels made from oil. They concluded that a crash program to develop and deploy alternative liquid fuels would have to begin 20 years in advance of the peak to avert major economic dislocations. The report is named after its lead author, Robert L. Hirsch. The full name of the report is *Peaking of World Oil Production: Impacts, Mitigation & Risk Management.*

kerogen – Waxy, hydrocarbon-rich substance found in *oil shale*. Kerogen must be extracted using heat. Additional heat and upgrading are normally required to produce oil suitable for refineries.

oil shale – Industry term for organic marlstone. It is not shale, and it contains no oil. Rather it is rich in *kerogen*, a waxy substance, which can be extracted and processed to make feedstock suitable for oil refineries. No commercial production of oil from oil shale has taken place to date due to the high costs associated with such production.

solar flare – An intense energy emission from the sun which takes the form of a large flare caused by an explosion in the sun's atmosphere.

supervolcano – A volcano which ejects thousands of times the quantity of material ejected by volcanoes recorded in human history. Such volcanoes are known to have erupted in the geologic past. The eruption of a supervolcano today could wipe out life on large swaths of an entire continent. For those in areas remote from the eruption, the material ejected from the volcano might partially block the sunlight for up to a decade which would hamper plant growth and thereby seriously curtail food supplies for animals and humans.

Chapter 16

biomass – Plant matter grown for fuel.

futures market – An exchange set up to allow producers and industrial consumers of major commodities—such as wheat, corn, oil, copper and gold—to agree on prices for those commodities before they are actually delivered. Speculators who neither produce nor plan to take delivery of those commodities often participate in such markets. Futures exchanges typically require less than a 5 percent deposit—called margin—against the total price of the goods. That means a small move in price can cause losses and profits to mount quickly. (See *short*.)

short (in the *futures market*) – A wager that the price of a specific commodity will decline. To go short, one sells a contract at the current price to deliver the commodity at some future date and hopes for the commodity's price to decline in order to pocket the difference when it comes time to deliver the commodity or buy back the contract.

Oil in Perspective

See sources below.

1. Number of days that 1 billion barrels of oil will supply the needs of the world: 12

2. Barrels of oil consumed in 2008 in billions: 31

3. Recent "large" discoveries of oil expressed in days of world supply (based on consumption in 2008).

    Kashagan (Kazakhstan): up to 153
    Gulf of Mexico Lower Tertiary: Between 35 and 177
    Tupi (Brazil offshore): Between 59 and 94
    Ngassa-2 (Uganda): 18

4. Decade in which U.S. oil discoveries peaked: 1930s

5. Year geologist M. King Hubbert predicted in a 1956 speech that U.S. oil production would peak: 1970

6. Year U.S. oil production peaked: 1970

7. Decade global conventional oil discoveries peaked: 1960s

8. Total energy inputs measured in calories required to produce one calorie of food in North America: 10

9. It takes energy to get energy.

    The estimated ratio of units of energy obtained to energy used to get oil from wells in the U.S. in 1930: 100 to 1

    That same ratio in 1970: 25 to 1

    That same ratio in the 1990s: Between 18 and 11 to 1

10. Average daily world output in millions of barrels of conventional oil (not including tar sands, deepwater, Arctic and other hard-to-get unconventional sources) from 2005 to 2009:

2005	73.72	2008	73.65
2006	73.43	2009	72.25
2007	72.99		

11. Average daily world output in millions of barrels of all sources of liquid fuels including ethanol and unconventional sources of oil from 2005 to 2009:

2005	84.58	2008	85.43
2006	84.64	2009	84.24
2007	84.50		

12. Percent increase in the price of oil from January 1999 through December 2009: 497%

13. Percent increase in the U.S. Consumer Price Index in the same period: 29%

14. Percentage of total U.S. energy derived from oil: 37%

15. Percentage of all oil consumed in the U.S. that is used for transportation: 71%

16. Percentage of transportation fuels in the U.S. derived from oil: 95%

17. Oil producing countries past their peak in production with year of peak:

United States 1970	Colombia 1999
Venezuela 1970	United Kingdom 1999
Libya 1970	Rep. of Congo (Brazza-
Kuwait 1972	ville) 1999*
Iran 1974	Uzbekistan 1999
Indonesia 1977 & 1993	Australia 2000
Romania 1977	Norway 2001
Trinidad & Tobago 1978	Oman 2001
Iraq 1979	Yemen 2002
Brunei 1979	Mexico 2004
Tunisia 1980	Malaysia 2004*
Peru 1982	Vietnam 2004
Cameroon 1985	Denmark 2004
Russian Federation 1987*	Nigeria 2005*
Egypt 1993	Chad 2005*
India 1995*	Italy 2005*
Syria 1995	Ecuador 2006*
Gabon 1996	
Argentina 1998	*Apparent peak

Note: Iraq has announced plans that would result in production exceeding its previous peak. Columbia may also experience a second peak equal to or greater than its first.

18. Oil producing countries almost certain to reach new production peaks:

Algeria	Kazakhstan
Angola	Qatar
Azerbaijan	Saudi Arabia
Brazil	Sudan
Canada	Thailand
China	Turkmenistan
Equatorial Guinea	United Arab Emirates

19. Percentage of world oil production in countries with declining, flat or volatile production: 60.6%

20. Percentage of world oil production in countries expected to reach new peaks: 39.4%

Sources:

1. Based on 2008 consumption figures from the U.S. Energy Information Administration.

2. U.S. Energy Information Administration.

3. Eni S.p.A., Chevron Corporation, Petroleo Brasileiro S. A., Tullow Oil PLC. Based on 2008 consumption figures from the U.S. Energy Information Administration.

4. Kenneth S. Deffeyes, *Hubbert's Peak: The Impending World Oil Shortage*, p. 138.

5. *Nuclear Energy and the Fossil Fuels* was the name of a paper given by M. King Hubbert, then a Shell Oil geologist, at a regional meeting of the American Petroleum Institute in San Antonio, Texas, held March 7 through March 9, 1956. Hubbert offered two predictions for the year of peak oil production based on differing estimates of ultimately recoverable oil in the lower 48

states, 1965 and 1970. U.S. reserves turned out to be closer to Hubbert's high estimate, and his 1970 prediction proved to be dead on.

6. U.S. Energy Information Administration.

7. Colin J. Campbell, *The Growing Gap* in the Association for the Study of Peak Oil & Gas (International) Newsletter.

8. Mario Giampietro and David Pimentel, *The Tightening Conflict: Population, Energy Use, and the Ecology of Agriculture,* 1994.

9. Cutler J. Cleveland and Charles A. S. Hall, *EROI: Definition, History and Future Implications,* Presentation before the annual conference of the Association for the Study of Peak Oil & Gas – USA, Denver, Colorado. November 10, 2005.

10. – 12. U.S. Energy Information Administration.

13. CPI Inflation Calculator, Bureau of Labor Statistics, U.S. Department of Labor.

14. – 16. U.S. Energy Information Administration, *Annual Energy Review 2008.*

17. – 20. Adapted from *Is Peak Oil Real?* by Praveen Ghanta which first appeared July 14, 2009 on his weblog, *True Cost,* and was later republished on *The Oil Drum.* The data was compiled from the *BP Statistical Review of World Energy 2009.*

Peak Oil In Brief

Are we running out of oil?

Strictly speaking, no. We are, however, running out of cheap oil. And ever expanding supplies of cheap oil are critical to world economic growth.

What do you mean by "we're running out of cheap oil?"

Since the beginning of the oil age in the 1850s, prospectors and oil companies have been extracting the oil that's easiest to take out of the ground. Now 150 years later, we are approaching the point where the flow of easy-to-get oil is starting to decline, and we are beginning to rely on oil that is much harder to extract and thus more expensive.

So, why is this important?

History shows that oilfields and oil-producing countries inevitably reach a point where the rate of oil production peaks and then begins an irreversible decline. This is not necessarily a serious problem for a country because it can import the oil it needs. But the world as a whole is projected to reach a peak in oil production somewhere between now and 2037 and then begin an irreversible though probably bumpy decline.

Why should I be concerned if the peak isn't until 2037?

Nobody is certain when peak oil will occur. The 2037 forecast is the official median estimate of the U.S. government.[1] But the government does not have a good track record of predicting oil peaks. In 1961 the U.S. Geological Survey forecast that U.S. production would rise until the year 2000. The peak in U.S. domestic oil production actually occurred in 1970, an event which, in part, led to the oil crises of the decade that followed.

Several independent oil geologists have made predictions that call for a peak in world oil production before 2020. A few believe we are already there. Although it is not clear that we have hit the peak yet, we seem to be getting close. Every reputable scientist agrees that at some point the rate of world oil production will peak and thereafter enter a permanent decline. A small but growing number of oil industry executives agree that the world is nearing its all-time oil production peak, though they shy away from using the term "peak oil."

Can't we just find substitutes?

In order to live anything like the way we live now, we will have to find substitutes for oil. Unfortunately, while we are technically capable of producing such substitutes, the infrastructure needed to make any of them workable is either impractical to build or far too costly. In addition, making and distributing some of the proposed substitutes—such as hydrogen or corn ethanol—would actually consume more energy than we would get back from them. That would put us into a deeper energy hole. Given enough time, we might work out these problems. But a 2005 U.S. Department of Energy report concluded that a crash program to find substitutes would have to start 20 years before world peak oil production arrives if we hope to avoid an economically debilitating shortage.[2]

This sounds like it could be serious. What can we do?

If a peak in world oil production is nearby, the entire human race will be faced with conducting a huge, emergency-style response. This would inevitably include drastic reductions in energy use and a complete reorganization of how we live and work. No doubt we would face economic hardship since oil is the basis of our economy and our lifestyle.

If a peak is further in the future, say, 15 to 30 years away, we have an opportunity to make a smoother transition to an alternative energy economy. It would still be essential, however, to start taking appropriate action now.

Even if we have a fair amount of time to act, we will likely need to go beyond simply finding substitutes for oil. We will probably have to increase the energy efficiency of the world economy radically, curtail some unnecessary energy-consuming activities, and rearrange the way we live and work to a considerable degree.

Won't solar, wind and nuclear power see us through the energy transition?

Solar and wind power are growing by leaps and bounds and show great promise as renewable energy sources. New nuclear power plants—despite their well-known environmental and safety problems—will almost surely be built in the United States and throughout Asia.

That said, the oil problem we face is going to express itself primarily as a liquid fuels shortage, i.e., a shortage of gasoline, diesel and kerosene (used for jet fuel). Cars, trucks, planes and ships now run on liquid fuels. It would be either impractical or far too costly to convert them all to run on electricity from windmills, solar panels or nuclear reactors. The emerging fleet of electric vehicles will help, but they won't even make a dent in the problem for a decade.

What about natural gas?

There is indeed a lot of natural gas left, much of it deep in shale deposits beneath the earth and in a special form at the bottom of the ocean. And natural gas may be part of the solution to our emerging oil depletion crisis. Already there is technology that can turn natural gas into liquid fuel for vehicles. But, as with other substitutes, there are considerable hurdles to overcome before liquid fuels derived from natural gas can be widely used. One of the main concerns is that a substantial amount of energy is used up just converting natural gas to liquid fuel suitable for today's vehicles.

As with oil, natural gas will also eventually reach a peak in production and thereafter decline. So, we cannot depend on it as a long-term replacement for liquid fuels. Some say the peak in the worldwide rate of production for natural gas will come between 2030 and 2040. (Possible deep-sea gas resources are not included in such projections.) Of course, if we start to use a lot more natural gas than we do today, the peak is likely to come sooner.

As for those natural gas resources at the bottom of the ocean, they are gargantuan. Unfortunately, we have no proven technology to extract them in the form they're in—essentially natural gas frozen inside ice. This so-called methane hydrate is hazardous in that it tends to explode. Even if we do perfect the technology for mining it, we don't yet know whether it occurs in concentrations that are large enough to be economical or numerous enough to meet our energy needs.

How about coal?

Even if we ignore the fact that coal when burned produces far more greenhouse gas than either oil or natural gas, there are serious questions about how much coal remains. We already know how to turn coal into liquid fuels that can power our various forms of transportation. But this would require a hugely expensive new infrastructure. It would also be highly polluting and take a long time to build. As with natural gas, a substantial amount of energy is used up during the conversion process.

In addition, we would be vastly increasing our rate of consumption of coal. That would bring the inevitable peak in coal production even closer than it is now. In fact, some analysts believe world coal production could peak as early as 2025. If that happens, we would be faced with figuring out all over again how to produce liquid fuels from different sources. We would be much better off looking for more permanent solutions.

[1] U.S. Energy Information Administration
[2] *Peaking of World Oil Production: Impacts, Mitigation & Risk Management* by Robert L. Hirsch, Roger Bezdek and Robert Wendling

Sources for More Information

Books

The Party's Over: Oil, War and the Fate of Industrial Societies
By Richard Heinberg

Out of Gas:
The End of the Age of Oil
By David Goodstein

News and Information Websites

Community Solutions
www.communitysolution.org

Energy Bulletin
www.energybulletin.net

Post Carbon Institute
www.postcarbon.org

The Oil Drum
www.theoildrum.com

Blogs

Casaubon's Book (Sharon Astyk)
www.scienceblogs.com/casaubons book

Resource Insights (Kurt Cobb)
www.resourceinsights.blogspot.com

DVDs

A Crude Awakening:
The Oil Crash
www.oilcrashmovie.com

The End of Suburbia:
Oil Depletion and the Collapse of the American Dream
www.endofsuburbia.com

The Power of Community:
How Cuba Survived Peak Oil
www.powerofcommunity.org

Reading Group Guide

- What made you want to read *Prelude*?

- In Chapter 3, Victor Chernov gives what is described as a "disquisition on the wonders of geology" (page 34) concluding that "geology is destiny." Later he and Cassie Young argue about the issue of peak oil while dining at the Iron Gate restaurant (pages 38-40). Victor states, "Technology is like fairy dust to you. You sprinkle some on the tar sands and magically their output goes up four times…You sprinkle some on the ocean and magically oil that is 30,000 feet down becomes easy to produce…Yes, Cassie, we have technology. But now geology is winning the contest between the two. Remember: geology is destiny." Do you agree with Victor that technology might be failing and that geology is destiny? Did Victor's comments deepen your concerns about the issue of peak oil and its ramifications?

- After talking with Conrad Turner, Cassie Young reflects on her doubts about the Mooney-3 well which is located in some of the deepest waters of the Gulf of Mexico (page 67). "It marked the opening of a new offshore frontier. But frontiers, she thought, are always full of unforeseen dangers and possible setbacks. And frontiers can sometimes be fatal." Discuss Cassie's position as an energy analyst and her transformation from one of her firm's true believers into a concerned skeptic. Do you think her conversations with Turner and Victor Chernov set the stage for this transformation and, ultimately, for the changes in her life and career? Why or why not?

- How important are Cassie's relationships with Victor Chernov, Paul Hendler and Evan Grant in terms of the novel's plotline? Did one or more of the relationships help move the story forward? How?

- Discuss the significance of fossil fuels (oil, coal and natural gas) and the allusions to the Roman god Vulcan and the Roman goddess Ceres (pages 87-88, 201). How does Cassie's view of these two gods change? Do you agree with her new view? Why or why not?

- After reading *Prelude*, do you have a better understanding of how world oil production occurs and how it affects societies? What specific information/passages provided in this novel helped you gain perspective?

- Did the romantic subplot of this novel enhance or detract from the story? Why or why not?

- As a suspense novel, how would you rate *Prelude* in terms of characterization, action, dialogue and setting? Did Cobb effectively use all four elements to keep you engrossed? Were there any elements that were more effective than another?

- Were you surprised at the ending or was it predictable based on the events leading up to the novel's conclusion?

- How relevant do you think *Prelude* is based on what you know about the energy issue? Do you know more about this issue than you did before you read the book?

- Did reading this novel change how you view your own life? Discuss changes, if any, you could make in your everyday life to reduce the consumption of oil-based products.

For additional resources visit *www.preludethenovel.com*

CPSIA information can be obtained at www.ICGtesting.com
Printed in the USA
LVOW091557170112

264291LV00020B/38/P

9 780983 108900